The family congregated at the house feeling victorious even though they had no idea what the outcome of the hearing would be.

In the kitchen, where they were eating, drinking, and relaxing, Tory imitated Meg at the hearing, standing and gesturing with her finger. "And that's what I call control!" Then howling with laughter, she fell back into her seat. "Oh girl! I almost died! I was holdin' it in... I had tears coming out of my eyes."

Everyone at the dining room table cracked up. Meg covered her face with her hands in delighted embarrassment.

SHADES OF BROWN

DENISE BECKER

Genesis Press Inc.

Indigo Love Stories

An imprint Genesis Press Publishing

Indigo Love Stories
c/o Genesis Press, Inc.
1213 Hwy 45 N, 2nd Floor
Columbus, MS 39705

ISBN: 1-58571-110-1
Manufactured in the United States of America

First Edition

Visit us at www.genesis-press.com
or call at 1-888-Indigo-1

DEDICATION

To Cathy and Eric...

May you and future generations work to rid the world of racism and help fill it with love.

CHAPTER ONE

In desperation, Meg felt behind her for the kitchen drain board. Though the edge of the formica countertop was cutting into her lower back, curiously, it didn't hurt. She was so focused on what she had to do that she couldn't feel her own pain. There, her hand fumbled in the drain board, searching for the knife resting in it from breakfast this morning. Did she have the guts to use it?

Yes, it's either him or me.

She touched the cold blade with her fingertips, then felt a sharp pain like a paper cut as it sliced superficially into the middle finger on her right hand. She remembered sharpening that knife this morning, right before she sliced her grapefruit, a lifetime ago. If she'd known then what was going to happen now… She carefully traced the blade down to its rubbery handle, then wrapped her fingers around it. Praying he couldn't see what she was doing, she summoned up all her emotional and physical strength.

I hate him.

Her actions had to be swift and she must not miss. The consequences would be too dear. She brought the knife around without his noticing and plunged it deeply into Bill's stomach.

Oh my God! I did it!

She felt the knife hit something hard. What was it? It was a sickening feeling. Bill's eyes widened, his mouth gaped. She sucked in a deep breath. His face was so close to hers, she could taste his sour breath in her own mouth. She felt momentarily dizzy, outside her own body. Her mind raced.

What if he doesn't die?

What if I'm stuck with him in a wheelchair or he's a vegetable or something?

What if he can still attack me?

With that, Meg pulled the knife out and purposefully stabbed him a second time, higher, as close to his heart as she could guess. The second time the blade went in a little easier. No hard obstruction.

Bill's eyes widened further and he moaned horribly. Blood trickled from his mouth as his body slowly sagged toward her. Meg shoved him backward with strength she didn't know she had, screaming a sound that echoed as though it came from somewhere else in the house. He fell heavily to the floor and lay there without moving.

Meg stood there, her breathing fast. Realization suddenly set in. Her hands shook and she began to sob. This was someone she had loved once. She started to raise her hands to her face, then saw they were blood-covered, especially the right one. She looked down at Bill's body. Blood was gathering in a large, dark pool at his side. The blood looked thicker than it did in the movies. And darker. There was so much blood that he had to be dead.

An eerie calm came over her in just a few short minutes. Her breathing returned to normal and she walked over to the phone and called 911. In a matter-of-fact voice, she said,

"Hello, my name is Meg Robbins. I've just stabbed my husband."

CHAPTER TWO

Months Later

Meg started the long drive home to Delaware with renewed hope. She had always enjoyed long drives, even as a child. Traveling alone was not a scary thought. It gave her a lot of time to think and clear her head. She could also stop whenever she wanted – a luxury she'd never enjoyed with Bill. He had installed a second gas tank on his Blazer so they wouldn't have to make any "unnecessary" stops. Never mind having to go to the bathroom or getting something to eat. Meg thought she had tested the limits of her bladder standing in bathroom lines in bars and at parties in college, but it was nothing compared to the discomfort that her husband had made her experience whenever they were on the road.

Marriage to Bill had also meant moving a lot. Bill didn't want roots and with his job as a freelance sports writer, he could move any time he wanted. Just when Meg seemed to settle into a town, Bill would declare that they had to move for some new job. In the thirteen years that they were married, they moved six times, usually near or into big cities where they'd blend in and people would mind their own business. It had made it difficult for Meg to settle into a teaching job and build up tenure. Now, since Bill's death, Meg couldn't return to her teaching job at all. Not within several square miles of Los Angeles, anyway.

Several years into the marriage, Meg had realized that the more she talked about her life apart from him, the more he reacted irrationally and they'd move. Having friends meant she had someone to confide in, and Bill refused to let anyone get closer to Meg than he was. He had been trying to control her friendships even in high school. He had to be not just the most important person in her life, but the *only* important person in her life. He even got jealous of her students. If Meg paid too much attention to them, especially if the student was experiencing personal difficulties, he'd flip. Once he'd even accused her of sleeping with a fourteen-year-old boy who had a tendency to show up at their house because he had a drunken and neglectful mother. He'd just needed to talk to someone. Meg's students got a lot of her attention, and she liked it that way. With no children of her own, she was one of those teachers who went above and beyond her normal duties. She was visible in the community; making visits to student's homes, sometimes unwelcome ones. She had discovered that seeing a student's home often explained a lot and helped her help that particular student. She cared about her kids and they knew it. Even though she was never long in any one particular school, she was always one of the favorite teachers. Though this also occasionally caused some jealousy amongst her peers, Meg didn't care. She'd earned the respect of the students and they could too.

Meg had started out as a junior high school social studies and math teacher, but when frequent moves became the pattern, she got certified for high school. She needed all the flexibility she could get in her job searches as they moved from state to state.

So, in an effort to avoid moving, Meg learned to hide a lot from Bill, feeding him only miniscule pieces of information about her day, enough to keep him satisfied, but not too much to get him thinking about moving again. It was like walking a tightrope.

They lived in Los Angeles the longest, a little over three years. She had friends there that he never knew about – mostly other teachers, even a few parents of former students. Her friends were curious about her husband, but they soon stopped asking questions because Meg remained so tight-lipped. They knew something wasn't quite right in the marriage, but then again, whose marriage was perfect?

Now she was moving again, this time alone. Behind her Honda Accord she was pulling a small U-Haul, which was only half full. Meg had overestimated how much of her old life she was going to keep. Finally, she'd decided to take only things of sentimental value, her clothes, and all her school materials, which she'd spent years accumulating and mostly paid for herself. She's learned the hard way that the paltry allotment given teachers at the beginning of the school year barely got a teacher through September. The decision to take it was a no-brainer. Over the years, she had collected some neat teaching stuff – stuff that would take too long to find again.

As Meg took the I-40 exit off I-15, she knew she'd be on this stretch for over twelve hundred miles. She put her car on cruise control and let her mind drift to the Harringtons, her loving family, and she fantasized about their imminent reunion.

∞

Meg was born and raised in Wilmington, Delaware, the only child of a general practice doctor and a real estate agent mother. Materially, she'd had most of everything. She wasn't exactly spoiled, but she didn't want for much either. She lived in a beautiful colonial-style home on a tree-lined street, but it was the atmosphere inside the house that Meg hated. Her parents weren't particularly warm people. Meg could count on one hand the number of times she remembered being hugged. Though her home wasn't a cold place full of anger, it was quiet, non-confrontational, and boring. Not many compliments.

Not many criticisms.

Meg never forgot that her parents never came to any school events – no science fairs, no concerts – nothing. They were too busy. It seemed that no one else had parents that were as busy as hers. That's what Meg told her friends anyway. Their indifference left a lasting impression on her, especially when she came to know the Harringtons and experienced what a *real* home was like.

The Harringtons moved to Wilmington when Dr. Harrington joined her father's practice. At the time, it was quite a shock to the predominantly white community when this interracial couple and their three children moved into the house just around the corner from Meg. Dr. John Harrington was African American and his schoolteacher wife, Sue, known to the family as Mootsie, was white. Meg's father was responsible for the Harringtons moving to the neighborhood and several neighbors never let him forget it. He didn't care, though, and Meg found herself admiring her father for the first time in her life.

Meg's parents threw the obligatory dinner party when Dr. Harrington joined the practice, but more than that, the two families hit it off right away. Neither of her parents was bigoted. Quite the contrary. Despite the fact they were white, her parents participated in the March on Washington. Meg found it a total contradiction that her parents could be so adamant about the equality of people, and be, at the same time, such cold people. She wondered if they had exhausted all their warmth on the cause. If so, it was worth not getting the warm fuzzies throughout her childhood.

One very important decision her parents had made was to send her to public school, despite the fact that they had more than enough money to send her to private school. They felt that attending school with children of all races, religions, ethnicities, and socio-economic groups was an invaluable experience. Among then were the

Harrington offspring, best friends she would have never met in private school.

It was easy for Meg to become instant friends with the Harrington daughter, Tory, who was twelve, the same as she, and Michael Harrington, who was thirteen. Luther Harrington was only seven and a bit of a renegade, but Meg enjoyed his antics. There always seemed to be a "Luther story" to tell. He was a source of simultaneous joy and worry to his parents.

More often than not, Meg got off the school bus with Tory and went directly to her house, which was so different from Meg's quiet, inactive house. Tory's house was loud, bustling, always smelling of good cooking, and full of love. Meg wanted to live there. She soon got her wish.

Midway through Meg's freshman year in high school, her parents were killed in a car accident coming home from a hospital fund-raiser. Unbeknownst to Meg, her parents had made John and Sue Harrington her guardians when they'd had their will updated a year before. A few hours after the accident, Dr. Harrington, known to the family and Meg as 'Pop,' told her and moved her into the Harrington household. They became her family in every sense of the word, and she felt like she totally belonged. Dr. Harrington looked after her as he would his own child, even sending her for therapy when she later confessed she thought she'd caused her parents' deaths by wishing to live with the Harringtons.

At first, Tory depended on Meg to help her fit in at junior high school. Though Meg wasn't homecoming-queen-popular, she was cute, quick-witted and smart and had many friends. However, she wasn't prepared for the resistance some of her friends gave Tory. She wasn't naïve; she knew that much of that resistance was based on race. But Meg didn't care what anybody thought. She stuck by Tory and slowly everyone accepted her.

Michael, a year older than Tory, shared her dazzling smile. Of the three children, he was the most serious and, at times, was a bit brooding, intense, and downright righteous. But once he got to know Meg, he warmed to her considerably and was quite funny, and, Meg decided, a bit vulnerable. She surprised herself when she started looking forward to seeing him and couldn't hide her disappointment when he wasn't home.

Luther was the rebel, always getting into trouble. When he was younger, it was physical – broken arms, bad sprains, usually from doing some outrageous stunt. Pop swore Luther was the reason that he had to become a doctor. Otherwise, he couldn't afford all the trips to the emergency room. When Luther got to be a teenager, he was seldom home, and when he was, he was like a tornado coming through the house. His irresponsible behavior caused him to butt heads constantly with the levelheaded Michael. Of everyone in the family, Meg knew Luther the least, especially after Tory, Michael and she went off to college. When he was eighteen, he got a seventeen-year-old girl pregnant and refused to take responsibility. Meg was not particularly surprised.

Pop was quiet, intelligent, and loving, a man of few words. He had a very dry sense of humor, and had a knack for one-line zingers. He had put himself through college and medical school by working two jobs, taking twice as long as usual to get through. Though it took him years to get established in their primarily white suburban practice, his patient base grew steadily because of his accuracy in diagnosis as well as his wonderfully easy manner. He even made an occasional house call. Meg admired him more than anyone in the world and trusted him implicitly. She relied on him in all her serious life decisions, beginning with her inheritance and the selling of her parents' house.

Pop was tall and stocky with skin the same color of Meg's favorite brown bear, which was fitting because there was no better place to be than in the safe embrace of one of Pop's bear hugs. Yes, Pop was the real deal.

Where Pop was quiet, Mootsie chattered endlessly and appeared to be the happiest woman on earth, even when Meg knew she had had a bad day. She was plain, yet beautiful. Her smile was utterly contagious. That smile lived on in all her children. Great in the kitchen, she not only taught all her children how to cook, but how to handle all household responsibilities. Ironically, the boys sailed through, but Tory never got the hang of the domestic chores.

Meg remembered a time when she'd found Mootsie sternly talking to Bill in the Harrington kitchen. It was rare to see Mootsie talk through clenched teeth, and when they saw Meg enter the kitchen, both of them pretended to be otherwise occupied. Reflecting on it now, Meg thought Mootsie must have really been giving him the dickens about something, probably something to do with Meg. Mootsie had never fully trusted Bill. Now they were both dead...

Meg shook the bad thought from her head. *The therapist said to focus on the positive...*

Mootsie had really had two full-time jobs, one as a teacher and one as a homemaker. Their house was a real home and she worked hard at making it so. She also had a passion for teaching. But when Luther started getting into more serious trouble, Mootsie had taken it as a personal failure as a mother and quit her job to pull in the reins on Luther. Though she subbed at the local elementary school, Meg could see she missed having her own classroom. It was Mootsie who had inspired Meg to become a teacher. Some of the teacher stuff that Meg now towed had once been Mootsie's, lovingly given to Meg when she was in methods classes at the University of Delaware. Meg cherished Mootsie's belongings, particularly since Mootsie's death from breast cancer three years before. Her death had crushed Meg more than that of her own parents. Remembering the funeral where Michael sang "Ave Maria" in his beautiful baritone voice with tears streaming down his face, Meg started to cry. She pulled over to compose herself.

Meg wondered what awaited her in Wilmington. She had shared sporadic e-mails with Tory since Mootsie's death, but Tory was busy as a very successful lawyer specializing in medical malpractice suits –protecting doctors, of course. She did Pop proud. Meg knew they'd have a lot of reacquainting to do.

And what about Michael? He had been engaged at Mootsie's funeral, but Meg had heard nothing about a wedding. Surely she would have been invited. Meg felt a twang of envy toward his fiancée, knowing what a great husband Michael would be. He was now a successful architect, which totally fit his personality – precise, orderly, and creative.

Meg had no idea what Luther was doing, and Pop had recently retired.

It suddenly occurred to her that she really should call Tory. She didn't want to catch them totally off guard with her arrival, and she figured with several more days on the road, maybe Tory could scope out an apartment for her.

Around seven that night, Meg found a hotel off I-40 and called Tory. Her townhouse number was disconnected. She called her work number, thinking she might still be there, and left her cell phone number with the answering service. Meg lay on the bed watching TV, afraid that if she jumped in the shower, she'd miss Tory's call.

An hour and a half later, the phone startled Meg awake. She was nervous, but excited. "Hello?"

"Hey girl!" Tory shouted. "Where are you?"

"I'm in a hotel somewhere in western New Mexico. I'm coming home." She paused. "For good this time, Tory."

"You're kidding! That's so great! How did you get Bill to agree to *that* one?" Tory's voice grew a bit snide at the mention of Bill's name.

"He's dead, Tory."

A long pause. "Oh, Meg. I'm sorry," Tory said sincerely. "How did it happen?"

Meg had rehearsed this one for weeks.

"It was a prowler. He was stabbed."

"Oh my God. Were you home at the time?"

"Yes. Listen, I'll tell you all about it when I get there," Meg lied. She had no intention of elaborating on Bill's death. "I was wondering if you'd be willing to look for an apartment for me."

"Sure! But if I can't find one right away, you can stay with Pop and Michael."

"Okay. Thanks. I'll call you when I get closer. I don't think I'll be in Delaware until Thursday."

"Okay. I am *so* excited!"

"Me too!" Meg said. "Bye!"

Meg hung up the phone and thought a moment. Pop *and* Michael? Michael was living back home? So he must not be married. Or maybe his wife was living there too. Why had he moved back in with Pop? For that matter, why was Tory's townhouse number disconnected? Oh well, she'd have her questions answered soon enough.

CHAPTER THREE

While Meg's journey had started out well, by the time she reached Ohio, she was tired and impatient and a day behind her planned schedule. When she reached Route 202 the next day, her heavy foot got her a speeding ticket near West Chester, Pennsylvania.

How ironic for her to drive across the country, to be so close and get this ticket now. The optimist in her had always believed that things like this happened for a reason. Perhaps a hideous accident had awaited her down the road if she kept speeding, and this ticket was her warning.

She called Tory while the ticket was being written by the police officer back in her police car. She told her she'd arrive in about forty minutes.

Tory let out a yelp, which could only be described as a cross between a coyote and an injured alley cat, then yelled, "Go to Pop's! We'll barbecue!"

Meg wondered what it was like to be one of Tory's co-workers and have to listen to her loudness every day. She started to giggle. The policewoman, who'd come back to the car to present Meg with her ticket, did not look amused, seeing Meg giggling all alone. Meg apologized and pulled, ever so slowly, away from the shoulder.

Exactly forty-eight minutes later, Meg pulled in front of the Harrington house. It was a beautiful Victorian-style house on Gilpin Avenue, near Trolley Square. Built in the early 1900s, the house had a wrap-around porch, six bedrooms, two fireplaces, two staircases and oodles of charm. She did a double take when she looked at the porch swing. Bill was sitting in it rocking and smiling. How... She squeezed her eyes shut, heart thudding, and then refocused. He was gone.

The older neighborhood was just outside the center of the city, but within Wilmington city limits. Its access to scenic parkland and the fact that it was still in the city, made it a desirable neighborhood for young professionals as well as retirees.

Before Meg had a chance to drink in the sight of the house any further, Tory came out of the front door, screaming at the top of her lungs. Meg now remembered why Tory had been captain of the cheerleading squad – her volume. Tory was barefooted, but still in part of her "power suit" from work. Meg realized it was only six p.m. and under normal circumstances, Tory would still be at work. But when her best friend and sister, whom she hadn't seen in a while, came to town, Tory left work early. She always did have her priorities straight. Michael came out of the house not far behind Tory and with a glorious smile. Pop came last, but was every bit as happy to see her as the other two. He walked with a cane now and when Meg saw him, she felt an instant pang of guilt.

How long has he had the cane?

Meg couldn't get out of the car fast enough. A few neighbors who had heard Tory's hootin' and hollerin' came outside their houses to see what the fuss was all about. Recognizing Meg and witnessing the joy of the reunion, they smiled. They were used to Tory. Meg waved to them as if she were a celebrity. One couple sat down in their rockers and prepared to watch. Either that or they were cooling down. It was hot this sultry August day and some of the old houses still had no air conditioning. Meg remembered that the two on the porch were the nosy ones who had always looked out if they heard so much as a car door slam. They were now enjoying the scene in front of them almost as much as the happy family.

Tory looked beautiful, as always. She wore a suit skirt of periwinkle blue and a plain white sleeveless shell. Her clothes fit her as if they were expensive, which they most likely were. Her smile lit up her whole face — a face the color of coffee with cream — Pop being the coffee and Mootsie being the cream. Tory had a luminous complexion that had barely seen a blemish even through puberty. Like Mootsie, Tory needed little makeup and, being a lawyer, she wore little in order to be taken seriously. Her hair was her father's, wiry, unruly, but worn shoulder length in a fashionable style. Tory threw herself into Meg's waiting arms, practically knocking her down.

"Hey, girl! I'm so glad you're here," she said in a surprisingly quiet voice.

"Not half as glad as I am," Meg whispered while in Tory's embrace.

Releasing Tory, Meg gazed upon Michael. He finally had grown into his tall frame. He had always been a bit lanky growing up, but now he had put on just enough weight to fill out his body.

My God, he's handsome.

His wavy hair was cut close to his head and he sported a new mustache and goatee — a perfect frame for his gorgeous smile. Meg had always had a little crush on Michael, but had never pursued anything, even though they were not related by blood.

Michael embraced Meg, much more gently than Tory had and rocked her, saying, "Welcome home!" He then stepped back and placed his hands on Meg's shoulders to look at her face. He suppressed an urge to run his hands through her smooth brown, shoulder-length hair. Her skin was sunburned just across the bridge of her nose. She still had a few freckles.

Noting the look, her heart skipped a beat. "You look so handsome," she stammered.

"And you look stunning, as always," he replied.

Meg felt her face flush and went to reach for Pop who was clearing his throat and waiting patiently. He, too, was beaming and embraced her in one of his famous hugs.

"There's my girl," he murmured in her ear.

Meg choked back a sob.

Why didn't I come home sooner?

Pop heard her sob and in order to break the seriousness of the moment, he lifted her off the ground slightly, making everyone chuckle.

"Pop, you shouldn't do that," Michael chided half-heartedly.

"Oh, she's as light as a feather!" Pop countered, referring to Meg's tiny frame.

"Where's Luther?" Meg asked as they walked onto the porch. She glanced at the swing. It was swinging slightly in the wind. Empty. When they entered the house, the screen door squeaked beautifully. Meg loved that sound. It was the sound of home. She took a cleansing breath.

"Oh, he's picking up a few more things for the barbecue," Tory answered. "Wanna beer?"

"Sure," Meg said, already beginning to relax. She followed Tory into the large kitchen; the place where she'd spent most of her time when she lived there. The same four stools sat by the counter, only now the seats were re-upholstered in an updated plaid.

Michael sat next to Meg on one of the stools, while Tory went to the refrigerator to get beer. Pop hobbled through a door in the back of the kitchen that Meg knew connected to a small in-law suite that had never been used. Meg had never known what it looked like in there. It had always been locked before.

"Pop can't do steps anymore," Tory said when she saw Meg watching Pop. Even now, Tory could read Meg's mind and answer her question before it was asked.

"Is he okay?" Meg whispered, looking concerned.

Michael answered. "He had hip replacement surgery several months ago – the result of a fall that he had. His hip was bad to start, but that made it unbearable for him. He also has arthritis, but he can still get around pretty well. He seems to be doing a lot better, but who knows?"

"What do you mean?"

"You know Pop. He'd never complain anyway. Doctors make the worst patients."

"How true. Why didn't you call me?" Meg asked.

"I did," Tory said. "Bill said he'd let you know. I knew when we didn't hear from you that the bastard, God rest his miserable soul, didn't tell you. But it was okay. Pop's surgery was very routine."

"I'm sorry about Bill," Michael said sincerely.

"Thanks." Meg felt so disconnected. She was incredibly happy to be there in that kitchen, yet for the first time felt as if she weren't a part of the family. It was her own fault. In an effort to hide things from them, things about her and Bill, she had distanced herself. Meg didn't want to be a downer or have anyone feel sorry for her. If there was one thing she hated it was pity. She realized that this was one of the reasons that she had been so secretive.

"It's okay, Meg. Everything's fine with Pop," Michael said, seeing the disheartened look on Meg's face.

"Well, I'm here *now*," Meg brightened. "And I'm so glad to be home." She put her arm around Michael and laid her head on his shoulder.

"Awww," Michael purred and returned her embrace.

"Wait for me!" Tory ran around the counter and put her arms around both of them.

I'm never leaving.

Meg had always treasured her family but never more than at this moment. Her eyes had started to well up again when the front screen door slammed and Luther yelled, "Where is she? I see CAL-I-FOR-NIA plates out there! Where is she?"

Smiling, Meg hopped down from the stool to greet her younger brother who was bounding into the kitchen despite having his arms full of groceries.

Luther howled as he saw Meg, and dumped the bags on the counter. "Dare she is and she looks *fine!*" Everyone laughed and Meg beamed as she and Luther hugged.

"You look wonderful!" she exclaimed. "Everyone does!" She glanced Michael's way and he didn't miss it.

"Gimme a beer, Tory. I am a *bar-be-cuing!*" Luther yelled, emphasizing each syllable.

"You?" Michael shouted. Tory and Meg simultaneously yelled, "Oh, no!" and "Oh, no, not you, Luther."

When they were teenagers and Luther was twelve or so, he had decided to add a "few drops" of gasoline to the charcoal just to "see what would happen." Michael, who was tending the grill, had lurched out of the way just in time, avoiding a ten-foot high burst of flame from the grill. But it caught the awning over the stone patio on fire, which Michael with great dramatics had been able to put out with the garden hose before any major damage was done. Luther had literally rolled on his back, howling with laughter at the sight of his brother freaking out. Michael had almost hit him that day and would have if Pop hadn't come out and stood between them. Pop had looked at Michael, angry and panting, at the charred, smoking awning, and then glared at Luther, who still had a few more giggles to get out.

"Oh, come on, it's a gas grill now, and I'm all grown up!" Luther protested, sounding much younger than his thirty-four years.

Michael chuckled and said, "Okay, little bro. Let's see if you can handle this. Don't let Meg's homecoming be ruined by the fire company having to come."

"We used to be on a first-name basis with the firefighters from the Wilmington Fire Company. Do you remember that?" Tory added, only half-kidding, referring to Luther's pyromaniac stage.

"Do I remember that? One of the firefighters was an usher at my wedding!" Meg joked.

"Ha, ha, ha," Luther said sarcastically.

"Oh, let them fight it out," Tory said to Meg. "Help me make a salad."

Michael and Luther walked out the back screen door, carrying burgers, buns, platters and utensils, still arguing good-naturedly about who was going to cook.

While Meg and Tory ripped the lettuce and cut the vegetables, Tory explained that Michael had moved back into the house after Pop fell down the last few steps of the back stairway. Apparently he had been lying there hurt for several hours before a neighbor heard him calling out. After the surgery, and on Pop's insistence, Michael had moved into the master bedroom upstairs. The in-law suite had been fixed up for Pop.

"Why Michael?" Meg asked.

"My hours are so long and, well, we know how dependable Luther is," Tory explained. "Luther has come a long way though. When Mootsie died, it was like a wake-up call to him. Now he's bartending and playing in a band part-time. It's not the occupation that Pop would have chosen for him, but he's pulling down a paycheck and he's been working at the same place for two years, a record for him! He's still with Jessica. They moved in together about a year ago. She has the patience of an angel! And she really loves him."

At that moment, it occurred to Meg to look at Tory's left hand. There she spied a simple, shining gold band. She abruptly stopped cutting carrots.

"What the hell is that?" Meg asked, not even trying to hide the fact that she was not only surprised, but also mildly perturbed.

"I'm married," Tory said softly with a sweet, slightly guilty smile.

"When? Who? Why didn't you tell me? Am I not in this family anymore?" Meg's voice was much louder than she intended. Pop was now standing in the doorway of his room. He was used to raised voices in this house, but he knew the difference between play and not.

"None of us were there, Meg," Pop said with a touch of accusation.

"Don't you start with me, Pop," Tory warned. She looked apologetically at Meg. "You remember Travis?" Meg nodded. "We went to Vegas on vacation and…"

"You were in Vegas and didn't call me? I could have hopped on a plane and…"

"I was *going* to, but it turned out to be my honeymoon and three's a crowd, if you know what I mean," Tory said playfully. "Pop was a little angry with me that he didn't have the chance to give me away."

"At least I got to give Meg away, even if it *was* to an asshole," Pop retorted. Meg couldn't help laughing. Rarely was Pop this talkative, but he was always this candid.

Meg eased off the beer a bit. She hadn't eaten since ten-thirty that morning, an English muffin and coffee, and she was quickly feeling the effects of the alcohol. She pushed the beer can aside.

"When?" she asked softly, resuming her cutting in order to avoid

Tory's eyes.

"Three months ago."

"Where is he now?"

"Eating out with some friends. I wanted tonight just to be the five of us. I didn't want to spring too much on you at once."

"Too late," Meg said, not unkindly. "Though I was in a bit of a fog when I met him at Mootsie's funeral, he seemed great. Her death hit me so hard. I'm sure he's perfect."

"Hell, no! But I love him to death! We've been together for a long time and I didn't have time to plan a big wedding, and he was getting impatient. He's so smart and stubborn and *silly*! He really keeps me on my toes. We fight all the time—but you know me, I love a good argument." The family joke was that was why Tory had become a lawyer.

Meg watched her friend and realized how happy she was for her. She was sad for herself, not getting to see them get married. She got off her stool and went to hug her.

"I'm happy for you, Tory. Really I am. I'm sorry if I reacted badly. I always assumed I'd be there, ya know?"

"I always assumed you'd be there too."

With the salad finished, Meg and Tory joined Pop and Michael in the rockers on the back porch. Luther had been deemed trustworthy enough to tend to the grill, and he did so with glee. He was dancing to a tune on a small radio he had on the rail of the porch –"Gettin' Jiggy Wit' It" by Will Smith. At times his gyrating bordered on the obscene. Everyone laughed except Pop, who just closed his eyes and shook his head. Then Meg joined Luther dancing and mouthing the words to the song, hips swiveling, eyes closed. Then, unexpectedly, Luther grabbed her by the small of the back and pulled her toward him, pressing the lower halves of their bodies together. He started his gyrating again, this time against Meg. Meg squealed a little-girl-on-the-roller coaster-squeal, and Michael yelled, "Hey, that's enough, Luther!" Tory was howling with laughter, Luther and Meg were giggling, but Michael just scowled.

Hmmmm, jealousy?

"Oh, you just wantin' it to be you!" Luther said to Michael.

Meg thought how typical this episode was of their personalities. Luther pushing the envelope, not knowing when to stop; Michael chastising him, taking it too seriously.

Meg went over to Michael, sat on his lap, and kissed him on the cheek. He flushed, so unexpected was her affection. He warmly wrapped his arms around her waist. But the serious moment had passed.

On the other side of the porch sat the same old cedar picnic table and they sat there and ate their dinner. Meg devoured hers with gusto. Burgers had never tasted so good and she complimented the proud chef.

During dinner, Meg told them about the interview she had on Monday with their old principal, Dr. Gardner. Meg felt fortunate that he was still at the high school all four of them had attended. Normally, she would have applied to the middle school, but she thought she stood a better chance with Dr. Gardner. Since he already knew her and liked her, perhaps he wouldn't dig too much into her past. He had an opening for a ninth and tenth grade social studies teacher. Interviewing Meg was just a formality, he'd told her while chatting on the phone with her two weeks earlier. It was already mid-August and he was gearing up for the school year. If she was lucky, she could be setting up her classroom by Tuesday.

After dinner, while Michael and Luther unloaded the U-Haul for her, Tory excitedly told Meg about the townhouse that she had found for her.

A townhouse? I can't afford that. I said apartment.

"It's in Trolley Square. You'll be so close!"

I really can't afford a Trolley Square townhouse.

"Great. Uh, I'll have to look at it." Meg tried to sound enthused.

"You'll love it!" Tory exclaimed.

That's what I'm worried about.

"I found out about it from a co-worker," she continued. "It's a foreclosure in beautiful condition. And it's available right away. It seems that the wife had a flair for redecorating and home improvements. The problem is that her hubby erroneously thought she was paying the mortgage. We're going to look at it tomorrow."

"Okay! Sounds great!" Meg said.

Well, it won't do any harm to look.

CHAPTER FOUR

After dinner, the family fell back into the routine of drinking coffee while cleaning up. Pop said he was tired, and went to shower and watch TV in his room.

Throughout dinner, Meg had found it difficult to keep her eyes off Michael. Had her feelings for him intensified? Had the time away made him feel like less of a brother and more like a possible suitor?

Tory's husband, Travis, stopped by after having dinner with friends. It was easy to see why these two were together – their affection was so great and their teasing endless. He wasn't a big man and was ordinary looking, but he was hilarious and sparkled next to Tory. Since he was a guidance counselor at the same high school where Meg was interviewing, she had a hundred questions for him, but thought it best to wait.

Luther and Michael seemed to like Travis a lot and Meg knew how important that was to Tory. Many a boyfriend of Tory's had been chewed up and spit out by one or both of her brothers. They had been remarkably accurate in their character appraisals too. This family was fiercely protective of one another. It wasn't a matter of sticking their noses where they didn't belong, although sometimes it could appear that way. It was love, pure and simple.

Meg also remembered Michael and Tory giving her similar treatment when she was dating Bill. Tory never hid the fact that she didn't like him and Michael's disapproval mostly consisted of eye rolls. But Meg couldn't see past the fact that Bill was a popular, blond hunk who went to Princeton on a football scholarship. She thought about how easily dazzled she had been. So young and ignorant.

If only they had stopped me from marrying Bill.

Not long after Travis arrived, Luther left the festivities, claiming to be needed at home.

"I'll bet," Michael teased.

With Tory and Travis in the kitchen getting cozy with one another, making Meg feel like a third wheel, she decided to move to the family room where Michael was. She had been waiting for the opportunity to be alone with him anyway. He was engrossed in an article from an architecture magazine. She grabbed their high school yearbook from the bookshelf and cozied up next to him on the couch. He smiled at her until he saw what she had in her hand. Then his expression went to mild despair.

"Oh, Meg, not the yearbook!" he groaned. It was from Meg's junior year, Michael's senior one.

"Oh, come on, chicken," Meg prodded.

First they flipped through the pages making the usual gossipy comments about people:

"Did you hear about her?"

"He's dead."

"He's gay."

"She's on her fourth husband."

And then a picture of Meg.

"She killed her husband," Meg imagined someone saying.

Their bare legs were pressed against each other. Each of them had on shorts and on this hot summer night, it didn't take long for their skin to start getting sticky. But neither one was about to move.

When Tory and Travis entered the dining room, which was open to the family room, they stopped dead in their tracks. Michael's arm was around Meg, and they were still looking at silly yearbook pictures. In reality, neither of them was actually looking at the pictures any longer. They were pretending. Each was totally distracted by the other.

Travis smiled as he cast a knowing glance at the couple on the sofa. Tory studied the situation and was instantly delighted. They had been trying to fix up Michael for a long time now.

"I assume this woman meets with your stamp of approval," Travis whispered.

She didn't need to answer. She had always thought that Meg and Michael would make a great couple, but Bill had always been in the way. Now he wasn't. As they continued to stand there unobserved, she felt strangely like a voyeur.

When Meg and Michael came across a candid photo of Michael with an afro and a very startled expression on his face, Meg started giggling. Michael was embarrassed. Even though they had seen that picture so many times before, it seemed different this time. Meg seemed different.

Michael hurriedly turned the page only to be greeted by another picture of him, this time with Meg. They were cheek to cheek, smiling.

"Aww, look at us!" Meg said softly.

With a slight chuckle in his voice Michael said, "I was in love with you, even then."

He'd barcly finished, when he realized what he had said. His eyes grew round, his smile disappeared, his head came up and he stared straight ahead, shocked at himself. So caught up in her presence, her proximity, her touch, he had just blurted it out. He couldn't believe it. Time stood excruciatingly still for Michael and he felt positively queasy.

Did I hear him right? She looked at him questioningly.

Yes. I definitely heard him right! Meg was afraid Michael could actually *see* her chest heaving; her heart was pumping so hard.

At that moment, Tory and Travis, who hadn't heard any of their conversation, decided to leave.

"We've got to go, kids!" Tory declared as she entered the family room.

Michael stood quickly, relieved to have an escape.

"Bye," he said to them quickly. He sheepishly walked over to the entertainment unit and scanned the CDs, not really looking at them. It was something to do. He wanted to tell Meg more. He wanted to run away. He wanted to kiss her. He wanted to disappear into the wall.

As Michael anguished, Meg was hugging Tory and Travis goodbye. They made arrangements to see the townhouse the next day, but Meg heard only half of what was said. She kept glancing over at Michael, making sure he didn't leave, making sure he was okay. As much as she loved Tory, at this moment, she couldn't get rid of her fast enough.

When Tory and Travis finally left, Meg cautiously approached Michael, who had his forehead propped on a shelf of the entertainment unit, staring straight down, looking defeated.

"Wanna talk about it?" Meg asked gently, her eyebrows raised. *Please, want to talk about it.*

He couldn't look at her. He had no idea how she felt. Was she just being warm Meg, or did her feelings mirror his?

"Look at me," she said.

He turned toward her now, but he still stared at his feet. She was standing so close. He thought this was a good sign. She wouldn't stand so close if she weren't interested. Would she? He gave up. It was already out. He might as well bury himself.

"It's always been you, Meg. Ever since we were teenagers."

His heart pounding, he looked up finally and saw that she was smiling, looking quite satisfied.

"Why didn't you ever tell me?" she asked softly. But she already knew the answer. Michael kept a lot inside, and although she'd known he loved her, she hadn't known *how* he loved her or how much. That and the fact that Bill was such a bully had probably sabotaged any hope of a relationship that Meg and Michael might have had.

"I don't know!" Michael said, exasperated. Then, changing his mind, he said, "Yes I do. *Bill.* It was always Bill for *you.*" He couldn't stand next to her. He had to move about the room. It was claustrophobic.

"Well, maybe if I'd known… " she said defensively. *Was I that stupid not to recognize it?*

A feeling of dread washed over Meg. *What if he doesn't feel like that now?*

She thought back to what he'd said: "*I loved you even then.*" Even then. *That means he still feels the same way, right?* Meg's mind was racing. Her eyes were shifting, blinking.

Michael sat down on the arm of the sofa. He didn't say anything. Meg had to confirm his feelings. She walked slowly toward him and stood between his knees. This time, he met her gaze.

"How do you feel about me now?" she whispered, swallowing hard.

Michael studied her face. She stood so close. His heart pumped wildly as he cupped her face in his hands and kissed her gently.

His kiss was more like a caress – so tender and sweet. Meg realized she was holding her breath.

He kissed her again, more urgently this time, a bottled-up kiss, changing the angle, deepening it. She returned the passion with all her heart. They embraced tightly, holding on for dear life. Michael breathed an enormous sigh of relief. It seemed to them that this was the perfect moment. It was the beginning.

They proceeded to make out like teenagers on the couch, smiling, talking, touching, and kissing. Michael told her how he'd broken up with his fiancée shortly after seeing Meg at Mootsie's funeral. All of his old feelings had returned and he couldn't go through with the marriage. He added that his fiancée also had the habit of telling little white lies, something he couldn't tolerate.

Meg's heart sank as she thought of the huge secret she was harboring. *It'll keep. I can't spoil this moment.*

They couldn't stop touching each other, gazing at each other. His loving touch was something new to her, so different, so exciting. He was exactly what she needed.

They talked about their feelings until late into the night. Meg told him how she'd almost asked him to the Sadie Hawkins Day dance in eleventh grade after getting into a fight with Bill.

"But then Sherie Brown asked you and I stayed home," Meg said.

"Oh yeah, Sherie Brown," Michael said with a laugh. "I had a terrible time. I don't why she asked me. She hung out and danced with her friends the whole time." He stroked Meg's face. "I wish you *had* asked me. Maybe I would've gotten up my nerve all the way back then."

Meg stared past Michael for a brief moment, zoned out.

"Meg?"

Meg shook her head slightly and blinked as if to wake herself up from a dream.

"I was just thinking how different my life would have been if it had been you instead of
Bill."

Michael's back straightened and he said in a deep, comedic voice, "It was all Sherie Brown's fault!" Michael had inherited Pop's flair for breaking up a serious moment just when it needed to be broken.

Momentarily distracted, Meg laughed softly. Then sobering, she said, "Seriously, there's some stuff I need to tell you about Bill."

"No, not tonight. We're not going to ruin tonight by talking about him."

Meg paused. She was relieved. "Okay," Meg relented as she cuddled under his chin. She'd tell him another day.

Eventually, Meg and Michael said goodnight and she went upstairs. Meg's old room was more of an impersonal guest room now, since she had taken everything with her when she moved out, except for the furniture. She didn't care. Her old, full-sized brass bed was there with her quilt in varying shades of blue and cream. Someone on her mother's side of the family had made the quilt, an aunt or a cousin. It was one of the few belongings she had brought with her from her old house when she moved in with the Harringtons. A number of things had been sold or discarded, though some had been placed in storage somewhere. She'd have to ask Pop about it. When she married Bill, he had been adamant that all their belongings be new.

The quilt made Meg think about the relatives she had gradually lost touch with since her parents' deaths. The reasons varied. Some of them lived too far away. Some were prejudiced and had disagreed with her parents' choice of guardians. Meg thought it laughable that they would think she'd be better off with a distant aunt, whom she'd met only once or twice, than with the Harringtons whom she knew so well and loved so much. She was so grateful for her parents' choice.

Earlier in the week, when Meg called to say that she was on her way, Tory had aired out the room and made up Meg's bed with powder blue sheets, as if it would somehow make Meg arrive faster if the room were ready. Michael had welcomed her home with a single red rose in a crystal vase on the nightstand. Now she bent down to smell it and smiled.

The room itself was small, but cozy. It had hardwood floors with a blue floral square area rug in the center of the room. The single window faced the front of the house, a fact Meg had loved. She could always see the comings and goings of everyone in the house.

Suddenly tired, she readied herself for bed and climbed between the cool, fresh-smelling sheets. She slept deeply and dreamlessly, so safe in this wonderful old house with Michael down the hall and Pop downstairs.

When Meg awoke, it was already late morning. She realized that, exhausted from her trip, she had barely moved all night on the too-soft mattress. Consequently, she was very stiff as she climbed out of her bed. She peeked out the door and down the hall to the master bedroom. The door was open, so Michael must be up. It was Saturday and she hoped he didn't have to go to work. Normally, she would have thrown on a robe and gone downstairs without a thought to her appearance. But things were different now. Even though it felt vain, she had to clean up and look good before she saw Michael. After she showered, she dressed in khaki shorts, a simple, white tee shirt, and brown leather sandals. At that point, she was so anxious to see Michael that she decided to skip the makeup altogether.

He's seen me worse than this. When I had the flu. Every time I cried...

She ran noisily down the hardwood back stairway that went to the kitchen. For the first time in years, she had awakened happy. She would be so disappointed if Michael wasn't in the house.

There he was, sitting there at the kitchen counter, drinking coffee and reading the paper. But he looked up, beaming, when he heard her noisy descent. She ran to him and wrapped her arms tightly around his neck.

"Good morning," she murmured as she kissed him.

"Yes, it is," he agreed. He was so relieved that he hadn't dreamt the entire preceding night's events.

"How did you sleep?" he asked.

"Like a rock! I love my old bed. Thanks for the rose."

"What makes you think it was from me?" he quipped.

"It was your style," she said while helping herself to coffee.

He smiled, pleased.

"What do you want for breakfast?" he asked, jumping off the stool and rubbing his hands together.

"You!" she whispered, setting down her coffee and slipping her arms around his waist. He gave her a warm succession of tender kisses.

During their embrace, Pop opened the back screen door with three tomatoes in his hand from his tiny garden out back. Meg and Michael were much too busy to hear him or care.

All they heard was Pop mutter purposely loud enough for them to hear, " `Bout damn time."

They dissolved into giggles in each other's arms.

Tory arrived as Michael was in the middle of cooking tomato and cheese omelets. Pop's chest puffed out with pride when they insisted on using his tomatoes. Three omelets stretched to four when Tory begged Michael to make her one too.

"You know I don't cook and I haven't had an omelet in months!" she pleaded.

When they sat at the kitchen table to eat, Tory sensed something in the air.

"What's with you, Pop? You look like the cat that swallowed the canary."

Meg looked toward Pop and started giggling. He was obviously going to burst with his secret about Meg and Michael.

"And what's with *you*?" she directed to Meg. "You've been all giggly and silly."

Michael smiled a knowing smile at Meg, pleased that he was the reason why. The brother in him also liked to annoy Tory and keep her in suspense.

"What the hell is going here?" Tory demanded.

"Michael and Meg are doin' it," Pop blurted.

Tory dropped her fork as Meg and Michael simultaneously yelled, "Pop!" Then they all roared with laughter.

So, thought Tory, she and Travis had assessed the situation correctly the night before. Something had happened. Something wonderful.

"Really?" Tory asked incredulously. Meg and Michael smiled broadly. "I'm so glad," she said softly and seriously as the laughter died down. Since Michael was closest to her, she leaned over and hugged him without getting up. Then, when realization set in, she screamed,

"Oh my God! My brother and sister are *doin'* it!"

Pop was laughing so hard, he was crying. Everyone was laughing.

"A little louder, Tory. They didn't hear you in New Jersey," Michael chided good-naturedly.

Meg smiled as she wondered what the neighbors must be thinking if they'd heard Tory's outburst. Her neighbors in California had never known anything about her – with good reason.

It never occurred to Meg or Michael to correct them – that they hadn't actually "done it," because they knew it would be true soon enough.

After breakfast, Pop volunteered to clean up so the others could get on their way townhouse hunting. Before Pop stood, Meg hugged him from behind in his chair and pressed her lips long and warmly on his cheek.

"I love you, Pop," she whispered in his ear. Pop looked smugly at Michael, loving every second of the affection. Michael loved watching it. Then Meg shared a smooch with Michael that made Tory place her hand on her chest and exhale, "Ohhhh."

Tory, Michael, and Meg walked the few blocks to the townhouse where they met the realtor. Tory was right. It was perfect.

Yeah. Too perfect.

The Trolley Square area was a very desirable, safe area of the city, not far from the

Brandywine River, Brandywine Park, and Rockford Park. A townhouse there cost twice as much as a similar size townhouse in another part of the city. It was important to Meg that she live in the city, so she could be close to school and feel a part of the community. Being this close to Michael would be great, too. Besides, this was her old stomping ground.

First of all, the off-street parking was a major bonus. Nothing was worse than trying to find a parking space in front of your own home and not being able to do it. Some people in the city resorted to putting trashcans or old kitchen chairs out at the curb to hold their parking spaces. Meg didn't want to have to bother with all that. This place had a driveway from the street toward the back of the property. No garage, but that was okay.

The townhouse was charming with its enclosed antique-glass front porch. From the front, the house looked small, but it was deep, long and skinny. It had three bedrooms, one and a half baths and a large kitchen in the rear. There was a door that led from the driveway into the kitchen and it was clear that it was the homeowner's main entrance. The small dining room was sandwiched between the kitchen and the living area at the front of the house. The living area was a little dark because of the porch in the front, but it wasn't a major drawback. The house was meticulously maintained, so Meg wouldn't have to do much but move in.

The floor plan was what the British would describe as "three up and three down." The largest of the three bedrooms was upstairs in the front with a glorious bay window. The two other bedrooms were smaller, but Meg already had plans to make one a study and one a guestroom.

What am I thinking? I should be looking for excuses why I can't get this place. I can't afford it. I have to fess up.

Michael was busy checking out every bit of molding, flushing the toilets, and running the garbage disposal—everything.

"Listen, Tory. This place is perfect for me. But I…"

Tory seemed more excited than Meg did. "Did you see the little slate patio in the back? It's so cute. You and Michael can sit out there and look at the stars…"

"Tory, I don't know if I can afford this place. How much is it?"

"$225,000."

"Oh."

Tory didn't want to pry into Meg's financial affairs, so she just paused a moment and asked, "When will you know?"

"Later today. I have to get out my books and crunch some numbers. Bill didn't leave me with much."

"Now why doesn't that surprise me?" Tory said disgustedly.

"Yes. He kept telling me how much more he made than me, and that was his justification for taking all those pro-athletes out to dinner, his BMW, his Rolex… And we spent unnecessary money on house furnishings because Bill wouldn't allow me to take any of my own things into the marriage. It was his way of erasing my past. Or attempting to, at any rate."

Meg shook her head. Tory studied her friend with concern, then looked around the updated kitchen.

"Things will be different for you now," Tory said with confidence. "You like this place though, don't you?" she asked softly.

"Are you kidding? What's not to like? We'll have to see." Meg was doubtful, but didn't want to disappoint her friend.

"You better decide quickly. These deals don't come up that often in this part of town."

Meg knew it was true, but she refused to be pressured into buying a place she couldn't afford. She had had too much of that with Bill. Her life was going to be different now. It had to be.

CHAPTER FIVE

That afternoon, Michael did go into work for a couple of hours, but made arrangements to go out to dinner with Meg. Tory went home to spend some quality time with Travis. They had been trying to have a baby even before the marriage, but had had no success.

"You work too much," Meg said.

"What about you?" Tory asked.

"I had two miscarriages," Meg confessed.

"Oh, yes, I remember one. I didn't realize that you'd had two. I'm sorry, Meg."

"No biggie. Some things just aren't meant to be. It's best that Bill's genes didn't get passed on to some poor innocent child," Meg said in a poor attempt at a joke.

Tory furrowed her brow in surprise at Meg's casual tone. No biggie?

After Tory left, Meg sat in the kitchen with her laptop, trying to find money she knew wasn't there for the townhouse. Pop was sitting on the front porch playing chess with Mr. Rosenburg, one of the neighbors. When he came in for a glass of lemonade, he saw Meg staring at the computer screen.

"Hey, baby," he said casually.

"Hi, Pop. Who's winning?"

"He is, but he cheats. Whatcha doin'?"

Meg smiled. "Tryin' to get blood from a stone. The townhouse is $225,000 and I don't see how I could comfortably afford it. Bill was a spendthrift and I wasn't left with much."

"I'll help you, you know that."

"No Pop…" She'd known he'd offer, but she couldn't accept. Before she could finish, Pop disappeared into the dining room. She could hear him going into the safe that was hidden behind a picture in there. It took him a while, but when he came back into the kitchen, he was holding an envelope.

"No, Pop, really. You've done more than enough for me."

"But this is *your* money."

Meg looked up. He had her complete attention. "What do you mean?"

"Now, don't get mad because I didn't tell you. But when your parents died, I had investors help me take care of the money your parents left you. Most of it went into your college fund, your wedding, and then you took a lot when you married." Pop sighed and looked at Meg. "But you didn't take it all. I kept some money for you in a separate account because I was suspicious of Bill and I just thought I'd hold onto some for you, you know, in case things didn't work out. If they did, I was going to give it to you in a trust fund for your kids." His eyes shifted nervously from the envelope and back to Meg. "I was just trying to do the right thing, Meg."

So, even Pop didn't have confidence in the marriage.

"How much?" Meg asked softly.

"Well, in 1975 it was only $50,000. But it must be worth three times that now. Enough for a nice down payment."

She could hardly believe it. Her jaw dropped.

"You aren't mad at me, are you?" Pop asked, still worried.

"Mad? How could I be mad? Pop, you have a way of saving me at the lowest points of my life!" she said sincerely. She got off the stool, hugged him, looked in his eyes and said, "Thank you, Pop." She stood still in amazement. "You know, it's about time I started taking care of *you*."

"Meg, no parent expects any kind of repayment. I consider you my daughter, therefore you're my responsibility."

"But I'm thirty-nine!"

"And look, you still need me."

Meg realized that, like everyone, Pop liked to be needed. Embracing him again, cheek to cheek, she whispered, "Always. How about I make you and Mr. Rosenberg a snack?"

"If you feed him, he'll never go home."

"Never mind," Meg laughed. "I'll make you some nachos."

Meg decided to take a late afternoon nap. Her cross-country trip and her emotional state the last twenty-four hours were catching up to her. After two hours, she felt someone cuddle up behind her, spooning her.

"Wake up, sleepyhead," Michael murmured in her ear. "It's time for our date. We have a seven-thirty reservation at the Columbus Inn."

Meg turned over to face him. She sleepily murmured, "Okay, handsome." She looked past his shoulder at the clock radio on the nightstand. It was one of the old ones in which the numbers flipped down. It was six-forty.

"Six-forty! I have to get ready!" she said as she jumped out of bed.

Michael leaned up on his elbow. "That's why I woke you up."

Luckily, the restaurant was close by. Meg wanted to shower and look magnificent. In reality, Michael would've thought she looked magnificent in a burlap sack.

"Out! Get out! I have to get ready!"

"Okay, okay," Michael said as he slid out of bed. He walked to her standing at the bedroom door, comically tapping her foot. He grabbed her hard, pulling her tightly toward him. It startled and delighted her. He kissed her softly and tenderly, purposely making it linger. Then he whispered in her ear, "To be continued," and swaggered down the hall to his room. Meg smiled broadly, because she knew it would be.

Meg dressed in a simple, black, sleeveless sheath dress with black heels. She couldn't remember the last time she'd dressed up like this and was happy to be going out. She couldn't stop smiling.

When she walked down the stairs, Michael was already waiting for her in the family room. He rose slowly from the couch, never taking his eyes off her. He realized his mouth was open and he closed it.

"Wow," was all he could utter.

"Thank you. Wow yourself," she said, looking at him up and down. He had on gray pleated pants, a black collarless shirt, and black jacket. "You look yummy."

"Yummy?" he protested.

"Yeah. Deal with it!"

They rode the short distance to the restaurant in Michael's green Range Rover. Located on Pennsylvania Avenue, the Columbus Inn was an old, stone colonial house converted into a fine restaurant.

They didn't pay attention to what they ordered or anything else about their surroundings. They were so wrapped up in each other, the whole restaurant could have burned down around them and they would not have noticed. They talked, drank wine, held hands, and occasionally smooched.

Meg told him all about what Pop had done for her with the investments. He told her about his latest project at work, a large home for an MBNA banking executive. When she expressed interest in seeing the plans, Michael realized how lucky he was for a woman to show interest in his endeavors. He wasn't used to a woman listening so intently. She told him vague stories about California, but when the subject of Bill came up, it was Meg who changed the subject this time.

"So, how is it living with Pop again?"

"Sometimes I feel ridiculous. I'm forty years old and living with my father." His eyes were downcast and he seemed truly embarrassed.

"I think it's wonderful," she said softly and admiringly. He looked up at her a little surprised. "He's your *father*. I'm so glad you were there when he needed you. I'll bet he fought you moving back in."

"Tooth and nail!" Michael chuckled.

"Well, you did the right thing."

He looked at her. She was amazing. What other woman would think that? He looked into her eyes for a long time. He had the urge to be alone with her immediately. Taking his money clip out of his pocket, he peeled away several bills and tossed them onto the table.

"Let's go," he said abruptly.

Meg didn't need to be asked twice.

Back at the house, they ascended the stairs, holding hands, without so much as a word spoken between them. It was understood where they were going and why. They walked into the master bedroom. It was a large, beautifully furnished room in tones of cranberry. There was a huge window seat in the front cupola, a circular, two-story, tower-like structure found in so many Victorian-style houses. The room was also equipped with a gas fireplace which Meg already envisioned using in the winter.

Michael took off his jacket, tossed it on a chair, and went to Meg, put his hands on her waist, and started kissing her neck. She had never felt this level of excitement. Tiny goosebumps covered her. She closed her eyes, but managed to utter, "Do you really think we should be doing this? After all, it's only our first date." Her last words were barely a whisper. She felt his soft lips, his whiskers on her tender skin. She positively tingled.

"We know each other so well that it's more like our *fiftieth* date," he said, not stopping the lip assault on her neck. His warm breath made her light-headed.

"Then that makes me a prude, doesn't it?" she teased.

"Mm-hmm," he murmured in the affirmative.

He unzipped her dress, peeled down one shoulder and her bra strap and let his kisses trail down to her shoulder. Meg untucked his shirt and slipped her hands up his bare back.

Before long, clothes were flying, amidst momentary clumsiness and giggles. They knelt on the bed in each other's arms, kissing passionately, unashamed of their nakedness. Michael's hands shook slightly. He'd dreamt about this day at least a thousand times, and it was happening. Meg kissed the palm of his hand, then each finger, flicking some with her tongue, nibbling others gently. He watched her do this, mouth agape, heart pounding.

She returned her attention to his handsome face, now etched with emotion. Her fingers gently touched his face as he closed his eyes. He kissed her palm as she went to cup his chin. Her eyes misted over as she took in the pleasure of simply being loved and wanted.

He lowered her to the bed and their tender touches soon began transforming into grinding needs. The endless kisses got deeper and more urgent. Michael held back for as long as he could, but unable to wait another moment, he sank into her at the same time as he sank into another kiss.

Meg's breath caught and a groan erupted from her throat.

My God, was that me?

Their lovemaking was alternately tender and passionate. They'd waited so long for one another. They took their time, wanting their first time to last forever. They explored, stroked, kissed and licked every inch of skin. All of their senses were fully alive.

It had never been like that for Meg. Never. The only person she had ever had sex with was Bill, and he was always business-like, as if he could do it with the TV remote in his free hand and still not miss any of the game or his rhythm. Sex had never lasted longer than ten minutes, including foreplay, and Meg had often been left unfulfilled. Until now, she'd thought that normal. Never had she experienced heart-stopping passion. She'd read about such passion in romance novels, but thought it must be someone's ideal, not something that anyone had actually experienced.

After they made love, they lay quietly in each other's arms, moist limbs intertwined, his skin just a shade darker than hers, allowing their heart rates to return to normal.

"You okay?" Michael finally asked. She was so quiet.

She looked up lovingly into his eyes, her own eyes glistening with tears.

"What's this?" he questioned.

"I just realized that at the age of thirty-nine, someone has made love to me for the first time," she whispered.

He looked at her in amazement. "I do love you, Meg, with all my heart."

"I love you too, Michael."

He felt as if he had died and gone to heaven. Never had he been happier than at this moment.

Meg was every bit as happy, but her thoughts turned bittersweet. "I can't stop thinking about all the time we missed. It isn't fair…"

"Meg," Michael interrupted. "There's nothing we can do about that now. We have nothing to complain about. Look at us *now*."

Meg smiled. Yes, things were perfect. "You're right," she said, cuddling back under his neck.

"Well, I'm sensible and you're full of emotion — that's why we make a good team."

"I think you have incredibly warm feelings," Meg protested. "You just don't let a lot of people see them, that's all. I also think that *I* can be *quite* sensible." They both paused to think this one over.

"Naaaaah," they said simultaneously.

More giggling.

Michael fell asleep, but Meg wasn't tired because of her nap earlier in the day. She picked up a book by the bed and read, hoping to make herself sleepy. Nope. It wasn't working. She looked at Michael asleep beside her and counted her blessings. He was exactly what she needed and she vowed to nurture this relationship. She stroked his dark, wavy hair and kissed him on the temple. Then she got a deliciously wicked idea. She slid down under the sheets and woke him up, the way every man dreams of being awakened. Michael was delightfully startled awake, smiling, moaning. They made love again, this time more urgently. So urgently, in fact, that he felt the need to apologize.

"What do you mean?" Meg asked. "Do you have any idea how sexy it is that you wanted me so much that you just *took* me? Never apologize for that, Michael. Each time will be a little different."

She was right, of course. But he was already concerned about not jeopardizing their relationship in any way whatsoever. Her words comforted him, though, and they both fell asleep, tucked neatly away within the confines of the other.

CHAPTER SIX

Sunday was special simply because she woke up in Michael's bed. Pop went to church while Michael stayed home to work. Meg slept in. She had not been able to go to church since Bill's death. It didn't feel right. So she did her praying at home and hoped God listened outside the church walls. *God is everywhere, right?*

Once she woke up and got ready for the day, she started a huge batch of Mootsie's famous spaghetti sauce. Mootsie's mother had been Italian, so her sauce was authentically good. It needed to cook a while, so she made Pop promise to keep an eye on it while she and Michael went for a walk in Brandywine Park.

Firmly enthralled with their new relationship, the couple strolled along the Brandywine River, pausing at times to sit on the rocks and smooch. Meg didn't want to leave this idyllic spot, but her interview on Monday was starting to weigh heavily on her mind.

"As much as I love this, I should get back to the house and get my résumé and portfolio in order for tomorrow."

"Do you need any help?"

"No," Meg said with a laugh.

"What's so funny?"

"Remember when you used to proofread my papers in school? You were s-o-o-o critical!"

"That's not true! Your grammar was terrible."

"No, Michael. You corrected stylistic stuff. Even the color ink I used bugged you!"

"Purple! You used a *purple* pen, and you dotted your *i*'s with big circles."

Meg laughed. She had forgotten about that.

"I'll behave. I promise," he said.

"That's what you said last night," she said, stopping to nuzzle his neck.

"Better watch out, or I'll tell everyone how you woke me up!"

"You loved it."

"Uh, yeah," as if that one was a no-brainer.

When they returned to the house, Tory and Travis were waiting with papers for the townhouse deposit. Pop had stirred and tended to the sauce like an expert while they were gone. It smelled great.

"If everything goes right, you can make settlement by the end of the week since the house isn't occupied," Tory predicted.

"Good! Hey, can you guys stay for spaghetti?" Meg pleaded. "I've made enough sauce for an army."

"Sure," they both answered at the same time.

"My woman starves me. She doesn't cook! I swear, if I have one more frozen dinner, I'm gonna marry Mrs. Swanson," Travis said.

"I don't see *you* cookin', Emeril," Tory retorted.

Meg loved listening to these two. They were so comfortable with each other.

"Do you think Luther and his girlfriend will come?" Meg asked.

"I don't know, I'll call. Luther may have a gig tonight," Tory said. "You ought to see his band sometime, Meg."

Meg went into the kitchen and filled a large pot with water. Tory came in on the cordless phone and said to Meg, covering the mouth-piece with her hand, "They can come only if it's soon. He does have a gig."

"Fine. Tell them to come over now."

Everyone pitched in so that they could eat soon after Luther and Jessica arrived. It was an old-fashioned Sunday family dinner and it was evident Pop was pleased.

Jessica was a young African-American woman of about twenty-three, Meg judged. She was quiet, sweet, and quite in love with Luther. It seemed like a very good match. From what Tory had told her, Meg thought Jessica must keep Luther grounded – at least as best as anyone could.

During dinner, Michael returned to the kitchen to fill the water pitcher, and Meg excused herself just because she wanted to be alone with him for a minute. Just when they were deeply involved in a passionate kiss, Luther walked in on them through the swinging door. He covered his eyes and dramatically screamed as though someone had thrown acid in his face.

"Aaauuughhhhhhh!!!"

Meg pressed her forehead against Michael's chest and smiled sheepishly. She had forgotten Luther didn't know about the two of them.

"Eewwww…What the hell is *this?*" he asked in disgust.

"What do you mean, 'Eewwww'?" Michael asked defensively.

"You two?" He paused. "Together? She's your…sister…it's *gross!*"

"We're not related by blood…I really don't care what you think," Michael responded, avoiding eye contact with his brother. Luther's eyes were shifting nervously between the two of them, his mouth hanging open.

"How? When…did this happen?" he sputtered.

"It *just* happened," Meg answered. "Right after I got home."

Luther's mouth was still open; he was unsure what to say. He started to say something, stopped, but then snorted, "Well, you needed to get laid anyway, Michael."

Michael had had enough. He grabbed the front of Luther's shirt with both hands and brought him to within inches of his face. Meg was startled at his reaction. Physically, Michael was an inch or two taller, but Luther was a bit more pumped up. In a fight, it would be a draw. "Is that all you think this is?" Michael hissed. "I will not have you cheapen this. Apologize to Meg, now!"

Meg felt she had to intervene. She touched Michael's forearms and tried soothing him with her words. "It's okay, Michael. He was just kidding around."

"Yeah, what she said," Luther said, still with an attitude.

Michael pushed Luther away as he released him. They continued staring daggers at each other. Luther smoothed the front of his shirt. Finally, he looked at Meg. "Sorry, Meg. Y'all just caught me off guard, ya know?"

"Sure, Luther. I guess it was a bit of a shock for you."

Luther and Michael resumed the staring contest.

"Maybe I should go," Luther offered.

"No!" Meg whined. "We haven't even finished eating yet. Michael?"

Michael finally looked at Meg and softened.

"No, Luther. You should stay," Michael said in a firm voice, more commanding than asking.

Meg went over and hugged Luther as Michael returned to the dining room.

"How did this get so serious, so fast? I've never seen Michael act this way about a woman," said Luther.

"That's because it's been brewing for a very long time."

Luther grinned from ear to ear. "And you're a *per-co-lat-ing* now!" Luther said, suggestively gyrating his hips and laughing.

Meg laughed and yelled, "Get back in the dining room, *you!*" She shook her head. Some things never changed.

Dinner resumed with lively conversation and pleasantness, even though Luther and Michael avoided speaking. Under the warm eye contact he kept getting from Meg, Michael slowly relaxed.

"Ya know, Meg, there *are* other people in the room," Tory teased.

"Oh, there are?" Meg asked, unashamed.

Travis pretended to gag on his finger, and Tory shushed him.

"I cannot believe how much this sauce tastes like Mootsie's," Tory complimented. "What a flashback."

"I was just thinking the same thing," Pop agreed.

Luther and Michael murmured agreement, but while Luther continued to eat hungrily, Michael stopped to look at Meg proudly.

"I should've paid closer attention when she was showing us how to make it," Tory continued.

"Yeah! You *should* have!" Travis said.

"Hush, puppy!" Tory said, not unkindly.

Pop rose from the table and hobbled through the family room out to the front porch as the bantering continued. Meg watched him, then decided to follow him. He hadn't finished his meal and Meg thought something could be wrong. He stood at the rail of the porch, seemingly staring at nothing.

"You okay, Pop?" Meg asked, trying to sound casual.

"Yeah," Pop answered quietly.

Meg just waited to see if he wanted to elaborate. She stared at nothing, too.

"Yesterday, you said something about me always saving you," said

Pop.

Meg just nodded her head.

"Today, you repaid me ten-fold."

"How, by taking Michael off your hands?" Meg tried to make light of the moment.

Pop smiled. "Well, that too! I meant the spaghetti."

Meg's brow furrowed. "It's just dinner, Pop."

He shook his head and smiled. "You brought Mootsie back in the house." His voice was barely a whisper. "I was feeling guilty that I was beginning to forget what she felt like, what she smelled like. Hmmm, remember that Chantilly lotion she liked?" Meg nodded. "She could've had any perfume she wanted, but she liked the drugstore stuff." He paused for a beat. "Oh, I'll never forget what she looked like 'cause we've got lots of pictures and everything to remind me. But the smell and taste of that spaghetti...I was actually lookin' for her."

"Oh, Pop, I'm sorry." Meg didn't want to be the cause of one second of heartache for this man.

"No, no. It's not like that. You got everyone together for Sunday dinner, which was something Mootsie would have done. Don't be upset. I see that look on your face, Meg. I'm melancholy, that's all. What I'm tryin' to say is that I'm grateful to you."

Meg was overwhelmed. She hugged Pop and welled up for the umpteenth time in the last two days.

Then Pop whispered in her ear, "I couldn't be happier that you're with Michael."

"Thanks, Pop. We're happy, too."

Tory came to the screen door then and said through it, "Everything okay?"

"Yeah, we're just talking about Mootsie," Meg said.

Tory pushed the door open and joined them on the porch. "It was the sauce, wasn't it?"

"Yeah," Pop said, now feeling a little foolish.

"Hey, supper's getting cold, Pop. Let's go finish," Meg prodded.

"I'll be in in a minute," Pop said, dismissing both of them.

Tory looked at Meg with concern, but Meg motioned her inside. "He's okay," she whispered.

Travis held court at the table, making everyone laugh, especially his brothers-in-law, with Tory stories. Jessica was laughing so hard she had to leave the room. Tory and Meg got back to the table in time to hear a story about Tory singing off-key in the shower, not knowing that a couple they were going out to dinner with was waiting downstairs listening to her the whole time.

"She's beltin' out this tune," Travis continued, imitating Tory singing in a terribly off-key voice.

Everyone was howling, including Tory. Travis really knew how to tell a story.

"You didn't come up and stop me, though, did you?" Tory accused her husband. But she let Travis carry on, loving the way he fit so well into her family.

"I don't know where you came from Tory," Michael teased. "You're the only one in the family who can't sing."

"Well, excuse me, Mr. Golden Pipes! Just because God gave you this amazing voice and you play piano so well, it doesn't give you the right to get all righteous with me, Michael Harrington!"

Meg felt the need to stick up for Tory. Everyone was picking on her. "Leave her alone! She enjoys her music and that's what matters."

"It's *how* she's enjoyin' it that we got a problem with!" Travis laughed.

It was true about the family being musical. Mootsie had insisted they all take piano lessons. She'd wanted each of them to be able to play an instrument and felt that the piano was the best place to start. Michael was the most proficient at piano, because he'd taken it, like everything else, so seriously. When they were younger, he had been so shy he'd refused to perform outside the house. The only reason he'd sung at Mootsie's funeral was that she had requested it while on her deathbed. Meg could play the piano well enough. Her parents had had her take piano lessons until she was twelve, and Mootsie had later persuaded her to take it up again. Tory was too impatient for piano. She'd wanted instant results and couldn't achieve a decent level fast enough, so she'd quit. Luther had played piano for only a short time before opting for drums, a better fit.

Pop came back inside, smiling at this lively table. Jessica had also returned, eyes red, shaking her head, her composure finally gained.

Luther looked at his watch. "Oooo, I've got to go!"

"Already?" Meg asked. "It's only seven-thirty."

"Got to set up," he said, referring to his gig. "Why don't you and your boyfriend here come down and take a listen?"

Meg didn't miss the touch of sarcasm in his voice. She looked over at Michael, who was tracing the rim of his wineglass with his index finger. He didn't look up.

"No, I can't tonight, Luther," said Meg. "I have to get ready for the interview tomorrow. I'm starting to push the panic button."

"Oh, yeah. Good luck with that," he said, sounding more courteous than sincere.

"Maybe we can come see you next weekend. Are you playing at the same place?"

"Yeah, but just Thursdays and Sundays. Gotta bartend on the other days."

Meg looked hopefully with raised eyebrows at Michael. Ignoring her prompt, he said to her, "Why don't you get working and I'll clean

51

up?"

"Yes, I'll help," Tory agreed.

"Me, too," Travis chimed in.

"Not me," said Pop. It appeared everything was back to normal with him.

Meg sat at her laptop at the partially cleared dining room table. Her résumé was in order, except she had to add her last job. What if they called her last school? She tried to imagine the answer they'd get.

"Oh, yes. Meg Robbins. She left after she stabbed her husband to death."

Maybe they won't call.

Flipping through her portfolio, she rearranged some pages and fixed the table of contents. She also made a few minor changes to her "Philosophy of Education." She'd changed jobs so often in the past that the interview process wasn't that intimidating. Then again, she'd never before had to hide the fact that she had killed someone. She was finishing up when Michael approached her from behind, wrapped his arms around her and kissed her on the cheek.

"How's it goin'?" he asked.

"I'm finished. I just need to print out a few pages."

"I'll do it for you," he offered.

"Thank you," she said, just inches from his lips. "You will be greatly rewarded."

He raised his eyebrows. "Give it to me –quick." He snatched the computer disk from her hand and ran from the dining room, not waiting to hear which pages she needed printed.

Tory sat down across from Meg. Having watched them, she said, "You guys look pretty happy."

"Oh Tory. He's so amazing," Meg gushed. "And *you*. You look like you have your hands full with Travis."

"Oh, *girl*…my life is never dull!"

"I really like him. He's perfect for you."

"Yes, he is," Tory agreed.

After Tory and Travis left, Meg joined Pop on the porch for coffee and a game of backgammon. Michael joined them later and watched. It was clear that he started to get impatient as the game dragged on.

"What's the matter with you?" Meg asked, noting his body language and his exaggerated sighs.

"I'm waiting to be greatly rewarded," he said. He appeared almost boy-like.

Meg smiled. He wanted her. It was mutual.

With the game unfinished and Pop winning, Meg quit and said, " `Night, Pop."

Pop watched them return to the house.

"I was winning!" he called after them.

CHAPTER SEVEN

After an early morning jog, Meg put some coffee on and showered. She hadn't slept well the night before thinking about the interview.

What if Dr. Gardner asks me about Bill? He knew Bill, too. I'll have to try to get him to focus on my employment experience.

Michael left for work early, so Meg took her time getting ready. Her teacher wardrobe consisted of long, flowing skirts; plain tops; cardigans; comfortable, pleated-front pants; and low-heeled, expensive shoes. The feet were the first to get tired and cheap shoes hurt and didn't last. No high-heels. No low-cut tops. No jackets. No short skirts. No heavy perfume. Like most teachers, she'd learned, sometimes the hard way, that these items did not work. Fluidity of movement was the key for her. Low-cut tops prevented her from bending over to help a student. Blazers were too constricting when writing on the board, or just moving around. Perfume was bad since there was almost always a kid with serious allergies.

Meg had had a short skirt fiasco during her first week of student teaching. Her cooperating teacher had asked her to hang some artwork high up in the hallway. Unfortunately, Meg's skirt was so short that when she lifted her arms to hang the artwork, there was an impromptu peep show. She was very embarrassed when the teacher stopped her and chastised her. She offered to do it the next day, but the teacher needed the artwork hung for open house, which was that night. So, after that, no more short skirts.

Today, Meg opted for something a little more professional than usual: a conservative navy blue pantsuit. It wasn't something she'd wear on a normal school day, but it was appropriate for the interview.

She was ready so early, she decided to look for Pop to see if he needed anything. The door to his room was open, but Meg knocked on it anyway.

"Pop?"

"Yeah?" He was around the corner watching *Good Morning America*. This was the first time Meg had been in the in-law suite. It was an efficient set-up. No wonder Pop liked it in here.

The room was L-shaped with a loveseat, recliner, TV and a small table for puzzles or for playing cards in the main living area. Against the wall sat a computer, which Pop loved to play around on. His secret screen name was Hot Brown Doc.

In the other part of the "L" was his bedroom. He had an oversized hospital bed, which he needed especially on his painful mornings. The bathroom was in between the two areas and had all the special equipment needed for an elderly person to care for himself.

Meg also noticed a door to the outside. Because the house was on a hill and the front steps were difficult for Pop, Michael had come up with the idea of tunneling through the hill from the street directly to Pop's room, thereby eliminating the steps for him and giving him his own entrance.

Meg hated the idea of Pop needing all the special equipment and accommodations. He wasn't supposed to get old. He was Pop. But these things helped Pop function on his own and that was important for his well-being. It was clear that Michael had had a hand in designing and equipping the room also. He'd spared no expense and it looked as though he'd thought of everything. Nothing was too good for Pop.

"What do you think?" Pop asked her as she looked the place over.

"This is great, Pop. But don't get too comfortable in here. I like to see you out and about."

Pop snorted. "Don't worry about me, Meg. I would go crazy if I couldn't get out every day."

"Good. What are you gonna do today?"

"I go to the senior center on Mondays, Wednesdays, and Fridays."

"Okay. I'll drop you."

"No, a shuttle comes to get me."

"But I can take you."

"Meg, it's covered." Pop was gently telling her to back off.

"Sorry, Pop. I'm just a little nervous about the interview."

He looked at her earnestly. "You're a wonderful teacher. You learned from the best. If Gardner is too stupid to give you a job, it's his loss. You'll find a job somewhere else. And don't worry about moving either. You stay here as long as you need to. I like having you around again."

Pop had no clue as to the true source of Meg's nervousness, but she hugged him anyway, smiling. "Thanks, Pop. I'd better go." She left through the kitchen and yelled, "Love you!"

"You better!" he yelled back.

It was strange seeing the old high school. Trophies now filled the once half-empty showcases in the lobby. Realizing she was a few minutes early, she lingered, looking for Michael in an old track picture. Dr. Gardner saw her through the office window and came out to greet her.

"Meg!" he said warmly.

"Hello!" She extended her hand, which he grasped and used to pull all of her toward him into a hug. Meg was caught off-guard, but laughed. They returned to his office, a place Meg had never had to visit in high school days. Luther, however, had known every inch of that office.

The interview was short and informal. Dr Gardner breezed through all the usual questions as he jotted notes on a legal pad. Meg asked about class-size and about the staff. At one point he asked, "How's your family?" Aware that he knew about her situation, Meg understood he meant the Harringtons.

"Great! I'm staying at the house now until I can find a place."

"And Bill?"

Meg paused and swallowed hard. "I'm afraid he's dead, Dr. Gardner."

"Oh my God! How?" He was genuinely upset.

"You know, I still have a really hard time talking about it," Meg said, avoiding the question in her best pathetic voice, her eyes downcast, her heart pounding.

"Oh! I understand. Boy, could he play football," he said almost dreamily. Then snapping out of it, said, "Well, Meg, if you want the job, it's yours."

"Yes! I'd love it!"

"Great! Let me show you your classroom."

❧

Meg had seen some bad classrooms in her life, but nothing compared to this one. It was on the first floor, at the end of a long hallway, near an emergency exit. When they walked inside, Dr. Gardner said apologetically, "You're a little low on the totem pole," referring to her lack of seniority, which would have ensured her a choice of classrooms.

Meg stepped in slowly. It smelled musty. It was filthy. Mismatching desks and chairs were strewn about. Ceiling tiles were badly stained, and some were missing altogether, exposing pipes and insulation.

"Wasn't this a science lab?" Meg asked, trying not to inhale the odor as she spoke.

"Yes, but it hasn't been for a long time."

She glanced at the filthy windows, which were nearly opaque, and noted that one had a spider-web crack in it. She glanced down at the orange carpet.

"Oh, this will be shampooed," he offered, almost with embarrassment.

There were still science cabinets lining the one wall. Right then and there, Meg decided to focus on the positives. If she didn't, she'd run away. The cabinets were good. They'd give her plenty of storage space. As for the location of the classroom, since it was far-removed from the others, she could feel free to play her music. Only the computer lab was next door, and it was not used all the time. Two other classrooms were across the hall, but the hallway would be a good sound buffer. Then there was the size of the room. Huge. Absolutely huge.

Okay, I have two and a half weeks to make this a place where my students won't need to get a tetanus shot before entering. But it's mine. All mine.

"So, how do you like it?" Dr. Gardner asked.

"It's perfect," Meg said.

Meg changed her clothes and arranged to meet Luther at the storage facility where Pop said her parents' things were kept. Since Michael and Tory were working, she had asked Luther to go with her because she didn't want to go by herself. She just wanted to see what was in the storage garage so she could plan accordingly.

The facility had garages of different sizes and Meg was surprised to see that hers was on the small side. Inside she found her parents' poster bed without a mattress, two nightstands, and two dressers. In addition, she saw the contemporary dining room set which she had always hated, an oak kitchen table and chairs, two recliners, which were musty and possibly ruined from being in storage for so long. Neatly stacked in the corner were four unmarked boxes, which Luther proceeded to put into his truck for Meg to sort through later.

"Are you interested in earning a little extra money?" Meg asked him.

"I'm *always* interested in money!" Luther said.

"Help me slowly empty this garage out. We could do a little bit every day."

"First of all, I'd rather do it all in one day, and second of all, Pop and Michael would never let me take any money from you."

Meg almost told Luther that they could keep it a secret, but the last thing she needed was another secret from Michael.

Luther sat there pondering, then said, "How about I take the dining room set? You hate it; I like it. There – we're even." He stood there looking as if he'd just solved the national debt.

"Deal!" Meg was delighted.

"Good! When do you want it moved?"

"I have to find out when the settlement is. I'll let you know."

"Okay. I want a hoagie. You wanna hoagie?" Luther's mind always seemed to be on his stomach, music, or sex –not necessarily in that order.

"Yeah, I'm starved. Is Trolley Pizza still there? I loved their hoagies."

"Oh, yeah. Let's go."

After lunch with Luther, Meg went to the hardware store and bought cleaning supplies and several cans of spray paint on clearance. The paint was a weird shade of blue, not really teal, not really royal, and the store was trying to get rid of it. She decided to clean the room and paint the chairs before moving any of her teacher supplies in.

That night, she cooked Chicken Marsala, hoping it was still Michael's favorite. Or was it Tory's? Oh well. She couldn't remember.

When he came home, it didn't matter what was cooking. They hadn't seen each other for hours and their greeting was long and R-rated.

They celebrated Meg's new job over dinner, just the three of them. Michael raved over the Chicken Marsala, even though she thought she'd overcooked it.

Pop enjoyed watching the two of them since even observing the most normal conversation between them showed how they felt about each other. It was good to see his oldest child finally in love.

Tory called and said that settlement was set up for Friday morning. She suggested that Michael could help Luther with the storage garage on Saturday.

That got Meg thinking about the boxes that Luther had put in the parlor. The parlor was a small room on the other side of the foyer, with French doors for privacy. It contained the bottom part of the

Victorian cupola and was the perfect space for the baby grand piano which sat there. In the remainder of the parlor, there were floor-to-ceiling bookshelves jammed with books, and two brown leather wing chairs. Off to the side was Pop's desk, which looked as though it wasn't used much anymore. In fact, this whole room looked unused. She loved this room. She remembered curling up in one of the chairs doing her homework while she listened to Michael play the piano.

"Come play the piano for me while I go through the boxes," she coaxed him after dinner.

"Okay, but I haven't played in a while."

"Too long," Pop said.

As Michael began to pick out notes, Meg sat on the floor and tore into the first storage box, which contained some silver items, including her parents' engraved wedding gifts. She stared at the items, slightly tarnished despite being in protective blue cloth, and felt no connection to them. No memories. The second and third boxes contained knick-knacks, some of which she recognized as being from her father's office: his framed diploma, a picture of Meg from freshman year that she'd always hated, a paperweight in the shape of a dog. She pondered that. They had never owned a dog, yet her father had a paperweight of one. Maybe he'd always wanted a dog. She wondered what else she didn't know about her father.

Meg also wondered who'd packed these boxes and how they'd decided what to keep. Probably Mootsie. Right around the time of the funeral, people had tended to do stuff for her and she'd just let them. She remembered how Michael had stayed home from school with her for a couple of days when she wasn't ready to go back. He'd just held her as she cried.

Michael's words from earlier echoed in her mind. *"I was in love with you even then."*

Meg smiled and looked over at him. He was playing different things on the piano: Mozart, Billy Joel, Scott Joplin. He hadn't lost his touch. She paused for a few minutes just to enjoy the music. He played with such feeling that he seemed to get lost in the music sometimes.

The last box was full of photographs, some loose, some framed. Her parents' wedding album. A photo album from her childhood. Flipping through, her hand went to her mouth as she studied old photos of herself at various functions and holidays. She looked happy, but without siblings, she was almost always alone. A few shots were with her dad, but only two were with her mom. Her mom hated having her picture taken, unlike Mootsie who would ham it up every time the camera was pointed in her direction.

Michael glanced at Meg and saw she was looking at an album of photos. He stopped playing and went to her. He sat behind her and leaned into her, looking over her shoulder. She was glad he was there and leaned back. They chuckled at some of the goofy shots of Meg but when she got to her awkward pre-adolescent years, she slammed the book shut and said, "That's enough!"

She peered into the box to see if there was anything else. Inhaling sharply, she pulled out a framed photo. She had forgotten all about this picture. Her father had taken it at the Harringtons' Christmas party, just weeks before the accident. He'd enlarged it and framed it for Meg for a Christmas gift. It was a candid shot of Meg, Michael, Tory, and Luther in various stages of laughter and hugging, and it was priceless.

"Look!" Meg put her hand to her chest.

"Oh, that's so good! I don't think I ever saw that picture," Michael said.

"My father took it. I forgot all about it. It has to be Christmas

1975. Well, this will have to be in a prominent place in my townhouse."

"We should get an updated one taken."

"Yes! That's a wonderful idea."

Meg realized that this was Michael's way of telling her to live in the present. What they meant to each other now and in the future was more important than the past.

Oh, if it were only that easy to move forward.

That week, Meg worked her tail off at school, cleaning her classroom and spray-painting desks and chairs that needed it. She was able to get the cracked window replaced after asking every day in the front office. As promised, the carpet was shampooed, but improved it only marginally. She met very few other teachers.

Every night, she returned to the house bone-tired. Every night, Michael gave her a back rub until she fell asleep.

Finally, by Thursday afternoon, the classroom was clean enough to move some of her stuff in. She recognized even more potential now, seeing everything without all the layers of grime and with a fresh coat of paint.

Friday came and so did the townhouse settlement. Michael insisted on a home inspection due to the age of the house. Meg agreed and everything went off without a hitch, leaving her time to clean the townhouse. Fortunately, it didn't need nearly as much elbow grease as the classroom had.

Friday night, Michael came by with Chinese food. He threw a tablecloth on the floor and set up candles for an indoor picnic. He forgot plates and glasses, but it didn't matter. They ate with chopsticks out of the containers and swigged wine directly from the bottle.

"This is so romantic, except for the fact that I feel like a scrub woman." Meg felt decidedly dirty and unattractive. "You're gonna love this, too. I conveniently forgot to order a mattress, so even with the bedroom furniture coming tomorrow, I don't have a bed. So if you don't mind…"

"Say no more. You can stay with me. Hey, I'm gonna miss you in my bed when you move in."

"What do you mean? We'll just take turns at each other's place."

Michael smiled and nodded in agreement. "Let's go back to the house and you can take a nice long bath while I put some of your stuff in the Rover for tomorrow."

"Thank you. I don't know what I'd do without you."

"Don't ever find out."

❦

The next day, Saturday, Luther and Michael emptied the storage garage in several trips. Meg ordered a queen mattress over the phone for delivery Monday. She cleaned some more and directed the guys where to put things. When they finished and looked around the house, it still seemed empty. But she couldn't face furniture shopping just yet. Things had started to overwhelm her. It was too much, too fast.

The murder.

The statement to the police.

The packing.

The driving.

The new love.

The job.

The townhouse.

The scrubbing.

The secret.

Michael found her sitting on the kitchen floor, back against the kitchen cabinet, in tears. He sat next to her and gathered her into his arms. He wordlessly comforted her, not asking what was wrong, but waiting for her to tell him.

"I don't have a potato peeler!" she wailed.

With furrowed brows, Michael looked at her in confusion. "I...I'll get you one, honey."

He hugged her, not realizing the extent of her exhaustion, both physical and mental.

Meg sobbed uncontrollably. He grew more concerned, and held her tighter. Finally, realizing that it wasn't just about a potato peeler, he asked, "What is it, Meg?"

"I don't have anything yet. I have too much to do," she managed to choke out.

"Okay, okay. Listen to me," he told her as he cradled her. "You stay with me for as long as you want to. No one is making you move in right away. He cupped her face, pressed his nose to hers and said, "Okay?"

Lip still trembling, she nodded and said, "Hold me."

He held her tightly, but he was worried. He wondered if there was something more, something she didn't want to talk about. But he didn't have to ask. He knew she would talk about it eventually, if it were important enough.

CHAPTER EIGHT

After a restful Sunday, due largely to Michael's insistence, Meg returned to school Monday morning with the intent of staying only a half-day.

For the first time, the door to the classroom across the hall from her room was open. She stuck her head inside and called, "Hello?"

A young blond-haired man was standing on a chair taping up new posters. Of average build, he looked to be in his mid-twenties. Meg didn't think she had ever seen anyone with skin so ghostly pale, especially in late summer.

"Hi!" he shouted from across the room. "Are you Meg?"

"Yes!" Meg answered, pleased that he already knew about her.

He jumped down from the chair, hand extended. "I'm Leon. Leon Burns. I teach eleventh and twelfth grade language arts."

"Nice to meet you. I teach ninth and tenth grade social studies."

"Yes, I know! I'm so glad you're here. I've been lonely down at this end of the hall. Well, actually, I have the asshole next door to me, but he doesn't count. That's a whole 'nother story anyway." He laughed at himself. Meg just smiled a fake first-meeting smile. Then he looked around as if he was going to tell her some big secret. He placed his hand by his mouth and whispered, "He's homophobic. Oh sure, he denies trying to get me fired last year, but I know it was him."

Too much information!

Meg felt the need to change the subject. "Wanna see what I've done to my room?"

The rest of the morning, Meg and Leon visited each other, lent materials, and shared snacks each had brought.

Meg had been told that she would be teaching American History of the 1800s to ninth grade and of the 1900s to tenth grade. She had three classes of each, with twenty-eight students being her smallest class and thirty-two, her largest.

Huge classes. But, I'll manage. Better than the thirty-seven that time.

She then realized she only had thirty desks. She and Leon went on a scavenger hunt for desks but no one was willing to part with any, especially for the new teacher. Finally, she just took two from the computer lab. Then she had problems finding where the previous social studies teacher had stored the textbooks. When she finally found them, they were in a utility closet on the second floor. They smelled like a combination of Pine-Sol and mold. She looked up and saw that the closet had a water problem, if the stained ceiling tiles were any indication. Why someone would keep books in here was anyone's guess. She and Leon hauled them down and Meg painstakingly wiped each one down and let them all dry and air out on the windowsill. It was while cleaning them that she noticed the copyright date of 1987.

Oh boy. No wonder they were so beat up.

She'd have to read them thoroughly and supplement her lessons with other interesting material. Normally, she did that anyway. She'd found that textbooks often had mistakes in them sometimes and they were too boring to stand alone. The age of the textbook alone wasn't as serious a matter since she was teaching turn-of-the century material.

Meg's lessons were her strong suit. Her students were rarely bored with the material because of the way she presented it. The only reason she used a text at all was because the school district mandated it. She had enough material for the nineteenth century to start the year, but a lot more for the early twentieth century.

She also liked to integrate social studies with other subjects, such as language arts, art, and especially music. Teachers from the "new school" were trained to do this as much as possible. "Old school" teachers resisted, not wanting to change the same lesson plans they'd had for a hundred years.

Music was Meg's thing. She liked to expose her students to many types of music, knowing that many children had heard only two or three different types. She played music in her homeroom, starting and ending the day with music. She also found ways to fit it into social studies. She called it her "music regimen," and it had proved very effective in the past. She fully intended to continue.

That day while she was organizing, a deliveryman rapped on her open door.

"You Meg Robbins?"

"Yes." Meg looked at him inquisitively, trying to remember what she'd ordered that was being delivered.

"Where do you want it?" he asked.

"Want what?"

"The piano," he answered, handing her a card.

Meg tore open the card which simply said, "Here's to many music-filled days and Michael-filled nights." Okay, he wasn't a poet, but she loved him anyway. She made a mental note to reward him greatly.

Meg moved on to planning her entire year. Her creative juices flowed as she got down to the nitty gritty of how she'd integrate art and literature into social studies.

As she shuffled the boxes of her extensive slide collection, she realized how beautifully the ones of immigrants at Ellis Island could tie in with her lessons from these decades, as would E.L. Doctorow's

Ragtime, which was set at the turn of the century. It had been her dream come true when *Ragtime* was made into a musical. Her lesson plans would include reading parts of the novel aloud as well as generous sampling of the music.

Before she knew it, it was lunchtime. She felt wonderfully in control, especially considering her emotions on Saturday.

She went to the mall for lunch and stopped at the kitchen store there. She bought so many kitchen necessities, including a potato peeler, that the salesperson had to help her carry packages out to the car. She still needed more, but it was a start. Buying everything new was an experience, but she didn't regret leaving everything from her old kitchen behind. It would have reminded her of the blood-filled room where her husband lay dead.

She took all her new purchases to the townhouse and awaited her mattress delivery. Once the mattress got there, she decided to leave even though she wasn't finished putting things away. She was going to follow Michael's advice and not push herself to the point of exhaustion again.

When she arrived back at the house, Pop was cooking some of his famous crab soup, which Meg loved. Though it stunk like the inlet down at the beach when she entered the house, it was nevertheless a good smell.

Michael arrived soon after Meg, and she excitedly told him about her progress that day. She wrapped her arms around his neck and said, "Thank you so much for the piano. You really shouldn't have."

"You're welcome," he murmured. She was about to continue talking when she noticed his distracted look. She cocked her head. "Something wrong?"

"I have to go away on business for a few days," he said. "Jack Whitman wants me to fly to Chicago so he can see the plans for his house thus far. He's not going to be home for several weeks and we have deadlines to meet. It'll only be for a few days. I should be home in time for the weekend." He looked at her apologetically. He hated leaving her after her emotional episode on Saturday.

"Oh, I'll miss you! When do you leave?" she asked, trying to mask her disappointment by sounding upbeat.

"Tomorrow morning. Could you stay here with Pop while I'm gone?"

"She doesn't need to," Pop said.

"I don't even have any sheets yet, Pop. Gimme a break," Meg said truthfully.

Meg and Michael retired early, wanting to stock up on several days worth of affection. She missed him already. And she felt guilty. Not telling him about how Bill had died was weighing heavily on her.

How will I tell him? How will he react?

"Michael, I need to tell you something," Meg started. Just then the phone rang and Michael answered it.

"Oh, yes, Mr. Whitman. Yes, I'll be out tomorrow. Let me get the plans." Michael got out of bed and took the phone into his old room, which was now his study. By the time he got back to bed, Meg was asleep.

Meg used the rest of the week to get organized, spending half days at school, followed by afternoon shopping. One night, she and Tory did a girls-night-out, shopping, eating dinner and talking girl-talk.

Tory made her buy a sexy nightgown — a tight, short, black lace number.

"Do you know how long this is going to stay on?" Meg laughed.

"Put it at the bottom of the bed in case of fire," Tory answered, smiling a devilish smile.

The evening felt as comfortable as when they were teenagers. She was grateful for Tory's calming effect. No matter what was happening, Tory made it seem like everything was going to work out.

Meg and Pop split dinner responsibilities, but on Friday they decided to go out. Meg was stunned by the looks she and Pop received at the steakhouse where they ate. She had gotten stares with Michael also, but not as many since he was lighter-skinned. Meg assumed people stared at Michael either because they couldn't get a handle on his race or because he was so handsome. But with Pop, people blatantly pointed and whispered.

"Look, people are wondering what you're doing with an old man," Pop teased, knowing that the age difference wasn't the only reason for the stares.

"I don't remember you going through this with Mootsie," Meg said.

"You must be kidding, Meg. I started dating Mootsie in 1956 in Richmond, Virginia. I had to ride in the back of the bus while Mootsie rode in the front." He smiled at her apparent ignorance.

Meg shook her head. She knew this had happened, of course. What kind of social studies teacher would she be if she didn't know all the details of the civil rights movement? But it was a different thing entirely knowing that this man who was so dear to her had experienced such prejudice.

"Couldn't she sit in the back of the bus with you?"

"Where would all the other Negroes sit?"

Meg pondered this and paused, staring at Pop. "I knew this stuff happened, Pop," Meg said, her face tight, her jaw clenched. "But suddenly it's personal, you know?" She looked down at her plate, then up at Pop again. "It got better for you when you moved to Delaware, didn't it?" Meg was hopeful.

"There will always be racists, Meg, no matter where we live. It's too bad all white people aren't like you, and like Mootsie and your parents."

Meg had been so wrapped up in her own selfish adolescence that she hadn't realized what Pop and Mootsie had experienced.

Partly because she was angry with herself, she grew increasingly agitated as the dinner progressed, even as they talked about other things. Finally, she threw her fork down.

"I feel like screaming at these people! How can you be so calm?" she asked him accusingly.

Without missing a bite, Pop simply said, "Experience."

"It doesn't bother you?"

"Not any more."

Pop changed the subject so that by the end of the meal, Meg had calmed a bit. While they were walking out of the restaurant in plain view of the other patrons, she took Pop's arm and planted a warm kiss on his cheek.

"Let them chew on that," she said.

"You're bad," Pop chuckled.

"Believe me, Pop, if it wasn't for the fact that it would be completely inappropriate, I would've French kissed you."

Pop almost fell down laughing on the steps of the restaurant. Meg giggled, too, attracting even more stares. Neither one cared.

That night, Meg slept in Michael's bed where she had slept all week. She had missed him terribly though he'd called her every night. Suddenly, she felt someone slide into bed with her. Startled, she sat bolt upright, only to see Michael smiling back at her. She squealed and threw herself into his arms. He laughed as she covered his face with kisses. Since it was the middle of the night, he had new whiskers growing, and Meg brush-burned her lips with her assault on his face.

"What are you doing home? I thought you weren't coming home until tomorrow!"

"I took the red eye," he said matter-of-factly.

"I'm so glad," she murmured against his lips. Everything was right in the world again for Meg. Michael was home.

Meg officially moved into the townhouse on Saturday afternoon, after sleeping in late with Michael. He was impressed at what she had accomplished with the house while he was gone.

Everything was new: a blue plaid sofa, a navy blue recliner, light oak end tables and a twenty-five inch TV. She had passed on using the recliners that were in storage in her house, but opted instead to use them in her classroom. One more lamp and a stereo were still needed, and a country-style oak dining set was on order.

The kitchen was almost complete, except for a microwave and some table linens. The most important thing in her kitchen was her boom box. She loved to cook and to listen to music while she did it.

That night, they ate pizza and drank beer in the den, while Meg chatted endlessly about her classroom and her co-worker, Leon.

"Leon? What's he like?" Michael asked.

"He's young, blond, nice, and good-looking."

"Really?" Michael asked cynically with raised eyebrows.

"Yeah," Meg teased, smiling.

"*How* good-looking?"

"Very. You're not jealous are you?"

"Yes!"

"You have nothing to worry about."

"Yeah, well…"

"He's gay, Michael."

"How do you know that?"

"It was one of the first things he told me, believe it or not. I think it's cute that you're jealous. No other man will ever mean what you do to me."

She cuddled next to him. He smiled, kissed her on the head and closed his eyes, satisfied.

⁂

That night they went to The Barfly, the bar where Luther worked. It was a nice place, as far as city bars go, one of those places that looks much better in the dark than in the light. It had two large bars, a sprawling dance floor, and smelled of stale beer that had soaked into the flooring. The clientele was a mix of people, different races, young and old. The place was getting crowded since it was a Saturday night, but Meg and Michael got there early enough to get two stools at the bar Luther was tending. Music supplied by a DJ played as background music since it was early.

They sat, drank beer, and talked to Luther whenever he had a moment. Meg couldn't help noticing what a flirt Luther was while working. Because of his good looks, he seemed to be able to get away with very sexually explicit behavior. She wondered if Luther was selling himself for tips.

If that were Michael flirting, I couldn't stand it.

When Jessica showed up with a girlfriend, Meg assumed that Luther would start behaving. But he didn't. Jessica looked over at him from her table a few times, then looked away. She couldn't stand it either. As if reading Meg's thoughts, Michael asked Luther, "Aren't you laying it on a little thick with the ladies?"

"Naaa, I always do this. This is *me*. If you don't like it, you don't have to watch," Luther said, challenging him. Michael's jaw clenched and a vein bulged in his temple.

"Nope. I don't." Michael suddenly rose from his stool and after draining his glass said, "Let's go," to Meg without looking at her.

"Let's say 'hi' to Jessica."

Michael didn't respond but followed Meg to Jessica's table to offer stiff, uncomfortable 'hi's' and 'bye's.'

Michael stewed all the way home, driving with teeth clenched. Finally, he exploded. "What is with him? Will he ever learn? I don't know what to do! He's going to get fired or lose Jessica or both!" Meg smiled at him. Michael made a double take at her, disbelieving her amusement.

"Why in the world are you smiling?"

"Because you sound like his dad. Leave him alone. He's a big boy now and not your responsibility. His mistakes are his own."

"But *I'm* always the one to bail him out of a jam, and I'm sick of it!" Then in a whincy voice, he imitated Luther. '*Michael, can you lend me money? Michael, can you pick me up — I'm too drunk to drive. Michael, I'm stranded at the beach. Come get me.*' He turned to Meg. "You know what else? I'm sick of you defending him. You've been doing that since we were kids."

"I just think that you need to pick your battles. You know, not get mad at him for every little thing."

They pulled into Meg's driveway and Michael made no motion to get out of the car.

"Are you coming in?" she asked.

"No, I don't think so."

Meg felt momentary panic. *What have I done? I spoke my mind. Hopefully he'll cool down. I just wish he'd cool down with me next to him.*

"Okay," she said softly, and leaned over to kiss him. He kissed her obligatorily, but no more.

Meg went to bed and tossed and turned for hours. Finally, she resorted to watching an old movie and drinking a warm cup of tea. But nothing could take her mind off Michael. He had quickly become her world, and she didn't know what to do now that he was angry with her. There was probably a lot she didn't know about Luther that had happened while she was gone all those years. Maybe she shouldn't have said what she had. All she knew was that she'd have to make it right.

Several hours later, she watched the clock until it hit eight. She wasn't going to wait a moment longer to see Michael. She had to see him and sped the short distance over to his house. She walked in as she usually did. The front door was unlocked. Since the house smelled like coffee, he was probably up. Unless it was Pop. Going into the kitchen, she saw Michael standing at the sink. He turned when the swinging door to the kitchen opened and looked at her. She couldn't get an automatic reading on him. While they stared at each other, Meg counted the ticks on the kitchen clock. One, two, three, four, five... Then he walked toward her, not taking his eyes away from hers. He fully wrapped her in his arms and whispered, "I'm sorry." Meg squeezed her eyes shut, sighed, and grew limp with relief.

"I'm sorry, too. I shouldn't comment when I don't really know..."

"No, you're right. I could be handling things better."

"He depends on you."

"He uses me."

She looked at him and pondered this.

"It wouldn't be so bad if he thanked me once in a while... Oh, hell, I don't want to talk about him anymore."

He embraced her again, this time for several minutes.

"I hope he doesn't mess things up with Jessica," Meg said finally, looking up into his eyes.

"See, that's what I mean. Now *you're* worried about it. Follow your own advice and let him go." He looked at her and brushed the hair away from her face. "I didn't sleep all night," he confessed.

"Me neither."

"Let's go lie down," he said, already walking toward the back staircase and leading her by the hand.

"Okay," she said. Nothing sounded better.

They lay down cuddled next to one another and were asleep the minute their eyes closed.

CHAPTER NINE

Though Meg's first impressions of people were usually dead-on, she tried not to size up her students on the first day. She also tried not to listen to teachers who had already taught them. She wanted to give each student the benefit of the doubt. When Leon tried to pass along rumors about a few of her incoming students, she refused to listen. She would judge for herself.

Meg never demanded respect from her kids, just because she was the authority figure. Things weren't the same as when she was a student in high school. Back then, the students had to think that the teacher was some super being who never had to do the things that mere mortals did. She'd never seen a teacher drink coffee, smoke, or even blow her nose. Now a teacher had to *earn* the respect of the students and quite often, it was an uphill battle.

Meg heard her students out in the hall before the bell rang that first day, laughing about the "fresh meat" waiting in the classroom. They knew she'd heard them, too. They were attempting to establish control right away.

But Meg didn't intimidate easily. After the bell rang, she asked a group of boys to come inside the classroom. One African-American boy shot a warning look at her. His brows were knitted so tightly that Meg was willing to bet that the lines between his eyes were permanent even when his face was relaxed. There was a lot of anger in that face. When he refused to come into the classroom, not wanting her to tell him what to do, she closed the door. The rest of the kids in her racially and ethnically mixed classroom looked at each other.

"What about Ronald?" one girl asked.

"And your name?" Meg asked.

"Taahira."

"Well, Taahira, one thing you have to know about me is that I only ask things once. The bell is your signal to come in and sit down. I asked the group in the hall to come in. Technically, that's two requests. Ronald doesn't appear to *want* to come in." She shrugged. "No big deal."

The students exchanged more looks, not knowing what to make of her. Meg took attendance and told the kids about her music philosophy. She then told them that each morning they would be writing in a journal pondering a question she'd give them. Although the journals would be personal, if anyone wanted her to read a page, they could post a flag on it. Otherwise, she explained, she would flip through to make sure the writings were current. They all groaned, as if writing that early in the morning would make their brains explode right out of their temples.

"I can't write that early in the morning," a boy named Geoffrey whined.

Meg remembered him as having been with Ronald out in the hallway. She looked at him and made an exaggerated pouty face, her lip so far extended that a bird could've perched on it. Everyone laughed, including Geoffrey.

Okay, this is going pretty well.

Meg wondered what Ronald was doing out in the hall, but she refused to give him the satisfaction by looking out. In fact, he was out there wondering what to do. There could be no graceful entrance now – only a grand entrance – yeah, totally attention getting. When he heard the music, curiosity got the better of him. He opened the door and sauntered toward a desk in the back of the room, leaving the door open – another power play.

Meg walked over to the door and shut it. She didn't speak to him; she refused to give him a stage. Ignoring him, she just listened to the song with everyone else and shuffled papers. When the bell rang, the students slowly rose out of their seats to go to their first period class. Eight remained since they had first period with Meg.

"Ronald, may I see you please?"

"Ooooooooooooo." The wail rose from the kids so predictably that Meg did it with them. Ronald walked as slowly as he could to her, making her wait.

"Hi, I'm Ms. Robbins." She extended her hand. He didn't. Meg lowered hers. "You'll have to go to the front office to let them know you're here."

"What?" The same angry face, this time with disbelief added.

"I marked you absent."

"You saw me in the hall. You knew I was here."

"If you're not in my room before attendance is taken to the office, you will be marked absent. Now you have to straighten it out." Meg never looked away from his eyes. To do so would be submissive. He tried staring her down, but she refused to look away first.

"Man, you're dissing me. I don't like people who diss me." He looked away first. He was still mumbling when he walked out into the hallway.

"See you third period," Meg called after him.

After a few weeks, Meg began sizing up the students. She was pretty sure Ronald was the leader of some sort of a gang or wanna-be gang. His "friends" were more than just a group of friends. They seemed to be afraid of him at times. He butted heads with Meg almost daily, mostly over minor things – pencil-tapping, loud gum-chewing, sharpening a pencil in the middle of a discussion. All of these behaviors were typical attention-getting ploys. Because of her teaching experience, Meg knew how to handle everything he threw at her. She ignored minor infractions, knowing that one day she'd earn his respect enough for him to stop on his own. The more obnoxious stuff – burping, laughing at inappropriate times – she handled privately. She saw him three times a day, twice for homeroom and once for social studies.

Ronald's cronies were quite an assortment and served as an eager audience for him. Geoffrey was a heavyset black boy with a rather pleasant disposition. He had a high-pitched voice and seemed to smile most of the time. It made him appear almost dopey. Meg wouldn't have guessed that he would be a friend with Ronald, but then she found out that they were cousins. Others in the gang tried their best to be angry, but Meg practically stood on her head to get her students to smile. Jesse was a lanky, light-skinned black boy who was quiet but didn't smile or make too much eye contact with Meg. Louis was amiable enough, but Meg had a distrust of him. He was a little too quiet, sneaky.

The girls were an interesting assortment, too. Meg felt an immediate attraction to Erika, but she wasn't sure why. She was a cooperative, sweet, African American girl with a timid disposition.

One morning in mid-October, Dr. Gardner came to observe her class, which was not unusual. In fact Meg had expected him earlier in the year, considering she was new to the school. She was used to being observed and had enough confidence in her lessons that she never really worried. Her lesson that day was America's entry into World War I. They discussed whether the U.S. should have gone to war in the first place. Meg played music of the period: George M. Cohan's "Over There," then a song called "I Didn't Raise My Boy to be a Soldier." These two songs showed different points of view about the war and patriotism.

The lesson went well, and Dr. Gardner told her so afterward.

"I've been hearing about your music. It works well. But we have a little problem. I've gotten three requests for transfers into your class from Jim Morrelli's class."

Jim Morrelli was the teacher next door to Leon, who barely grunted hello when Meg passed him in the hall. He was a middle-aged, balding white man, who apparently came from money, but had opted to be a teacher, despite his wealthy background. He let anyone who would listen know what a sacrifice he'd made when he could be doing just about anything else.

"Jim's not too happy about all the requests. He thinks you put the kids up to it," Dr. Gardner said.

"Well, I didn't, of course. How is this *my* problem?"

"Maybe you're being too easy on the kids."

"I'm not easy on them. They are learning. And I'm a good teacher. Maybe he's not," Meg said matter-of-factly. She was starting to simmer.

"I'm going to have to make a policy of no transfers."

"Fine. Do what you have to do."

Given her look of irritation, Dr. Gardner looked hesitant about continuing. "There's something else."

"What?"

"You can't play *Ragtime* in your class anymore."

"Ragtime music in general or *Ragtime* the musical?" Meg asked incredulously.

"*Ragtime* the musical."

"What? Why not?"

"I got a call from a parent about one of the songs having the phrase 'SOB' in it. Is that true?"

The baseball song. Meg couldn't believe it. "Yes, but... Do these parents hear what their kids are listening to at *home?* They listen to incredibly vulgar music. Or hate music. The song the parent is talking about is a parody. It's funny! But it also makes a point about the different ethnic groups that were starting to flood the country at the time."

"But it does have 'SOB' in it?"

He wasn't listening. She paused, beginning to get frustrated. "Yes. I thought the kids could handle it." He didn't appear interested in the explanation.

"You can't use *Ragtime.*"

"No, Dr. Gardner. I won't use the baseball song, but if you forbid me from using the whole CD, it will ruin my entire unit."

He pondered this. "Okay. There are no other bad words, are there?"

"Not that I can think of."

After he left, Meg sat stewing. The usual problems: You don't hear from parents at all sometimes. They don't come to open house. They don't return phone calls. The minute they hear one slightly objectionable thing, they're on your case. It was so typical, yet it still angered Meg.

"Unbelievable," Meg said out loud to an empty classroom.

The same day that Meg was observed by Dr. Gardner, Meg got a visit from the band director, Marcus Taylor, a young hyperactive black man with, normally, a very pleasant disposition. Meg felt that band teachers, including Marcus, were a very special breed of people with unlimited amounts of patience – patience surpassed only by the amount of Excedrin in their desks for all the headaches that went along with it.

Marcus and Meg had talked many times in the teachers' lounge at lunch, mostly about jazz, until Leon would whine that he didn't know who they were talking about and force them to change the subject to pop music.

But today Marcus was not happy.

"What in the hell do you think you're doing?" he yelled.

Meg was taken aback. She couldn't imagine what she had done to upset him. She mentally went into rewind, but just came up empty. "What did I do?"

"Four sophomores in the past week have come to me wanting to join the jazz band."

Meg was excited. "That's great!"

"No, no, it's not!"

Meg shook her head and repeated in a low voice, "No, no, it's not," as if repeating it would somehow make her understand.

"All of my new students are usually freshman and I'm prepared for them, instrument-wise, before the school year starts. Or they already are playing and have an instrument. I don't have instruments for these sophomores. And *they* sure don't have the money to buy or rent their own instruments."

"Oh." Meg rubbed her forehead. This was turning into a helluva day. "Is there anything I can do?"

"Yeah, find me some instruments!"

"What kind do you need?"

"*Jazz band* instruments," he said as if she were stupid. "You know, trumpets, trombones, saxophones…"

"Okay, okay, let me see what I can do."

He nodded firmly, his brow still furrowed, puzzled about how to end the confrontation now that she had offered to help.

"By the way," he said, "Sammy Carpenter wants me to call him 'Tricky Sam' after…"

"Joe 'Tricky Sam' Nanton," Meg said, giggling.

"This is before he's even *touched* a trombone! I told him when he could play like 'Tricky Sam' Nanton, then I'll call him that. *Sheeeiiiiitt!*"

Meg was laughing so hard now that Marcus couldn't help laughing too. He couldn't stay mad at her. She was one of the good ones. And she was going to get him some instruments.

CHAPTER TEN

The first few months flew by. Some of the kids had really warmed to Meg, especially Erika and Maria. They hung around her desk constantly peppering her with questions, wanting some inside info. The boys stayed more distant, but seemed less angry. She actually saw Ronald smile once. After class, she approached him and said, "You've got a great smile, Ronald. I wish I could see it more." Caught off guard, he actually smiled again.

One day Meg got to school early enough to play the piano in her classroom. She played for a while before she realized she had an audience of students standing in the doorway.

"You play good!" Brandy said.

"No, I play *well*. I'm okay I guess." They approached her at the piano.

"Yo, Ms. Robbins, can you teach me some piano?" Geoffrey asked, quite sincerely.

Truthfully, Meg didn't have time to give him piano lessons, but she found herself saying, "Well, Geoffrey, I have some beginner books and I can show you the notes. Can you read music?"

"No."

"Oh. Have you considered joining the band here at school?"

They all burst out laughing, so much so that it took a minute for them to calm down.

"Yeah, but nobody *cool* is in the band!" Jesse finally said.

"Maybe not yet," Meg said. "But if *you* joined, there would be."

More laughter, only more hysterical this time.

"Anyway, Geoffrey, I get here at seven-thirty and I don't go home until around four-thirty. That gives you a little time before or after school to fool around on the piano, but I can't guarantee that I can help you every day."

"Okay, Ms. Robbins! Thanks!"

Ronald shook his head in half-hearted disapproval. However, Geoffrey seemed undeterred, if his smile was any indication.

From that day forward, Geoffrey showed up sometimes in the morning but more often after school and pecked away at the piano. Meg had never seen such tenacity. She was worried when Ronald started staying with him, afraid he'd interfere in some way. But Ronald dozed in a recliner, pestered Meg, and periodically showed actual interest in what Geoffrey was attempting to play.

A few days later, Meg was returning to her classroom when she was stunned to see Ronald by himself playing a simple tune from one of the books Meg had lent to Geoffrey.

"You know how to play?" Meg asked, not masking her surprise in the least.

"No," he said, not looking at her.

Then what am I hearing?

Meg just stood there with her hands on her hips staring at him. She was afraid if she talked too much, he'd stop.

"I just picked it up, ya know? I sing too."

Meg raised her eyebrows. "Will you sing for me?" she asked

almost breathlessly.

"No."

"Someday?"

No answer. Meg decided not to push any further.

Teachers didn't visit students' homes much anymore, but Meg liked it. Her visits commenced in October and continued into November. Some families, like Maria's and Brandy's, were welcoming. Others seemed suspicious of her intentions, and at too many of the homes there were no answers when she knocked at the door. She knew some of the parents worked two and three jobs just to have food on the table, and she understood that when they weren't working, they were probably sleeping. She figured the last thing they wanted was a teacher knocking at the door.

But Meg got some idea of her student's living conditions. Their homes ranged from Trolley Square townhouses like her own, to total squalor in unsafe areas. Ronald's stood in a well-known drug dealing area. His house had badly peeling paint and a doorknob that looked too filthy to touch. While she waited for a response to her knock, she smelled something unpleasant, maybe the general decay of the neighborhood. As she gave up and turned away, Meg got a creepy feeling. She remembered that this was the neighborhood that a five-year-old boy had been gunned down in a barbershop while having his hair cut.

She'd really wanted to talk to Ronald's mother about music, about his potential. He was showing a real talent for both music and math and often stunned her with his insightful comments in class discussions. Meg was dying to read his journal but he never flagged his pages for her to read. She knew there was something more to his tough-kid exterior, something cerebral, something aching to get out.

Then the day came in the midst of a discussion about what motivated Coalhouse Walker's violent behavior in *Ragtime*. Was it Sarah's violent death? Was it the trashing of new Model T? Ronald surprised Meg yet again with his insight. Without raising his hand, Ronald spoke out.

"It's not about things or any certain person. Not really. He just wants to be treated like the white man. He wants due process. He wants them to pay for the way he was treated. He's educated and a trained musician. He was all hopeful in the beginning and all. But now he sees how it *really* is. He's finding out that no matter how hard he tries to better himself, as long as his skin is black, he won't get treated the same in court or anywhere else.

At that moment the bell rang and the students packed to leave the classroom. Meg sat perched on the corner of her desk looking at Ronald in astonishment.

Soon, November rolled around, bringing Meg's fortieth birthday. Michael planned a family dinner celebration on Sunday at the Green Room at the Hotel duPont, even though her actual birthday was Monday. Meg decided to fight forty with everything she had. She attacked with a dark green, tight-fitting dress that she'd especially picked for the somber occasion because it didn't make her *look* forty. It showed off her slim figure, but wasn't too daring for the conservative crowd at the Hotel duPont.

Before dinner, when Michael came to pick her up, he took one look at her dress and whistled his approval, looking her up and down.

"I'm gonna have to give you your present now," he said. "You'll understand why when you see it. He reached inside his inner jacket pocket and took out a small box wrapped in silver paper with a white bow. She tore it open excitedly. Inside the wrapping was a red velvet box, which creaked slightly when she opened it. Inside sat two beautiful emerald earrings surrounded by diamonds —a perfect match for her dress. Leave it to Michael to think about giving them to her now so she could wear them.

"Oh, Michael!" she whispered. "They're breathtaking!"

"I'm glad you like them." He smiled, knowing that he had made a good choice.

"Emeralds aren't my birthstone, ya know, not that I'm complaining in the least!"

"I know. They're *mine*." In response to her loving smile, he placed his hands on her waist and drew her toward him. "Happy birthday," he murmured against her lips.

The whole family assembled at the restaurant, dressed to the nines. Meg was pleased; this was the perfect birthday celebration. In the few short months since moving home, she hadn't had the time to make many new friends, so a party didn't make much sense. Meg ordered Michael *not* to have the waiters sing "Happy Birthday" at the restaurant, not that they would've at this posh restaurant. She despised the public singing, not only for herself, but for other people as well.

Leaving the restaurant, Meg saw Jim Morrelli, eating dinner with a woman. She stopped at his table.

"Oh hi, Jim," Meg said, as nicely as she could muster.

"Hello," he said coolly. He looked directly at Michael and Pop, dissecting them with his eyes. The others were already out in the hotel hallway getting their coats.

"This is Michael Harrington and Pop, Dr. John Harrington." She nodded at Jim. "Jim Morrelli."

Since the Morrellis were eating, Michael and Pop just nodded politely, rather than making an attempt to shake hands.

"Jim is also a social studies teacher at the school," Meg explained.

Meg's eyes shifted to Jim's dinner companion. She was determined to outwait Morrelli. He would introduce his wife to them if they had to wait there all night.

Jim's eyes shifted around the room, undoubtedly looking to see if anyone he knew had seen people of color stop at *his* table. Finally he said, "This is Marcie, my wife."

"Nice to meet you," Meg said. *You poor thing.*

Sensing Meg's tension, Michael said, "We really have to go."

At the coat check, Pop asked, "What's up his ass?"

Michael said, "He's a bigot."

"*And* he's homophobic, *and* he doesn't like me," Meg finished.

"Oh, is that all?" Pop said. "See, Meg, I told you eating out with the Harringtons would be an adventure."

"I like adventure!" She wasn't going to let Jim Morrelli spoil her birthday.

The cake waited back at the house and the group descended upon the house noisily. Meg remembered that Mootsie used to say, "Everyone knows when the Harringtons are home!" And it was true, but the neighbors were used to it.

Pop had seemed tired at dinner, and shortly after they got home, he asked Meg to come into his room. He gave her a pin of Mootsie's, one which he remembered her wearing to school a lot. Meg also remembered it well. It was a simple ring of small pearls set in gold.

"Oh Pop, thank you. I always loved this pin."

"Well, it's a teacher's pin."

"I love it."

Pop went to bed right after that, saying he'd had a long day. The rest of the group gathered in the dining room, around the cake, then in the family room.

Tory couldn't help teasing Meg. "So, old lady, how is it being forty?"

"Your time is coming!" Meg retorted. Tory would turn forty in a few months.

Meg plopped down on the sofa next to Michael. "Boy, this really sucks," she said under her breath. Then realizing that she didn't want Michael to misinterpret, she said, "Oh, dinner, and the cake – everything was wonderful! It's the *number*."

"It's *only* a number. You're as young as you feel," he said.

"Oh, yeah? I feel ancient," Meg said pathetically.

He snuggled up against her and murmured, "I know how I can make you feel younger."

Meg smiled, knowing this was so true, and kissed him warmly.

"Aww, come on y'all," Luther said with his mouth full of cake. "I'm trying to eat here!"

Michael rolled his eyes and sighed dramatically.

Meg whispered without moving her lips, like a ventriloquist, "Not important. Move on." But despite her comment, Luther's attitude was starting to bother her now.

Meg asked Luther if he knew of anyone that had spare musical instruments that could be donated to the school. She had to start finding them for Marcus.

"I don't know. I'll ask around," Luther promised.

When Jessica walked over to hand Meg a gift, Luther went into the kitchen. They apparently were not speaking. At dinner they had been cordial, but in the way strangers are. Once home, Jessica had stuck close to Tory and Travis. Meg opened her gift from Luther and Jessica, a couple of jazz CDs Meg had been looking for. As Michael got up to put one of them on the CD player, Meg went into the kitchen to thank Luther. He was alone, leaning on the kitchen counter, drinking a bottle of beer and spinning the beer cap on the counter.

"Everything okay, Luther?" Meg asked.

"Yeah," he said softly.

"You sure? You and Jess seem a little distant."

"We all can't be like you and Mikey," he said sarcastically, then swigged from the bottle.

Meg's eyebrows furrowed. "Do you have some sort of problem with Michael and me being together? You keep making these little comments and I'm starting to think that you're serious."

"Naaa. I'm still not used to it yet." He was avoiding eye contact.

"Still? It's been three months."

Luther didn't respond. He only kept drinking.

"Luther, what is it?

"All right, ya wanna know what it is?" He raised his voice.

"Yeah – I wanna know!" Her volume equaled his.

"I think Michael should be with a black woman." He met her eyes directly.

Meg couldn't believe it. She stared at him, mouth agape, not knowing what to say. "What?"

"Yeah, that's what I think."

"How can you think that? Mootsie was white – your own mother."

"And Pop and Mootsie had all sorts of problems with people being all judgmental and stuff. It was hard on them. Black people accept us as their own. White people never do – they say, 'Oh, he's black,' or 'He's mixed.' Black people say, 'Hey, he's a brotha, – even though they know we're not 100%. It's a matter of acceptance."

Now Meg really didn't know what to say. She understood what he meant. She wondered why this difference existed. She opened her mouth once, twice, to say something.

"And I'll tell you something else," Luther continued. "As a couple, you're gonna have trouble being accepted by either group."

"We don't care about that. We love each other." Meg realized her voice was barely a whisper.

"Oh, Meg, you're livin' in some white la-la land."

Meg was stunned at Luther's words. Was there truth in what he said? Unable and unwilling to continue the conversation, she slowly walked out of the kitchen with her mind reeling.

"What's wrong?" Tory asked, noticing her pallor.

"Nothing. I think I just need something for my stomach," Meg lied.

"I'll get you something," Tory said, and disappeared upstairs.

Jessica quietly asked Meg, "Did you just talk to Luther?" She'd heard Luther's view and disagreed with him, and she'd known it was just a matter of time before he imposed his view on Meg or Michael.

"Yeah," Meg whispered. Their eyes met.

Jessica's jaw tightened, and she stormed into the kitchen. Before long, Meg heard loud voices, although it was unclear what was being said.

Michael joined Meg in the dining room. He put his arm around Meg's waist, unaware that anything was wrong.

"Take this old lady home?" she asked.

"Stop," he chided. Then his eyes examined her. "Of course I'll take you home."

The ride to Meg's house was silent. By the time they got into her kitchen, Michael could stand it no more.

"Did I do something wrong? What's the matter?"

"No, it's not you."

"It's not the age thing is it?"

"No, not really." She sat down at the kitchen table. He pulled a chair close to her and took her hands in his.

How can I tell him without starting a fight between him and Luther?

She took a deep breath. "I don't want you to get mad at Luther again," she said.

"Luther said something to upset you?"

"Yes, but…" Meg stopped talking when she saw Michael's face tighten.

"Don't get mad. Please?" The last thing she needed was to keep another secret from him, she realized.

"Just tell me," he said more gently than she would have expected.

Without looking at him she said, "Luther thinks you should be with a black woman."

Michael furrowed his brows, then burst out laughing, not expecting this in the least. But, with Luther, the unexpected ought to be expected. He shook his head as if to clear the cobwebs, then said, "What?" He was still laughing.

"Yeah." She finally looked at him. "He thinks you're better accepted as a black man and things are easier if you date black women."

"I *have* dated black women, white women too. They all had one thing wrong with them."

Meg looked at him, waiting.

"They weren't *you*," he said softly. Meg melted. She already felt better. "How can he think that way considering the way we were raised?

"I know. I was surprised, too," said Meg.

"Why would he tell you this on your birthday?"

"I asked him if he had a problem with us being together. So he told me." Meg looked down at her feet. "I think he's just looking out for you, Michael."

Michael's thoughts shifted from Luther to Meg, sitting there in front of him looking dejected.

"So you don't agree with him?" she asked.

"Oh, come on, Meg, you know me better than that. I've never seen you act insecure before."

"I've never had this much to lose before."

He stood and pulled her to her feet. "I fell in love with *you*, Meg. Your color isn't an issue." He looked deeply into her eyes. "I love *you*."

She closed her eyes. His words soothed her. "I love you too, so much," she said.

"Come on, let's go upstairs. I owe you forty spanks."

Meg raised her brows, smiled, then bolted from the room, running up the stairs screaming with Michael at her heels.

CHAPTER ELEVEN

The next morning, Meg was officially forty. She didn't think anyone at school knew and she wanted to keep it that way.

About ten minutes before the morning bell, Geoffrey walked in. Meg assumed he was there to play piano. Instead, he walked up to her desk and placed a large glass vase in front of her. Inside the vase, he placed a single daisy and said, "He loves you." She looked at him for clues, but he walked over to his desk and sat down with the usual dopey grin on his face.

Okaaaaaaaay…

Taahira then walked in with a daisy in *her* hand. She placed the daisy in the vase and said very dramatically, "He loves you *not!*" Meg started to laugh.

Okay, they found out it was my birthday. This is a cute way to give me flowers.

And so it continued:

Maria: "He loves you."

Jesse: "He loves you...not!"

Meg was giggling and her eyes were tearing up at the same time. Students marched in, a seemingly endless stream, with a daisy until the vase was full, ending with Louis saying, "He loves you." All homeroom students were accounted for except for Ronald.

He was probably too cool for this.

"Oh my goodness, thank you all so mu…" She stopped when she saw a figure coming in. It was Ronald, or at least she thought it was

Ronald. His face was obscured by the largest bouquet of red roses she had ever seen. She stopped laughing and stood up, her mouth literally hanging open.

These kids can't afford these!

Ronald jauntily walked over and carefully set the vase of forty roses on her desk and looked at her with a silly smirk, not hiding how much he was enjoying this. Then he smiled at her knowingly, glanced out the window and pointed.

There was Michael leaning against his car, beaming. She went to the window and tried to raise it. It was stuck again.

Dammit, not now!

The boys helped her pry it open. It cracked and moaned, but finally pulled up. As soon as she peered out the window, smiling, he shouted with gusto, "He loves you! Happy birthday!"

Forgetting about her audience, she shouted back, "She loves you, too!"

He looked at her once more, then jumped into his car and sped away.

Meg remained staring after him, stupefied, in love.

Ronald cleared his throat. Meg finally turned and the whole class sang, "Awwwwwwwww!" Meg felt herself turn beet red and, giggling, covered her face fully with both hands. She felt completely juvenile, deliriously in love. This man amazed her on so many levels. He was a contradiction within himself, so stiff and proper, so silly and funny, so sensual and loving.

"Oooooo, Ms. Robbins, that was so *romantic!* He's so handsome, too. I wish somebody would do that for me!" Maria said, wanting Louis to hear. They were a new couple.

"Shut up! That dude was driving a Range Rover! You know how much they cost?" Louis protested.

"Daisies don't cost much!"

Meg had to intervene and gain some control of her own classroom. "Okay everyone, sit down, now."

"Ms. Robbins, I didn't know you were with a *brotha!*" Ronald exclaimed, obviously pleased.

Luther's words resounded in Meg's ears: "Black people accept us as their own…even though they know we're not 100%."

Ronald continued, "You know what they say, don't you? Once you go black, you can *never* go back!" Howls of laughter from the kids, except for David who was rolling his eyes.

"Yeah okay, Ronald. Now, go sit down," Meg said only half-heartedly, still with a laugh in her voice.

The class was loudly buzzing and Meg was overwhelmed. The bell rang, jolting her back into reality. As movement started toward the door, Meg yelled, "Freeze! Is everyone here?" she asked quickly, realizing that she hadn't taken attendance.

The students yelled, "Yes!" and they kept moving.

"Okay, get outta here!" She was still beaming.

Several girls stopped to hug Meg. Though she never pushed, Meg was a hugger and they knew it. Who didn't need a hug now and then?

Later that day when Meg had Erika in class, she noticed a black crescent under her eye, which she had attempted to cover with makeup. She must have missed it earlier in the birthday confusion. She frowned, remembering that earlier in the year there'd been bruises on Erika's upper arm as if someone had grabbed her too hard. At the time, Erika explained that her half brother had gotten too rough during some horseplay. Now a black eye. Meg got the class busy, then asked Erika out into the hallway.

Meg decided to be direct. "Do you want to tell me about the black eye?"

"What? Oh! This!" she said, touching it as if she had forgotten all about it. "My brother and I were just goofing around."

"Again?"

"Yeah," she said sheepishly, forgetting that she had used that excuse for the bruised arm. "He was having a fight with my step dad and I tried breakin' it up and I got hit by accident. I don't know which one did it."

"I don't understand, were you goofing around or was there a fight?"

"A fight."

Meg paused to see if she'd add any more voluntarily, but she waited in vain. "Erika, if there is anything you want to tell me or anytime you want to talk to me, please do it."

"I'm all right, Ms. Robbins," she said in her little voice.

Meg didn't think so.

"Hey, Meg," Travis stood up and hugged her warmly. "I'm embarrassed that you had to make an appointment. It's college application time, the busy season for guidance counselors," he apologized.

"It's okay," Meg smiled.

"Is this business or pleasure?"

"Business. Do you know anything about Erika Woods?"

"Erika Woods," he repeated thoughtfully, looking up at the ceiling. "Sophomore, good student."

"Yes," Meg agreed. "Any problems at home?"

"None reported. To tell you the truth, Meg, I don't even know what she looks like. I've never had her in this office. I could check with

Janice, the other guidance counselor. Hold on."

He picked up the phone and the muffled buzz in the next office could be heard through the walls.

"Janice, have you ever spoken to Erika Woods?" Pause. "No? Know anything about her? Not really? Okay, thanks." He replaced the phone and shook his head. "What's up with her, Meg?"

"I think she's being abused."

"Physically?"

"Yes."

"Why?"

"Bruises on her arm. Black eye."

Travis looked in his file cabinet and pulled out a sheet of paper with numerous carbons of varying color.

"No, Travis, could you just document it, but not turn it in yet? I want to fish around."

"Okay, if you're not sure."

"Oh, I'm pretty sure. It's her safety I'm worried about."

"I assume you talked to her."

"Yes. She made some excuses."

"Could they be plausible?"

"I suppose…"

"It would be good if you could persuade her to come see me or Janice, if she's more comfortable talking to a woman."

"Okay."

Meg left Travis' office feeling confused. She'd thought she might get answers.

The only thing she could do was wait and hope that Erika would open up to her.

❦

Meg loved initiating serious discussions with her students. Some topics were meant to be light and some got pretty heavy.

One of the heavier debates in Meg's homeroom came the Wednesday morning that she posed the question, "What race or ethnic group do you think is more accepting of others and why?"

David opened the discussion by saying that white people had been dominant throughout history, but since the Civil Rights Movement, blacks had advanced. But it was David's view that blacks had advanced only because white people *allowed* them to. So, therefore, whites were the most accepting people.

Ronald stared at David.

Oh, boy. I hope everyone keeps his or her tempers in check.

Meg worried that David was well on his way to being a racist, no doubt under the influence of family. "Okay," she said. "Who else?"

Ronald said with disgust, "I disagree. Blacks treat people better because we've been there, you know? We've been treated like shhh…crap and it don't feel good. Since we know what it's like, *we* treat people better."

Not exactly eloquent, but point well taken.

Then Brandy had her hand raised. "I agree with Ronald. I'm biracial, but black people say I'm black even when they know I'm mixed. And that's all right with me, ya know? I never heard any white person call me white. But that's okay, too. I mean, I don't care."

"That's because you don't *look* white," Justin said. David snickered.

So there it was. Luther's theory.

But then Louis interjected, "Well, I don't know. I mean I'm mixed. I don't know how much…"

"That's `cause you don't know who your daddy is!" Ronald cracked. The class, even David and Justin, broke out in peals of laughter.

"Ronald, Louis had the floor. No interruptions," Meg said.

Louis wasn't rattled in the least. He had heard it before. "Anyway, I don't feel like I'm accepted by either group. The whites don't think I'm white and the blacks don't think I'm black. I think I'm really accepted only by other mixed people."

"Whatchu talkin' about Louis? You're in our posse. You know that," Jesse said.

"Yeah, but I don't feel…" He shrugged. "I don't know."

So, Luther's theory had some holes.

Earlier in the year, Meg had had to literally pull boys off each other during discussions, with the help of Geoffrey, who by sheer size could break up any fight. At other times, kids screamed at each other, at volumes that made the windows rattle. That Maria could really yell.

Sometimes Meg would stand at the front of the class during these episodes and start talking in a really low voice, so that they'd strain so much to hear her that they'd have to quiet down. Sometimes it worked and sometimes it didn't. When it didn't, she had to use her "teacher voice." She didn't like using the teacher voice. She used it maybe five times a year. It was a voice that came from somewhere deep within and had the decibel level of a Who concert.

Meg's main goal with these types of questions was to encourage students to express their views clearly and concisely and without physical contact. "People who use their fists aren't smart enough to use their words," she would tell them.

David raised his hand again and directed his comments to Ronald. "How can you say black people are more accepting? You cluster together like you're afraid of white people. Everything's *brotha* this and *sista* that. You don't let whites in."

"Okay, hold on," Meg intervened. "What color are you, David?"

"What?" he asked her distrustfully.

"What color is your skin?"

"*White*," he answered as if she were brain-dead. He and Justin snickered.

"No, David," she said as she picked up a piece of notebook paper from Erika's desk and held it against his skin. "*This* is white. Your skin isn't white. What is it?"

"I don't know," he mumbled. He didn't like where this was going.

"Ecru? Pink? What?"

"I don't know!" he said, this time more angrily.

Meg scrambled to her cabinets looking for something. She didn't want to lose the interest of the kids. She had a point to make. They were looking at each other, speaking softly, questioning her intent. There it was, her "Big Box" of crayons – 96 count.

She took the box to David's desk and opened it. "Now, what color are you?" Some of the kids snickered. David looked around at them, disliking this.

Meg didn't want to belittle him, even though she despised his thinking. "It's okay. Look. I'll match up my own skin color. Let's see, I guess I'm closest to peach. What do you think?"

He shrugged and said, "I guess." She held crayons to his skin. "It looks like you're between peach and apricot." More snickering.

"Let's see what you are, Brandy." She compared crayons to Brandy's arm. "It's not a perfect match, but it's 'tan'."

More kids wanted to try it:

Sepia.

More tan.

More peach.

Burnt sienna.

"Let me see what I am, Ms. Robbins," Geoffrey asked excitedly. After trying ten shades, Geoffrey declared, "This is it! This is it!" He rolled the crayon between his fingers to read the color on the side. "*Brown?* After all that, I'm *brown?*"

The class howled and so did Meg.

"Let's take all the crayons that we matched – even the colors that were kinda close," Meg said. She lined them up in a row from lightest to darkest on Erika's front row desk, then laid a long piece of masking tape over them. Picking up the tape with the crayons stuck to it, she held it up. "What do you see?"

"Lots of color," Erika said.

"I don't see a white crayon," Meg said.

Then Ronald chimed in, "There's no black one either."

"No, there's not," Meg said, smiling. "Ladies, when you buy makeup, what's the common color in all foundation?"

"Brown," Ashley said.

"Yes," Meg said softly. "We're all some sort of shade of brown, aren't we? I don't know…it's comforting to me. It makes me think that we all came from the same place."

Some students smiled, pensively. Others did not. David slammed his journal shut.

The bell rang at precisely the right moment. Andrew, a very likeable Caucasian boy, came to Meg to critique her lesson. "That was cool, Ms. Robbins," he said.

Then Ronald shouted from the door, "Yeah, but I ain't goin' around sayin' I'm *sepia*!"

CHAPTER TWELVE

The Harrington family was busy preparing for Christmas. The plan was for the whole family to spend the night at Pop's house on Christmas Eve, and everyone was getting into the spirit.

Meg and Tory spent an exhaustive Saturday shopping, without finishing. The problem was that they'd buy one gift, then one thing for themselves.

"That's the way it's supposed to work!" Tory said. "That's why I like holiday shopping! One for them, one for me!"

"You have to leave something for people to buy you!"

"Oh, believe me, I'll think of something!"

The following morning Meg came downstairs at her house and announced to Michael, "*You* should shop with me."

"I hate shopping," Michael whined.

"With me? Oh, come on, it'll only be one afternoon. Get into the spirit."

He turned up his nose at her and opened the porch door to get the newspaper. She'd started toward the kitchen when Michael called, "Meg?"

She turned around and saw Michael standing frozen at the open porch door. She walked quickly toward him, concerned. Had she been vandalized? She always forgot to lock the porch door, figuring that as long as the door going into the house was locked, she was safe. Michael had told her repeatedly she was asking for trouble.

She looked at his face, then followed his eyes to a bundle on the floor. It was a person. A sleeping person wrapped in a blanket. It was cold on her porch, not as cold as outside, but just about. Meg started toward the bundle, but Michael stopped her.

"Wait. We don't know who it is," he whispered.

"We need to get a better look."

"Maybe we should just call the police."

Just then, the bundle moved and a face emerged.

"Oh my God, Erika!" Meg went to her and knelt beside her. She smelled like kerosene. A lot of her students did who were of lower income. Kerosene heaters provided cheaper heat. "Are you all right?"

"Oh, hi Ms. Robbins," she said sheepishly. "I'm sorry about this. I...I...was just scared."

"Come on in, it's cold out here. This is Michael."

"Oh, I remember him from your birthday." Erika smiled. They nodded hellos to one another. Michael disappeared into the kitchen while Meg sat Erika down on the sofa. She put her arm around her shoulders and examined her face. No black eye this time. No marks at all. Nothing visible anyway.

Erika remained hunched, looking at the floor, embarrassed, unable to meet Meg's eyes. Meg waited patiently for her to say something. Finally she said, "It's my stepfather." She paused, as if that was enough.

"He hits my mom. Last night he was real mad. He was drunk and...he..." She started crying. Michael walked in with a tray of hot chocolate but stopped when he saw the crying child in Meg's arms.

Meg looked up at him helplessly. He walked over and set the tray down on the coffee table and hurriedly went back upstairs.

"Does he hit you or your brother?" Meg asked.

Amidst sniffling and sips of hot chocolate, she shook her head no. Meg didn't believe it.

"What did he do last night?"

"He was yelling a lot about how my mother was good-for-nothin' and how she was a whore and how she doesn't even know who my father is. She knows, Ms. Robbins…she knows."

She burst into fresh tears, the hot chocolate teetering back and forth from rim to rim inside the mug. Meg took the mug from her hands and placed it on the coffee table, then gripped Erika's two hands in her own and whispered words of encouragement.

"It's okay. Everything's going to work out. What would you like me to do? I *should* report him. He didn't hurt *you*, right?" Meg probed.

"Oh no, Ms. Robbins! You can't report nothin'! He'll kill me if he finds out I told you! Please!" She was really getting worked up now, sobbing and wailing.

"Okay, okay," Meg said. "How about if I talk to your mother?"

"I…I…don't know. Maybe."

"Where does she work?"

She swallowed hard. "At Laird's Bookstore on Market Street."

"Okay. Does anyone know you're here?"

"No. I just ran. I never seen him so mad…" New tears. Meg couldn't close the floodgates now if she tried. But that wasn't necessarily a bad thing. She held her until she calmed.

"I'm gonna call your mother." Meg picked up the phone and paused.

What if he picks up the phone? She'd have to take the chance. It was ringing.

"Hello?" It was a woman. A sleepy woman.

"Yes, hello, Mrs. Woods? This is Meg Robbins."

"Yes," more awake. More alert.

"I just wanted to let you know that Erika's with me and she's okay."

"Oh, thank God. I was worried. I must've just dozed off." She was talking funny, as if she had just had dental work done.

Yeah, dental work done courtesy of her husband.

"Are you okay, Mrs. Woods?"

Pause. "Yes."

"Okay. If it's all right with you, I'll give her something to eat and bring her home."

"I'll come and pick her up now."

"It's really no trouble…"

"No! I…mean…uh…I have to go out anyway." She obviously didn't want Meg anywhere near her house. It was probably trashed.

Meg got Erika a donut from the kitchen. Five minutes later, Erika ran out the front door when she saw her mother's car approaching, blanket flying in the breeze like Superman's cape. The car scarcely slowed down as she jumped into the front seat.

Meg stood at the front door, still in her bathrobe. "You're welcome," she mumbled to herself.

Michael, fresh out of the shower, came up from behind and hugged her. "Everything okay?"

"No. I'm afraid not." She turned to him. "She's abused."

Michael looked disturbed and peeped out the front door as if he expected to find Erika still there. He had never been exposed to abuse of any kind. It was difficult to register. He finally turned to Meg.

"Are you sure?"

"Yes, I'm sure."

"Are you going to report it?"

"I've already spoken to Travis about it, but we decided to wait until I was sure. I think it's time I talk to her mother."

"Is she doing it?"

"No, the stepfather."

"It's horrible. She's a cute thing," Michael said.

"Yes. And one of my best students."

"I don't envy you. A teacher's job is never done, is it?"

"No. I worry about them all the time." She looked up at him and hugged him.

But Meg's thoughts couldn't leave Erika.

She decided not to tell Travis about Erika showing up at her house. She knew that he'd have to report it, and she wasn't sure it was in Erika's best interest. She wanted to talk to Erika's mother first.

The Monday after the incident, Meg went to the bookstore, but it was closed up tight. She returned on Tuesday. Laird's was a small bookstore and Meg wondered how it was staying in business with all the big bookstore chains opening. It reminded her of the movie *You've Got Mail.*

There was a woman up on a ladder when Meg entered the store, apparently the only person in the store. Meg assumed it was Erika's mom.

"Mrs. Woods?"

"Yes?" She was an attractive woman but upon closer examination Meg noticed her swollen mouth. There was something familiar about her. She gingerly came down the ladder, like an old woman with aches and pains, not a vital woman in her thirties.

"Hi, I'm Meg Robbins," she said with her hand outstretched.

"Oh, Ms. Robbins, I'm sorry about Erika coming over like she did."

"Oh, no. It's okay. Erika is a great girl. Are *you* okay?"

"Yes," she laughed, as if it were a ridiculous question. "Why?"

A customer came in and they had to lower their voices.

"Erika told me that your husband hit you Saturday night. And I can see by your mouth that she's telling the truth. That's why she came to my house. She was afraid."

Donna lowered her head and whispered, "I know." Then she met Meg's eyes. "But you know these teenage girls, they exaggerate. Everything is a big drama with them," she said with surprising nonchalance. "Listen, I can't talk. I have customers," she whispered.

"Okay, can we meet somewhere?"

"No, I can't." She busied herself with straightening books that didn't need it.

"Mrs. Woods, I don't mean to pry. I'm just worried about Erika. Perhaps if her father is on the scene…"

Get out of that house. Leave! He may try to kill you next!

"*I* can handle my daughter," she said firmly.

Meg paused, groping for the right words. "I didn't mean to offend you. I'm going to give you my home number. If you ever need me, please don't hesitate." Meg jotted down her number on a paper bookmark on the counter. She looked at Donna again and cocked her head. "I keep thinking I know you from somewhere. Did you go to Thomas Garrett High School?"

"Yes. Class of `84."

"Oh. I'm class of `79."

"I do have an older sister who looks a lot like me."

"Oh, that must be it." Meg smiled. "It was nice meeting you. You're doing a great job with Erika. She's a wonderful kid."

"Thank you."

Meg felt so helpless. She knew that this man was going to go too far one day. How could she make the woman leave when she didn't want to? What kind of a woman was she?

All I have to do is look in the mirror.

When Meg got home that day, there were two instruments on her porch: a trumpet and a saxophone. "Yes!" Meg said out loud to no one in particular. Luther had come through.

She promptly took them to a music store and left them to be overhauled, knowing she would have to pay for it out of her own money. It was worth it.

Friday, as usual, a group of teachers ordered out for lunch. Meg sat with Leon, Marcus, and Lynn Smithers, the young blonde choir teacher, who was a great singer in her own right.

At first, Meg had thought she was a phony-baloney because she was "up" all the time. Others mistook her friendliness for flightiness, but Meg had discovered otherwise. Lynn was real.

The teachers were eating, making small talk, when Regina Walker, a math teacher, approached the table and said to Marcus, "I need to tell you something."

Marcus looked up at her, waiting. "What? These guys are all right. You can say it in front of them." Regina looked at them, then sat down, quite ready to dish.

What Meg didn't know was that Regina, an African American

with a graduate degree, was the highest paid teacher in the school. She'd been hired away from another district because she was a teacher who could get results from children when no one else could. People dropped in to observe her almost weekly. Getting her to sign on the dotted line had been a major coup.

Though Regina liked to complain a lot, for the most part her bitching was therapeutic. She vented, and it was over. Despite her gruff exterior, she enjoyed teaching, and was a good person.

"What's up?" Marcus asked her.

"I heard Jim Morrelli use the word 'nigger,' " she said.

"It doesn't surprise me. He's an ass," Marcus said, still eating and shaking his head.

"Who was he talking to?" Meg asked.

"That's the interesting part," Regina continued. "Lester Smith."

All eating at the table stopped as they tried to take in that little tidbit.

"Smitty? Get outta here!" Marcus was clearly taken aback. "What did *he* say?"

"Smitty saw me and didn't respond at all. Like a deer in the headlights, ya know?"

Lynn murmured, "I can't believe it."

Lester Smith had been vice principal for three years. He was young as vice principals go, but he was visible, friendly, and now it seemed, a possible racist.

"Are you sure you heard right?" Marcus asked her.

"Yes, Marcus. I've had plenty of practice hearing the word 'nigger.' "

"Well, it's getting to the point where you don't know who your friends are," Marcus declared.

After lunch, Meg, Marcus and Leon went to the office to check their mail. Inside her mailbox, Meg had a message from Mr. McHale, David's father. "Uh oh," Meg said.

"What's up?" Marcus asked.

"David McHale's father wants me to call him."

"David McHale, David McHale," Marcus repeated. "I don't think I know him."

Meg tried to think what David's father could want. "I'm gonna call right now. I don't want this hanging over me for the rest of the day."

She punched the phone number on the message slip with sweaty palms. She hated to guess why parents wanted her to call. Unfortunately, it was rarely good news.

Marcus leaned on the counter to listen. He could hear only Meg's part of the conversation:

"Hello, Mr. McHale? This is Meg Robbins, David's teacher. I had a message to... What? That's right I did tell him that he wasn't white."

Marcus raised his eyebrows at Meg. She smiled at him.

Lester Smith started to walk through the main office where Meg was standing, but stopped when he saw her. Out of her view, he listened carefully.

"Peach. I think he was peach. Peach or apricot."

"I'm not insinuating anything, Mr. McHale. Only that if taken literally..."

Marcus was fascinated now. He leaned on the counter and listened. When Leon walked over to ask about a flyer in his mailbox, Marcus shushed him. Now Leon began listening too. So, still, was Lester Smith, though unobserved.

"Caucasian works better, but you're missing my point..." Meg rolled her eyes at Leon and Marcus.

"I don't have black kids either." Marcus stood bolt upright and

Meg almost let out a giggle.

"All my kids are brown."

Leon looked at Marcus and mouthed, "What?"

"All my kids are brown, even David. No, I'm not unstable… Yes, I am lumping the kids…well, what's wrong with lumping?"

Meg listened further, her hand tight on the receiver.

"I'd appreciate it if you wouldn't use that word. It offends me… My boyfriend is really none of your concern. Aren't you getting off the subject?" Meg flipped the bird into the mouthpiece of the phone. "Fine. I will refrain from calling David a color. I'll call him Caucasian."

Tight-lipped, she listened some more.

"Fine," she said, and slammed the receiver down without saying goodbye.

"What a *prick!*" she whispered.

It wasn't until they were walking back to their classrooms that Marcus asked, "All your kids are brown?"

Meg told them the whole story with her homeroom and the brown crayons.

"Meg, your lesson was naive and simplistic…" Marcus started.

"Hey – " Meg started to defend herself.

"Now wait a minute. Naive. Simplistic. But sometimes that's the only way to get through to kids. I think you done good." He gave her a hug that Leon, the perpetual hugger, had to get in on.

"Burns, did you just touch my ass?" Marcus asked.

"No!"

"I think you just touched my ass!"

Meg was laughing and Leon was fiercely defending himself when they realized they were right outside Jim Morrelli's door. He came out of his classroom and gave them "the glare." They all instantly shut up

115

as if they were his students. Then Marcus snapped his heels together, gave him a Nazi salute, and continued marching down the hall to his basement classroom. Meg walked quickly down the hall to her room, holding back a huge guffaw. Leon laughed right out in the hall. He didn't care anymore.

The next morning in class, Meg wrote the word *tolerance* on the blackboard. Then she said, "In your journals, define it for me."

Some students wrote right away. Some sat and pondered. When it came time for discussion, Meg was surprised how little the kids had to say.

Maria said, "Tolerance is like, letting somebody do stuff."

Jesse said, "I wrote that tolerance is like, not being able to take a drug because your body got used to it."

"Okay, good. I hadn't thought about that definition, but that is one," Meg said.

Then Geoffrey said, "I wrote that tolerance is respecting somebody for what they believe in, like, you know, their religion or whatever."

Meg approached Geoffrey smiling and planted a kiss right smack in the middle of his forehead, leaving a big red lip mark. All the kids giggled at Meg's reaction and at the lip imprint. Geoffrey smiled, even though some kids were giggling and pointing at him.

The rest of the day, Geoffrey walked around with the lipstick mark on his head like a badge of honor. He loved it.

CHAPTER THIRTEEN

The night of December 23, Meg went to the house to prepare some food ahead of time for Christmas Eve dinner. Pop was out playing bingo, so Meg had the house to herself. She was in great spirits, dancing around the kitchen in tight black pants and stocking feet to Marvin Gaye's "How Sweet It Is." Being alone, she had the music cranked up and was peeling potatoes, swaying her hips provocatively, singing loudly but not that well and totally lost in the song.

Little did she know Michael was standing in the doorway, smiling broadly, watching her every move, his eyes resting most of the time on her butt and hips. When she turned around to put a potato in a bowl, she saw him, screamed and jumped simultaneously, and threw the potato clear across the kitchen.

"Michael!" she screamed.

Michael was laughing hysterically now. "I'm sorry!" He put his hands up in mock surrender. "I'm sorry!"

Meg was laughing, too, now at her own embarrassment. She turned scarlet and placed both hands over her face and doubled over, giggling.

Michael sauntered over to her and placed his hands on her waist. "That was one lucky potato," he teased, kissing her tenderly. "It looked like you were undressing it."

"I guess I was!"

Looking over at the CD player, he lifted his eyebrows. "Marvin Gaye?"

As he walked to the CD player, Meg snapped him on the butt with a dishtowel.

"Yes," Meg said with a leftover giggle.

Michael hit a button until he had the track that he wanted. The sultry music began for "Precious Love." The beat was incredibly erotic and sexy. He rushed over to the lights and turned them down, then wagged a 'come here' finger at her.

Her heart skipped a beat. She walked over to him slowly, provocatively. He smiled in appreciation. When she reached him, his hands instantly wrapped behind her and slid down to her butt. He had been dying to touch it ever since he'd walked in the door. He pulled her hips toward his tightly, holding her there. She smiled into his eyes, wrapped her arms around his neck and drew the rest of him close. Then he started moving and grinding his hips into hers to the beat of the music. He was so sexy he sizzled. She was instantly excited, her heart racing.

He kissed her long and seductively. She returned his passion, first kissing him, then letting her lips trail down his neck, then nibbling his earlobe. He closed his eyes and let out a sigh of appreciation. She knew how to excite him, knew what he liked. They danced for a few more minutes, kissing, their hands everywhere on the other.

Michael slid his hands inside her pants and slowly, teasingly, began to peel them down. Meg looked at him, startled at first, being in the kitchen, then completely turned on. Plates, bowls, and food in the way didn't stand a chance. Everything flew haphazardly to the floor, some skittering, some breaking. They tore off essential clothing. They were both bent in half over the kitchen table, Michael's front to her back, urgently propelling her, exciting her in ways she'd never dreamed of. It was sex so primitive and carnal that had it been kicked up just one more notch, it would have scared her. As it was, she thought she might black out.

Once they were spent, they both collapsed face down on the table, he still on top of her, unable to move, their breathing as heavy as if they'd run a marathon. They were helpless to move for several minutes. Finally, Michael kissed her shoulders and stood, knees wobbling. They wordlessly gathered their clothing and carelessly put it back on. Michael collapsed in a kitchen chair and Meg sat on his lap.

Finally, Meg spoke first. "That was…"

"Yeah," he agreed.

After a long pause, she tried again. "I've never…"

"Me neither."

She looked at him then, and finally regained her senses. "You know what we have to do, don't you?"

He looked at her, curiously. "What?"

"Forget that ever happened."

"What?" he said, scanning the floor in long sweeping glances.

"What are you looking for?"

"Your mind. I think maybe I jolted it right out of your head."

She smiled and said, "No, seriously. *That* will be the one we'll always strive for, you know?"

He nodded and smiled.

"And that's not good, 'cause *that* may never happen again," Meg said.

Michael pondered this for a moment, nodding. Then he looked at her lovingly and said, "What if it does?"

She looked into his eyes and they both broke out in ear-to-ear grins, laughing and hugging.

The next morning, Michael went bounding down the back stairs, Meg one step behind. At the bottom of the stairs, Michael stopped short and Meg ran right into his back.

"Michael!" she scolded. Then she peered over his shoulder to see why he'd stopped.

There was Pop sitting at the kitchen table, eating his Wheaties in the precise location where just hours earlier they'd had intoxicating, very memorable sex.

Meg started laughing against Michael's neck, knowing what he was thinking.

"Good mornin', you two," Pop greeted them.

"Morning, Pop," Michael said with a slight giggle in his voice.

"Morning, Pop," Meg said, composed but smiling. She kissed Pop on the cheek and joined Michael by the coffee maker.

Michael mumbled to her, "This is great. Every time I look at the kitchen table now I'm gonna get a woody."

"Shhhhh," Meg smiled.

God, please let me always be this happy. Let me keep him this happy too.

Meg decided then and there that she was at the point of no return. She loved Michael more than anything and could not risk losing him, ever. She was never going to tell Michael about her past. She'd let too much time pass. Now he'd never understand or forgive her. She was officially going to put it behind her. Forever.

Christmas Eve was the best one in Meg's life. The only thing that would've made it better would have been for Mootsie to be there.

Luther came alone, Jessica having gone home to Baltimore. He didn't let on that things hadn't been right with Jessica for a while now, particularly since she'd seen him kissing another girl at the bar. In an attempt to avoid questions, he told everybody that he and Jessica had celebrated before she left, and that she'd be back for New Year's.

Dinner was wonderful. Meg added fish as a second dish when she remembered that Mootsie had always insisted that they had to eat fish on Christmas Eve. Meg didn't remember why, but added fish, feeling that if she didn't, it would be bad mojo. During dinner, Michael leaned over and said, "Good potatoes," and smiled devilishly. Meg smiled back, shaking her head, remembering the preceding night's events.

After dinner an argument commenced between Luther and Tory concerning when they should open their gifts. Luther wanted to open them that night, Tory was insisting on Christmas morning.

"What do you think, Meg?" Tory asked, expecting her support.

"I don't care, Tory. Whatever you decide is fine with me."

Tory looked at her disappointedly. "Michael?"

"I don't know. We've always done it on Christmas morning."

"Oh, of course, any vote against me," Luther said.

Meg sighed. *Here we go again.*

"To tell you the truth, Luther, I really don't care. You and Tory decide," Michael said.

Meg smiled at Michael for avoiding another fight with Luther. He was so relaxed tonight, so content.

"What do you think, Pop?" Luther asked.

"Well, I think we could start new traditions. I don't think anyone in this room believes in Santa anymore, so maybe opening presents tonight would be a good idea."

"There's no Santa?" Travis said in mock terror.

Tory smacked him with the backside of her hand in the stomach and Travis bent over in pretended pain. She was still brooding, though, over not getting her way.

"Hey, Tory, help me get the desserts?" Meg asked. Wordlessly, Tory joined Meg in the kitchen.

"You know, I'm sure Christmas is tough on Pop without Mootsie. So, maybe making some little changes will help him," Meg said.

"I know. I thought of that. But *I* need to remember her *and* her traditions." Tory's voice started to break. She paused for a moment, not looking at Meg. "I miss her." Her chin started to waggle and she started to cry as if she had been holding it in for some time.

Meg went to her and held her. "I miss her, too."

"I'm so glad you're here."

"Me, too." She propped her forehead against Tory's. "Listen, maybe we can save a few gifts to open tomorrow…"

"No, no, it's okay. I'll live."

Meg stood back. "You know, Mootsie lives on in you in so many ways – in your smile, the way you snort when you laugh sometimes. Your whole attitude – it's Mootsie."

"Yeah?" Tory asked softly. She was pleased with the comparison.

"Yeah."

They hugged again, Tory laying her head on her sister's shoulder. "I love you, Meg."

Meg closed her eyes. "Love you, too."

After a moment, Tory pulled herself away and said, "Oh, I've gotta pull myself together. This is mostly hormonal, ya know."

Meg looked at her, eyebrows raised. "Oh?"

"I'm pregnant," she said, smiling.

Meg sucked in a huge gust of air in order to scream, "Oh my God!" in utter jubilation. "Ohhhh…Tory!" Meg started doing a little dance, hopping from one foot to the next. Tory was giggling when everyone came running into the kitchen.

"What? What's wrong?" Michael was first in, trailed by everyone else.

Meg waited impatiently with her hands over her mouth for Tory to speak.

"I'm gonna have a baby," she announced.

Travis held up his arms like Rocky and yelled, "That's right! I did it!"

Everyone laughed and shouted their approval and hugs went all around.

"When are you due?" Meg asked.

"Not until July," Tory said.

"I shoulda known something was up when you turned down the wine. You *love* your wine!" Luther said.

Pop finally spoke. "I'd say this was the best Christmas gift for the family, ever."

Tory embraced her father. "Oh, Pop, I wish Mootsie were here to enjoy this moment."

"She is, baby. She is," he said through tears.

That night Meg and Michael exchanged gifts privately with a fire going in the fireplace in the bedroom. Torn wrappings and bows were strewn all over the bed and floor. In addition to the usual clothes, books and CDs, Meg gave Michael a gold ID bracelet. But instead of his name or initials on it, Meg had had the jeweler engrave simply, *Meg's*. He belonged to her and she wanted everyone to know it.

"You see, it's possessive," Meg teased.

"I see that," Michael said, kissing her.

He gave her a gold necklace with a pendant in the shape of the eternity symbol. It expressed his feelings perfectly. She put it on immediately, swearing to never take it off.

That night, a dream from Christmastime several years before had Meg tossing and turning:

She had just set up the Christmas tree. The fire was burning pleasantly in the fireplace. Music was playing softly in the background. She had a bottle of wine with cheese and crackers ready. Bill's car pulled up and she stood by the tree, eagerly waiting to surprise him.

He walked in scowling. "Is that a live tree?" Bill asked, pointing to the beautifully decorated Christmas tree.

"Yes," Meg said proudly. "Doesn't it smell great?"

"If I wanted to smell pine, I'd go in the damn mountains."

Meg's smile disappeared. Her Christmas mood was deflating by the second.

"What a frickin' waste of money. I thought I told you to get an artificial tree. Pine needles falling all over the place…"

Meg said nothing, knowing it was best.

"I'm going out," he mumbled, and stalked through the front door. Just that quickly, he was gone.

The dream ended with Meg whimpering in her sleep and awakening to feel Michael's arms tighten around her. She sighed heavily, shrinking into him. But, it was a long time before sleep found her again.

CHAPTER FOURTEEN

Christmas vacation had always come at a time when Meg needed a break. With the New Year, she returned to school rejuvenated. Michael had taken several days off and they'd spent them going to museums, eating out, strolling the mall with their Christmas exchanges, and, of course, trying to recreate that night in the kitchen. It didn't happen, but it was a whole lot of fun trying.

Erika didn't return to school after Christmas break. On Friday, Meg decided to call her house during her lunch period. It wasn't unusual for a teacher to call to see why a student has been out and she felt justified. There was no answer at home. No answering machine.

Meg asked the students if any of them had heard from Erika but no one responded. After class, though, Andrew approached her desk.

"Ms. Robbins?"

"Yes?" Meg looked up.

"I think...I..."

"What's up, Andrew?"

"I...I think...I think that Erika gets beat at home," he finally sputtered.

The back of Meg's neck prickled. "Really? What makes you think that?"

"She has bruises and stuff. I mean lots of kids get hit, ya know? But not like her. It happened last year, too, but no one talked about it. I like her a lot and I'm really scared for her. She doesn't deserve it."

"No one does, Andrew." Meg was just as upset as Andrew, but she knew her immediate job was to reassure him. "I know what you mean about Erika. I have had my suspicions. I've been looking into it, but that's between you and me for now, okay? I don't want to cause her any further embarrassment."

He nodded and smiled slightly. He knew if anyone could help Erika, it would be Ms. Robbins.

Stopping at Laird's Bookstore to see Donna Woods, Meg pretended to look for a book. Donna was unpacking a box of new books, but approached Meg after a couple of minutes. "May I help you? Oh…Ms. Robbins."

"Hi, Mrs. Woods. I was just looking for John Grisham's latest."

"Over here." She showed her an end display. Meg pretended interest, but in fact, Michael had given her the book for Christmas.

"How's Erika?" she asked casually.

"Oh, she's fine. She'll be back Monday."

No explanation. She had the flu? Nothing?

"Good. We missed her. Tell her some of the kids asked about her." Meg thought it best to leave it at that.

"Do you want the book?"

"Oh, no thanks. I have that one after all."

Donna Woods was no dummy, Meg knew. She'd understand that Meg was checking up on her and was unlikely to let the matter drop. What Meg didn't know was whether that would be a worry or a comfort to Donna.

Thursday that week, outside Meg's classroom, Ronald, Jesse, and Louis were singing at Ronald's locker. Meg came out to hear, smiling. She'd heard them rap before, and they were pretty good. But Meg wasn't as "up" on rap as she was other forms of music, beyond her two Will Smith CDs. Today, they were playing around with harmony and they weren't bad at all. Unfortunately, Jim Morrelli came out then, glaring at them, visually telling them to shut up. It was the end of the school day, so they weren't disturbing anyone —except Jim Morrelli.

"Come into my room," Meg invited, wanting them to continue.

"No, it's okay, Ms. Robbins," Ronald said.

The three of them walked away, leaving the school. Meg stared after them, then at Jim Morrelli's door.

"Dammit!" she whispered through clenched teeth.

The next few months passed without any noticeable marks appearing on Erika, and she had no absences. Although she was glad Erika seemed to be fine, Meg knew that it didn't mean she *was* fine. Mentally, physically, or sexually.

God, please don't let him be sexually abusing her, too.

Meg found herself becoming obsessed with Erika's problems. It was like waiting for a bomb to explode. She talked it over constantly with Michael. He was a great sounding board, but even he was growing tired of her constant worrying.

"You have to just let things happen, as hard as that may be," he said.

"Let things happen?" she asked.

He has no clue what it's like.

He continued, "Number one: You may be wrong about her. Number two: If you *are* right, I don't want some psychotic abuser coming after you because you revealed him. And number three: You must have some sort of protocol at school about this."

Meg nodded.

"Then follow protocol and let the system deal with it."

Meg nodded and thought about it. It was typical of Michael to want her to follow the rules, but she knew things were always very touchy in the lives of abusers and their families. Her best of intentions might make things worse for Erika and her mother, once the abuser sensed trouble.

"Maybe I'll talk to Travis about it again." Then she looked over at Michael on his side of her bed. "Have I been neglecting you?"

The thought had never really crossed his mind, but he took advantage of it and pathetically said, "Yeah!"

She smiled and cuddled next to him thinking how secure she felt, how loved. Then she thought of the nights endured by Erika and her mother. She remembered how terrifying it was to go to bed at night, to sleep with one eye open, to jerk awake with every noise in the house. Meg wrapped her arms around Michael tighter, but, once again, it took her a long time to fall asleep.

Geoffrey became fairly proficient on the piano. Impressed with his determination, Meg provided him with fun sheet music at his ability level. A handful of kids regularly stayed in Meg's room after school to hang out and listen. For some, it was far better than going home.

Once in a while, the same three singers from the hallway would sing in Meg's room. They weren't great, but they weren't terrible either.

"You guys should experiment with different sounds."

"Oh, no, here she goes," Ronald said. He had known that she'd intervene sooner or later.

"Oh, I don't mean you should stop doing what you're doing. Your harmonies are good enough for a barbershop quartet. But you'll need a fourth person. Geoffrey, can you sing, too?"

The loud burst of laughter from the three of them startled Meg.
It isn't that stupid!

"Straight up, Ms. Robbins, you want us to sing *Sweet Adeline* or some shit like that?" Louis asked.

"Watch it," Meg warned at his profanity. "There are *other* barbershop songs, but, yeah, something like that." She scratched her head with the end of a pencil, thinking. "The only stuff I have is from *The Music Man*," she said. "There's a barbershop song in it, 'Lida Rose'."

"She's trippin'. Could you see *us...* " Ronald managed to sputter.

She looked at all of them laughing at her. "Have you ever seen an *unhappy* barbershop quartet?" She couldn't compete with the laughter. "Oh, forget it! It was just an idea. I thought it might be fun." She didn't want to discourage them from their own music. What they did on their own time should be up to them. She'd take charge of what they listened to in the classroom.

Although it took a lot of schedule juggling and the use of parent volunteers, Thomas Garrett High School developed a program which allowed teachers to observe each other during a one-week period. Teachers could sign up to observe the teachers that they had always wanted to see teach. It was a great idea and all the good teachers looked forward to it. Regina's blocks filled up first, then Meg's. She was flattered – flattered but a little nervous. Jim Morrelli signed her list. In return, she signed up for his class.

"Why in the hell would you want to observe *him*?" Leon asked.

"I don't know. I'm curious. I felt sorry for him. No one had signed up for his class. But mostly, I'm curious."

The observations were staggered so only one teacher observed at a time. It was nice that way, more personal. There were times when Meg could pause and explain what she was doing, or include the other teacher in her lesson. She made sure that week was planned particularly well. The observing teachers filled out a critique at the end and supposedly, if they offered suggestions, the teacher being critiqued had to consider the criticism without taking it personally. Meg's critiques were all top-rate, but she noticed Jim Morrelli had not filled one out.

All her friends observed her at sometime during the week, all of them enjoying her lessons and her music. She observed them, too, and was particularly fascinated by Regina. She had a blast.

"You know what you are, don't ya?" Marcus asked. "A frustrated music teacher."

Meg laughed. "Naaa, I really like social studies – and music too!" Marcus shook his head and laughed.

She got to observe Jim Morrelli later in the week. She'd assumed that he'd be terrible, but he wasn't half bad. He was traditional, whereas Meg was not, but she thought he was animated and interesting. Of course, it was possible that he was on his best behavior but Meg was impressed nonetheless. Since she was his only observer, she *had* to fill out a critique. She gave him good marks except for the way he'd handled a discipline problem. He publicly humiliated an African American boy for not having done his homework, and Meg couldn't help wondering if it was racial, or if he treated all the students that way. So, she wrote on the critique, "Perhaps your energies would be better spent marking down the missed assignments and let the student suffer the consequences come report card time."

When Meg went out to her car after school, she noticed a piece of paper tucked under her windshield wiper. She pulled it out, smiling, thinking that it was probably a note from Michael. It would be just like him to leave her a note like that. When she unfolded it, the blood drained her face. The note simply said, 'Nigger-lover.'

She thought of Pop and how he would handle this situation –with class and dignity. Because of the timing of it, she was certain it was Jim Morrelli, but she wasn't going to let him get to her. Meg threw the windshield note out the day she received it. She also decided to keep it to herself, and not stoke the fire already simmering in Regina and the others, who were openly hostile to him.

There had been no further sightings of Lester Smith with Jim Morrelli, but Lester joined the lunch group ever so often in the teacher lounge. It was obvious that he was hanging around them only to be nosey.

Regina stewed about the earlier incident until she couldn't let it fester in her any more. She finally confronted Lester Smith and asked him about Morrelli using the "n" word.

"He actually played dumb," Regina later told the group. "He said he didn't know what I was talking about – that he would never condone a teacher using that word." Regina was extremely agitated, her voice getting louder with every word.

"If they're friends, you didn't expect him to admit it to *you*, did you?" Marcus asked.

"No, but now he knows that *I* know – and that's what I wanted," Regina said, pointing her finger at no one in particular.

"You go girl!" Lynn cheered.

Everyone stopped look at Lynn, in utter embarrassment.

"What? What did I say?" Lynn asked.

Regina smiled and patted her on the shoulder. "Nothin' girl-friend. Nothin'"

CHAPTER FIFTEEN

By April, Tory's pregnancy was progressing beautifully. Travis doted on her and scolded her when she worked too late.

Meg helped her shop for maternity outfits when her clothes started getting too tight. The first time she saw Tory's little protruding belly in the fitting room, she stopped chattering and stared in amazement.

"What?" Tory asked, slightly offended.

"Oh, Tory! Look at your belly! It's so cute!"

"Yeah, well, it isn't gonna be cute in a few more months. I've gained ten pounds already. I'm gonna get big. My bootie is already as big as a barn."

"Oh, stop exaggerating. It'll be so worth it."

"Yes," Tory said with a smile. "We can hardly wait. This is one baby that will know how much he or she is wanted."

"Oooo, I can't wait to get my hands on that baby...!"

"Remember what I said about no baby shower. I mean it, Meg. I hate those things. Avoiding a shower was another good reason to elope."

"I know, I know!" Meg rolled her eyes.

The shower was already scheduled for June.

When Meg and Tory returned to Pop's, they didn't notice George Carr in the blue sedan parked across the street. Some time ago, he and his friends, Jim Morrelli, Lester Smith and new friend, Joe McHale had discussed the problem of Meg Robbins at one of their weekly poker games. In their eyes, she was a dangerous influence on the kids, so she had to go. They were going to make it happen sooner rather than later. Since George was an ex-police officer, he'd taken on the task of following Meg, waiting on her to give him some clue, something they could use against her. But, instead, he'd found her incredibly boring to watch.

Noting Tory's belly as the women carried shopping bags into the house, he shook his head and muttered to himself disgustedly, "They're multiplyin' again. Jesus Christ."

He pulled away from the curb when Meg and Tory entered the house, riding home deep in thought. If they couldn't find anything on her, they'd have to set her up. But how? They couldn't get caught. That was not an option. What would be the least risky way?

Stopping at the end of his driveway, he opened the mailbox and pulled out a large, thick envelope with a Los Angeles return address. Unable to wait until he got into the house, he excitedly ripped into the envelope. He studied the first few pages for several seconds then smiled and smacked the envelope delightedly in his hand and said, "Bye, bye!"

The following week, Meg's world turned upside down.

It all started with a call from Dr. Gardner saying that he wanted to see her. It was after school, around four-thirty. Most of the teachers were long gone, but not Meg. She was, however, getting her things together to leave. Geoffrey was still there and Meg had to ask him to leave. He whined, but then, he whined every day when it was time to go home.

When she walked into Dr. Gardner's office, he looked weary. Lester Smith was standing to the side of his desk, abnormally straight. Meg grew instantly uneasy.

What's this, an ambush?

"Hi," she directed to Dr. Gardner. "Are you all right?" He looked tired, worn out.

"No, Meg, I'm not." He sighed heavily, took off his glasses and wiped his face with his hands. "Sit down, please. I received some disturbing news today."

Meg sat in a chair opposite Dr. Gardner's desk. "Oh?" Meg swallowed hard and felt beads of sweat beginning to form on her upper lip.

"Do you want to tell me how your husband died?"

Oh, shit…

"He…he was stabbed," Meg said quietly.

"By whom?"

Meg didn't answer right away. Her eyes shifted nervously between Lester and Dr. Gardner. She knew that they already knew the answer.

"Me," she said, eyes downcast.

They exchanged glances, not expecting it to be this easy.

"Did it occur to you to tell me this during the interview process?"

"It occurred to me that I'd never get the job if I told you that," she said, not intending to sound flip.

Lester finally spoke. "So, you *lied!*"

"Not exactly. I guess it's more like I avoided the truth. But there were circumstances…"

"Under what circumstances can you murder a human being, then come into to teach a classroom full of *children?* These parents assume these kids are safe when they come to school!"

Lester was spitting out the words as if she were a vile creature.

"They *are* safe. I would never, ever, hurt them or anyone else."

"Oh, it's *so* reassuring to know that this will never happen again," Lester said sarcastically.

Dr. Gardner intervened. "Okay, listen, Meg. We know that the charges against you in California were dropped, but you are going to have to go before the school board here if you want to keep your job. You lied on your application and during the interview process. You'll have about three weeks to get some information together that will help you."

Meg started to well up. "And what about my classes?"

"Until then, I'm afraid you're suspended. We'll call you with the exact date of the hearing."

The room started to close in on her. She imagined that if she had ever used drugs, that this was what a bad trip would be. The walls were melting. Their voices were on the slowest speed on the turntable. She was in a fog.

"Meg?"

She stood too suddenly and saw little rainbow spots before her eyes. "Is that all?"

Dr. Gardner looked truly sorry. Sorry for her or sorry he'd made such poor judgment in hiring her? Meg couldn't tell. "Yes."

She'd started to leave when a thought occurred to her. She turned to them and asked, "May I ask how you found out about this?"

"It sort of fell into our laps," Dr. Gardner said.

"From whom?"

"I cannot say, Meg."

She purposely looked at Lester, who was avoiding eye contact. She'd started to leave again, when Lester asked, "Where are you going?"

"Back to my classroom."

"You have to leave the building now," he demanded. Dr. Gardner looked embarrassed.

"I have to get my jacket and purse," she choked out. They were treating her like a criminal.

What do they think I'm gonna do, plant a bomb?

"I'll escort you," Lester said.

They walked down the hall in silence. Meg suddenly couldn't wait to get out of the building. She wanted to grab her stuff and run like hell. Lester waited like a prison guard at her door.

"What are my kids going to be told?"

"That you're on a leave of absence."

Meg nodded. As she left her classroom, she turned the lights off and looked back, wondering if she would ever be back. As they passed Jim Morrelli's room, Meg saw the knowing look, the slight nod, between Jim and Lester. Mission accomplished.

Meg sat in her car for an hour, alternately crying and getting angry. She didn't know what to do next. Go home? Michael was there; she'd have to explain the red eyes and her mood. Everything would have to come out. She didn't have the luxury of a choice anymore. Besides Dr. Gardner and Lester Smith, who else knew?

Suddenly the blood in Meg's face drained. She started her car and carelessly peeled out of her parking space.

Michael. She had to get to Michael before they did.

She pulled crookedly in front of the house, not attempting to straighten her car out. He was home. His car was there. She ran up the front steps, tripping twice in the process. She burst through the front door shouting, "Michael?"

She was about to call again when she saw him standing in the family room. "Oh hey." She tried to sound casual. "Why didn't you answer me?"

He just stood there glaring at her. He didn't speak.

"Michael?" His face was rigid, his back straight. When he still didn't speak, she knew. He knew.

She began shaking her head, whimpering, "Oh no, Michael…"

"Just tell me if it's true," he finally said, not looking at her.

"I…I…" She swallowed hard, her breathing rapid.

"Come on, Meg." He raised his voice. "Either you did or you didn't."

This can't be happening!

She started to sob, "Yes."

"Yes, what?"

"What?" she asked incredulously.

"I want you to tell me what you did." If Meg didn't know better, she'd think he was enjoying watching her squirm. She started to shake.

Why is it so cold in here?

She started sobbing harder. Then in her quietest voice she said, "I stabbed Bill."

"What?" he cupped his ear. Meg would never have believed he could be so cold.

She yelled this time, still bawling, "I stabbed Bill! I killed him, all right?"

She was out of control now, beside herself, consumed by racking sobs.

He turned from her, unable to watch. He was seething. More than that, he was hurt beyond comprehension. He'd thought they shared everything. This woman he loved so much was someone he suddenly didn't even know. He stood with his arms folded, his back to her.

When she finally gained some composure, she said, "Michael…let me explain…"

"What did I ever do to you except love you?" He caught himself on his own sob. Then, coldly, "Get out."

"What? Wait, can't we talk? There's so much I need to tell you…"

"It's a little late for talking *now*, don't you think?"

It was true. She didn't know how to respond. Her thoughts suddenly shifted to Pop.

"I need to go see Pop."

"You stay away from Pop!"

My God, he's treating me like a leper.

"I think he should hear this from me."

Michael burst into sarcastic laughter, his eyes wide. "Oh, you do? *I* deserved to hear it from you," he roared.

Meg stood there whimpering. Never had she heard him yell like that. "Get out!"

"Michael…please…" She walked toward him.

"I said *get out*!"

Meg jumped at the volume of his voice. She turned and fled from the house, blubbering as she ran to her car, barely able to see through the tears. She pulled away from the curb without looking first, not caring if a car was coming. Nothing mattered anymore.

Michael watched her from the window. Then he sat down and covered his face with his hands and broke down.

Over the next few days, Michael walked around like a zombie. He barely spoke to Pop. He had committed himself completely to Meg. He'd never let his guard down so much with anyone. Nowhere near. He had even been trying to figure out the perfect time for a marriage proposal.

This was Meg, the woman he'd wanted since he was fifteen, the woman who was everything he had ever wanted. No matter how had he tried picturing her killing someone, he couldn't do it. She was the most loving and gentle person he knew. She couldn't even *say* anything bad about another person.

He wondered how he would have felt if she'd told him right when she got home. He didn't know. It was a moot point now.

Pop was growing more concerned. He knew something was going on with Meg because she wasn't around. She and Michael had been inseparable. Now Michael was depressed. Whenever Pop spoke to him, he was short, to the point. Finally, Pop couldn't stand it any longer and asked, "Where's Meg?"

Michael avoided eye contact and said, "I don't know."

Pop wondered what that meant. Why didn't he know? He decided to call Tory to get to the bottom of things. She had a way of doing just that.

When Tory got Pop's phone call, she thought he had to be mistaken. Michael was probably just in one of his dark moods. Certainly nothing could be wrong between him and Meg. But Pop and Tory decided to intervene just the same. They sat him down the following Saturday morning.

Pop started. "We need to know what's wrong."

"Nothing," Michael said, avoiding their eyes.

"Don't tell us nothing, Michael. Meg hasn't been around. You're hardly talking to anyone. What's happened?" Pop pleaded.

"We're not seeing each other any more."

"Why? What happened?" Tory sputtered in disbelief. Pop was right.

Michael didn't want to tell them. It was something so awful.

"Please, son. Maybe we can help," Pop said gently.

Michael looked down. "No one can help, Pop."

"What the hell happened?" Tory was growing impatient.

Michael paused, then said matter-of-factly, "It turns out that Meg killed Bill. She stabbed him to death. It never occurred to her to tell me," he said, his voice cracking.

Tory and Pop looked at each other in stunned silence for several seconds. Finally, Tory sputtered, "Holy shit. What was her explanation?"

"Explanation? I don't need an explanation. The fact is she didn't tell me. I had to hear from someone at the school." Michael could say no more. He stood up. "I can't do this." He quickly left and went to his room.

Tory and Pop sat for a long time in silence. Finally Pop, trying to justify Meg's actions, said, "Well, I'm sure he had it comin' to him."

Tory sighed deeply. She was worried about her brother. He was devastated. How could Meg do this to him? Then she got angry. She stormed from the house. She was going to fix it for the brother she loved and the sister she'd thought she knew.

∽∾

Meg stayed in bed, eating nothing, drinking little. She cried more than she ever had in her life. Her eyes were swollen almost shut. She kept popping Excedrin PM to sleep. "For pain with accompanying sleeplessness..."

Yup, that's me.

How could things have changed so drastically for her? One morning she'd awakened next to Michael, gone to school and, just hours later, lost her job, and more importantly, the man she was meant to be with.

She wondered about Pop. What would he say? Did he know? Certainly by now he did. And Tory...she was sure to be angry with her. Would Luther be glad? Probably. Meg could hear him now. "I told you so, Michael..."

Her students. Surely they were suspicious. Meg hoped they wouldn't try to visit her. A few of them knew where she lived.

Who did this? It had to be Jim Morrelli. Maybe Lester Smith, too. It certainly would have explained the look that passed between them when Lester was ceremoniously escorting her out of the school.

I did it to myself.

Who told Michael? Whoever told him had really wanted to devastate her. But why? Racism? Jealousy? Why would they go to these lengths? It was hard for Meg to comprehend that level of hate.

When Meg got up to use the bathroom she was dizzy and grabbed the bedpost. She had some choices to make. She could call her old therapist. She could start collecting the information Dr. Gardner had told her she'd need. She could even kill herself. She quickly dismissed that idea. Not only was it was against her faith, but she'd always considered it a selfish act, bequeathing your pain to others.

Carefully she made her way down to the kitchen and brewed herself a cup of tea. Food didn't interest her. As she mindlessly dipped the teabag at the kitchen counter, the doorbell rang. She had no idea what time or even what day it was. She looked at the clock on the microwave: one-thirty. Maybe it was Michael at the door. He had a key, but under the circumstances, maybe he would ring.

She peeked out the window. It was Tory.

Oh, Tory. What am I going to say to you?

When she opened the door, the first thing Tory did was look her up and down. Meg could tell by her body language that she was upset. Wordlessly, Meg stepped aside for Tory to enter.

"You look like hell," Tory said.

"I feel worse," Meg managed.

Tory paused and looked at the floor, having trouble coming up with the right words. "I, um, I came here to really tear into you, but I wasn't prepared for the way you look," she said firmly and honestly.

"Is Michael okay?"

"He's not talking much. He's in a lot of pain," she said.

Meg's face contorted with her own pain, realizing how much she had hurt the person she loved most in the world. She sobbed openly.

Tory stood there, not knowing what to do. Suddenly, Meg got another dizzy spell and reached out for anything for support. Tory grabbed her. "Hey, whoa! When's the last time you ate anything?"

"I can't."

Tory was at a loss. She was so angry with Meg, but seeing her like this was difficult. She still loved her and cared about her despite everything that had happened. "I'm gonna get you something to eat and then I'm leaving. This isn't the time for a discussion," Tory declared.

"No. Tory, please don't leave. Can't we talk?"

"No, Meg. It's Michael you should talk to."

"But he doesn't want to talk."

"You'll have to wait until he's ready."

"Are you sure he'll ever be ready? He was so angry. I've never seen him like that."

"I don't know," Tory whispered truthfully.

"Pop knows?"

"Yes."

"What did he say?"

"I forget. Something like, 'Well, I'm sure he deserved it.' " Tory took Meg's arm. "Come on, let's go in the kitchen."

She made Meg some toast and sliced an apple. While Meg ate in small bites, Tory watched her.

"You really did it?"

Meg lifted her eyes. "Yes."

"I should go," Tory said abruptly, standing up.

Meg stopped chewing. "I had to, Tory."

"I don't think I want to hear any more." She started for the door.

"Tory?"

"Yeah?"

"Be there for Michael. Take care of him."

"I will." She picked up her keys and left.

Meg dropped the apple in her hand. She couldn't eat any more.

CHAPTER SIXTEEN

At Thomas Garrett High School, Meg's students continued to wonder what was going on. She hadn't mentioned any leave the last time they had last seen her. At first, they simply thought she was sick.

The substitute was an elderly retired lady, who mostly tried to keep order. She gave them "busy work" to do and insisted on quiet at all times. Fortunately she was hard of hearing and missed all the whispering. She also didn't see all the notes passed right under her nose.

Meg's teacher friends were curious too. Leon questioned Dr. Gardner about the leave of absence.

"It was rather sudden. Maybe you should talk to her," Dr. Gardner suggested. Dr. Gardner had never been in this position. He didn't know how much he should or could divulge.

Leon then asked Marcus if he knew anything.

"Are you sure he said she was on leave?" Marcus asked him.

"Yes. Something is definitely wrong," Leon said.

Meg started slowly getting herself together, ever so slightly. She finally picked up the phone when she heard Marcus' voice on the answering machine begging her to pick up.

"Meg? Meg! Where have you been? What the hell is goin' on?

We've left you a hundred messages!"

"Marcus, is there anyone there around you?"

"No, I'm alone. I'm on my cell phone. It's my free period. What's goin' on?"

"I'm suspended, Marcus."

"What? What kind of bullshit is this? What for?"

She rearranged her thoughts to give him the shortest version possible. "Marcus, listen to me. My husband was an abuser…"

"What? What does this have to do with…"

"Marcus," she interrupted. "He beat me and in defending myself, I killed him."

Silence. "He was going to kill me," she whispered.

This was more than Marcus had bargained for. He'd figured she was ill or there'd been a death in the family. "Jesus Christ, Meg." He was trying to understand. "And you never told them here at the school?"

"No. No, I didn't. What's worse is that I never told Michael and someone got to him before I could."

"Oh, Meg. This is a pickle. Are you all right?"

"No, not really. I'm coming off three days of crying in bed."

"Morrelli!" he suddenly shouted. "Morrelli's behind this – that racist, homophobic, Nazi son-of-a-bitch! *He* did this!"

"I don't know. I think so. Jim and Lester Smith."

Calming a bit and thinking of his friend, Marcus said, "What are you going to do?"

"I have a hearing in two weeks or so. I have to present my case, so to speak."

"I'm comin' over," Marcus announced.

"No," she said firmly. "I'm not ready yet. I need to be alone. Maybe in a few days?"

"Okay. You know Leon is gonna go ballistic when he hears all this."

"I know. I'm really sorry, Marcus."

"What for?"

"I don't know. You're my friend and I didn't tell any of this to you either."

"Hey, don't worry about it."

"You're the first one who let me tell my side. Thanks," she said, her voice cracking.

"You mean Michael doesn't know everything yet?"

"No, not about the abuse. I made a huge mistake not telling him from the start. It's my own fault."

"You're sure you don't want me to come over?"

"Yes, thanks."

"I'll call you tomorrow."

"Okay."

"Chin up, Meg. Don't let the suckas get you down."

Meg smiled slightly and hung up.

Rumors began spreading amongst Meg's students concerning her absence.

"She's got AIDS."

"No, she needs a heart transplant."

"I heard she's been arrested."

"I heard she blew her old man away."

Marcus, Leon, Regina, and Lynn didn't know whether to let the children gossip or tell them the truth. If they told them the truth, it might somehow cause Meg problems when her hearing came up. No doubt parents would get upset. But was it better to let rumors go on? They were consuming the students, interfering with classes and everyday routines.

They struggled with the notion of telling a core group of Meg's students the truth in hope it would squelch all the rumors.

On the other hand, they were viewed as Meg's friends; "friends of the enemy" as far as the school was concerned. Any move against policy might get them suspended too.

"Sometimes you just have to stand up for what's right," Marcus said.

"Look, I love Meg, but I can't be out of work. My husband isn't working and I just can't take any foolish risks," Regina said.

"Like defending a friend?" Marcus said.

"Look, here…"

"Okay, stop you two. Regina's right. There must be a way that we can help her without getting ourselves in trouble," Leon said.

"If we told Meg's kids, we'd have to tell them not to tell anyone how they found out," Regina said.

"No, that's putting the kids in the middle," Lynn said.

Marcus remained still, thinking. Then he said, "If they found out from an anonymous source…"

"Naa, they'd know it was us," Leon said.

"This is so frustrating," Lynn said.

They sat in silence.

"I still can't believe she killed him," Regina whispered. "Our sweet Meg. He must've been a bastard."

Lynn was welling up. They sat longer in silence, coming up with no real solution.

"Somethin' bad went down," Ronald declared to his friends during lunch at school.

"She deserted us," Geoffrey said, moping. He hadn't played the piano since Meg's suspension. The substitute wouldn't let him. She left the school as soon as the kids did.

"Do you think she's coming back?" Louis asked.

"She better," Jesse said.

"Why didn't she say anything to us? She's always been straight up," Ronald said.

"Let's go ask Mr. Burns. He'll know," Geoffrey suggested, with a glimmer of hope.

"Yeah," Ronald agreed, wishing he had thought of it first.

Ronald, Geoffrey, Louis, and Jesse visited Leon Burns after school that day.

"Yo Mr. Burns, can we talk to you?" Ronald asked from the doorway.

"Sure, Ronald." Leon had been expecting this visit, but wasn't sure how he was going to handle it. He knew Ronald from his reputation and from detention. "What are your friends names again?"

"This is Geoffrey, Louis, and Jesse."

Leon nodded to them. "What can I do for you boys?"

"We want to know where Ms. Robbins is," Geoffrey said timidly.

"I thought they told you. She's on leave."

"Have you talked to her?" Ronald asked.

Leon looked down, not answering.

"Please, Mr. Burns. We just want the truth," Jesse pleaded.

"Look, guys, I don't know how much I can tell you. I have an obligation to Meg…Ms. Robbins. And I could get into trouble from the school for divulging too much."

"You're off the clock, aren't you?" Ronald asked.

"Yes, but I'm still on school property and even so…"

"Suppose we accidentally run into you at say, the corner of Sixteenth and duPont Streets," Ronald said with lifted eyebrows.

"Come on, we gotta know," Louis pleaded.

Leon pondered this and let out a hefty sigh.

"Okay. Screw policy. I'll be there in fifteen minutes. In front of the smoke shop."

Leon knew that these kids had come a long way, largely due to Meg's influence. They loved Meg and Leon felt an obligation to *them* now.

After the meeting with Leon, the foursome stood on the street corner, stunned.

"I can't believe it!" Geoffrey said.

"She smoked her old man!" Louis said.

Jesse was smiling slightly. "I think it's cool. She got away with it, too."

"It ain't cool if she don't have her job," Ronald said.

"No, it ain't cool for us either," Geoffrey sulked.

"Can you imagine anyone wantin' to hit *her?*" Ronald asked incredulously. The role reversal was evident. They felt the need to protect the teacher and friend who had come to mean so much to them in such a short period of time.

"Some people are just like that, ya know?" Jesse said. "They just hit people."

"So, what do we do now?" Jesse directed his question to Ronald.

"Can we go to that hearing?" Geoffrey asked.

"Probably not. And that's almost two weeks away. I feel like doin' somethin' now," Ronald said.

"We could ask Ms. Robbins how to smoke the principal and get away wit' it," Jesse laughed.

"That ain't funny, man," Louis said quietly. "I bet she's low."

"Yeah. I don't like thinkin' of her low," Geoffrey said. "She was always so happy…"

They stood there in silence. Ronald was leaning against the building and looking down. Then he raised his head slowly, looked at the other three and said, "I got it."

The next day after school, Ronald went into the front office.

"What is it, Ronald?" the secretary asked.

"I left a couple of my books in Ms. Robbins room. It's real important. The room is locked."

Dr. Gardner came out of his office. "What is it, Shirley?"

"He needs something in Meg Robbins' classroom."

"Well, Ronald, since I haven't had much trouble with you lately…go ahead, Shirley."

The secretary rolled her eyes out of Dr. Gardner's sight and reached for a ring of keys. "Come on," she said.

Ronald followed her and looked to see if Geoffrey, Jesse, and Louis were all in place in the hallway. They were to create a diversion.

Ronald brushed the side of his nose with his index finger as a signal, something he'd had seen men do in a movie he'd watched on AMC.

After eleven keys, the secretary got the door open. All the while she was mumbling about how she had to get the keys marked and how she had too much stuff to do to be doing *this*. As soon as Ronald walked into the room, a racket in the hallway caused Shirley to run out the door.

"Hey! Stop that right now!"

The others were pretending to have a fistfight. As soon as Shirley disappeared from Ronald's sight, he went to work. He ran to the drawers where he knew Meg kept the CDs and cassettes. Grabbing them, he jammed them into his oversized book bag, then went to the classroom door and peered out.

Geoffrey, moaning dramatically, was on the ground and Jesse was pretending to punch him in the stomach. Louis was standing over Jesse, cheering him on.

"Stop it! Stop it this instant!" Shirley was yelling. "I'm going to get help." Just as she ran off in the direction of the main office, Jim Morrelli came out of his room and the four boys scrambled up and bolted to a designated back exit.

It was just too easy.

Pretty fun, too.

❧

Several days later, Lynn Smithers gathered her belongings to leave school for the day. As she pushed her chair in and flung her purse on her shoulder, she looked up to see Ronald, Geoffrey, Jesse and Louis in the doorway of the choir room.

"Mrs. Smithers?" Ronald asked.

"Yes?"

"Um...I'm Ronald. You're friends with Ms. Robbins, right?"

"Yes."

"We were wondering if you could help us with something..."

CHAPTER SEVENTEEN

Nine days to the hearing and counting. The days went by painfully slow. Meg had a dull headache all the time. She'd lost a lot of weight, eating only enough for existence. She watched TV, though she would have been at a loss to say what she'd seen. Sleep was her only escape.

She had left Michael two phone messages, pleading to talk with him. It was clear he was letting the answering machine screen his calls.

One night, she was awakened by the shrill ring of the phone. It was eleven o'clock. She had been sleeping for an hour. She groped for the phone on the nightstand.

"Hello?" she said groggily.

"Hi, Meg." It was Luther.

"Luther?" Meg was instantly awake and worried.

"Yeah, sorry. It sounds like I woke you up."

"It's okay. Is anything wrong?"

"Yeah. Is Michael there?"

He doesn't know?

Meg paused, caught off-guard. "Nnn…o, he's not."

"Damn," he whispered. "There was no answer at the house and I assumed…"

Meg glanced at the clock on the nightstand. "Wait. No answer at the house? That's weird. Pop's never out past ten. He's a morning person."

"I know."

"Where are you?" Meg asked.

"The police station."

"What? You haven't been arrested, have you?"

"I mouthed off to this cop for giving me a speeding ticket."

"Oh, Luther."

"Look, I can't spend the night here. Could you please come down and bail me out?"

Meg rubbed her eyes. "Sure. How much?"

"Three hundred plus seventy-five for the ticket. Sorry, Meg. I'll pay you back."

"It's okay. I'll have to stop at the ATM. You know something, Luther? Sit tight. I'm gonna go by the house first and see if everything's okay with Pop."

"Okay, but hurry. I can't stand this place."

When she stopped at the house, lights were on downstairs, but Michael's car wasn't there. She decided to go to Pop's private door. Lights were on and the TV was blaring. Though she knocked loudly, no one came. Trying the main door of the house, she knocked but no one answered there either. When she returned to Pop's door and knocked again, this time she heard Pop yell, "Come in!"

Come in? It's eleven-thirty and you don't even know who it is!

She opened the door. "Pop?" she called, walking further into the room. There he was, sitting on the loveseat.

"Pop?"

He looked at her and smiled. "Oh hey, Sue. You're late!"

Meg's brows furrowed. "Pop?"

"Yeah?"

"You just called me Sue."

"The kids are in bed."

"What kids?" Meg was concerned now.

"Our kids, silly!"

Does he think I'm Mootsie? Something was definitely wrong.

"Pop, it's me, Meg."

"I know who you are!"

Pop's eyes looked funny. Not really glassy as if he had a fever. Just different. He drained a glass of water that was sitting on the end table.

Meg picked up the phone to call Tory.

"Hey, Travis. It's Meg."

"Tory can't talk, Meg," he whispered defensively.

"Something's wrong with Pop."

"What is it?"

"I don't know he's incoherent. I think I'm gonna call 911."

"Okay. Call us back," Travis said calmly.

He sounded so calm on the phone that Meg knew he didn't want to upset Tory in her condition.

Meg dialed 911.

"911. Is this an emergency?"

How do I answer that?

"Um, yes, I think so. My...uh...father is disoriented."

"Is he on any medication?"

Meg looked around. "Uh, I don't know."

A pause from the operator. What kind of daughter doesn't know if her father is on medication? "But he's conscious?"

"Yes, he just keeps calling me Sue and, I don't know...acting like it's thirty years ago."

"Okay, we'll send the paramedics."

Meg gave her the particulars and ten minutes later an ambulance arrived and whisked Pop off to the hospital.

Before she went to the hospital, Meg stopped at the police station to pick up Luther. She waited at the desk for the paperwork, nervously tapping her pen on the counter. When the paperwork was placed before her, she glanced at it and noticed the speed at which Luther was traveling. Fifty-eight in a fifty-five mph speed zone.

"He was going fifty-eight in a fifty-five?"

"Yes. That's *speeding*," the police officer said to her, as if she were a child. He was a burly, balding man who looked as if he had been behind the counter for too long.

Meg stared at him. "And no one was going faster than that?"

"We don't have records of what all the other cars were doing."

Since when do you get pulled over for going three miles per hour over the speed limit on an interstate? Meg wondered. But she didn't have time to argue. She was worried about Pop and needed to get to the hospital.

Luther was released to her and on the way out to the parking lot, Meg said, "Fifty-eight in a fifty-five?"

Luther just looked at her. "Welcome to my world. *You* know why I got pulled over. That's why I mouthed off."

They got into Meg's car as she gave him the lowdown on Pop.

"He was calling you *Sue*?" he asked, disbelieving.

"Yeah. I'm worried."

"Well, step on it, girl. Let's get to the hospital."

On the way, Meg had Luther call Michael and Tory from her cell phone.

Once they got to the hospital, Luther inquired at the desk and was told that Pop was being "worked on." Only minutes after they arrived, Michael came tearing in.

"Where is he? Is he all right?" He directed his questions to Luther, only glancing at Meg once or twice.

"We don't know anything yet." Luther repeated what he had said on the answering machine about Pop being incoherent.

Tory and Travis came rushing in then.

More repetition.

The emergency waiting room was almost filled. A TV was on in the corner, but no one watched it.

Meg stood alone, outside the group. Outside the family. She could see Travis off whispering to Luther. Then Luther's stunned face. Stares at Meg.

She sat down, elbows on her knees, looking down. She knew Luther was finally being told about everything. She couldn't look at Michael. It hurt too much.

After an eternity, the doctor emerged. "Mr. Harrington?" Meg stood but stayed where she was, straining to listen. The family huddled around the doctor.

"Yes?" Michael answered.

"Your father will be fine. It was his blood sugar."

"You mean he has diabetes?" Michael asked.

"Yes. Have you noticed anything different about him lately?"

"Well, he has been more tired."

"How about increased thirst or labored breathing?"

"I don't know." Michael felt guilty. Wallowing in his own misery, he had not been aware that something was wrong with Pop.

"Can you get diabetes this late in life?" Tory asked.

"Yes. It's called adult-onset diabetes. A normal blood sugar level is between 90 and 130. Your father's was 800. That would account for the confusion he experienced this evening."

The family exchanged looks of concern.

The doctor continued. "Whoever found him tonight quite likely saved his life. He was close to acute circulatory collapse."

They all glanced at Meg. She was listening intently, but turned away swiftly when all eyes went to her. She stuffed her hands deeply into her loose-fitting blue jean pockets.

"What can we do for him?" Michael asked.

"First, he should lose a few pounds. Of course, we'll be giving him a special diet, and since he was a doctor, I'm sure that giving himself insulin injections won't be a problem."

"Exercise?" Tory asked.

"No exercise while his ketones are high. Let's get them under control first. Oh, and stress. Stress can trigger an episode."

Michael looked at Meg again.

"When can we see him?" Luther asked.

"Soon. Only family for a few minutes."

Michael approached her. She crossed her arms defensively; afraid of what he was going to say. Her heart pounded. She rubbed her arms as though she were cold.

"You can leave now. The family will stay," he said to her coldly.

Meg looked as though she had been slapped. No words could've hurt her more. She was no longer considered family. Luther quickly stepped up behind Michael in support, peering over his shoulder.

Meg looked up into his face, back straight despite how she felt inside. "I'll go, Michael. Not because you want me to, but because I know that Pop's going to be all right."

Michael and Luther stared at her, waiting for her to leave. Tory and Travis were whispering softly. Meg turned to leave, feeling a huge sob welling up in her. She moved toward the automatic doors and suddenly broke into a full sprint. The sob exploded from her outside the doors.

Michael took a step toward the door. Luther, still looking a bit bewildered at what he had just learned about Meg, placed a hand on his shoulder, stopping him. Seeing her made Michael hurt all over again. He had an overwhelming urge to run after her.

"Come on, man," Luther said gently.

Michael closed his eyes. He didn't feel good about himself. He turned with Luther and joined the family.

Meg visited Pop the next day shortly after visiting hours started at eleven o'clock. She figured she'd have the least chance of running into Michael at this hour. Pop had a private room. She knocked on the already-open door and he looked toward her, smiling. She pulled a chair up to his bedside.

"Hi Pop," she said softly.

"Hi baby," he said.

"How ya feelin'?"

"Pretty good."

"Good. I brought you these." She gave him flowers and the newspaper.

"Aww, thanks."

She set the flowers on the windowsill and put the paper on the nightstand.

"I hear I was calling you Sue," Pop said.

"Yeah." She held his hand.

He sniffed a laugh. "You must remind me of Mootsie."

"That's the nicest thing anyone's ever said to me."

"Oh, I'm sure Michael has said nicer things to you."

Meg looked down. "Not lately. Pop, I'm so sorry about everything."

At that moment, Michael started to walk through the open door, spotted Meg and flattened himself against the wall right outside the door. Neither Pop nor Meg saw him.

"Now, Meg, I'm sure you had good reason…"

"Listen, Pop, let's talk about it later. I don't want to cause you any more stress."

"You? Naaw, you didn't. The doctor thinks all of this may have been building during Mootsie's illness. All the chemo and seeing her deteriorate – that took a lot out of me."

They sat in silence a moment, deep in their own thoughts.

Pop continued, "I'm glad you came over when you did. Tory says you saved me."

"Oh…I don't know."

"Thanks, baby."

"You're welcome," she whispered.

"So, when are you gonna make up with my firstborn?"

Michael grew tense on the other side of the doorway. He wanted to interrupt them, but he also wanted to hear her answer. He strained to hear Meg's voice. It was barely a whisper.

"Oh, Pop, I miss him so much. I made such a terrible mistake. He won't talk to me."

Michael closed his eyes and leaned his head against the wall.

"You have to *make* him talk. You know how stubborn he can be."

Meg nodded. She laid her head on Pop's chest. Pop gently rubbed her back.

Hearing nothing, Michael cleared his throat loudly, then turned the corner into Pop's room. He was carrying a bag of Pop's belongings.

"Hi Pop!" he said cheerfully. "Hello, Meg," he said formally, as if she were a stranger.

Meg sat bolt upright, visibly stiffened. She was afraid he'd throw her out again.

"Hi," Meg said as she stood. "I better go, Pop. I'll be back, okay?" She kissed him on the cheek.

"Okay. Remember what I said."

"Bye," she whispered to Michael as she slipped past him. She'd started walking down the hallway when she heard Michael call.

"Meg?"

She froze and slowly turned.

Please don't say anything to hurt me again.

He cautiously approached her. "I forgot to thank you for what you did."

Meg nodded, saying nothing, looking at the cinder block wall next to her. He noticed the eternity chain still around her neck. He pulled down the cuff of his shirt so she wouldn't see the ID bracelet he refused to remove.

He continued, "I also wanted to apologize for what I said…you know…about family."

She didn't know what to say. Not 'it's okay' because it wasn't. It had really hurt. She looked up into his eyes.

What's this? Are his eyes pleading?

"Michael, we really need to talk."

He nodded. "Yeah," he whispered. "But, I…can't…I just can't…" He spun and walked swiftly back to Pop's room.

Meg stood there for a long time. Pop had said make him talk. But how?

She left the hospital confused but hopeful. He had spoken to her civilly. It was an improvement.

When she got back to the townhouse, she went to change into

some jeans. She was from the old school which taught that if you go to visit someone in the hospital, you dress nicely. It bugged Meg to see people dressed in sweat pants or baggy jean shorts in any place that called for higher standards.

Searching for her favorite pair of jeans, she went to a different closet, opened it, and froze. Bunches of Michael's clothes hung there. They had taken to leaving clothes and other necessities at each other's houses. She caressed one of his flannel shirts, then pulled it off the hanger and rubbed it against her face. It smelled like him. She started to cry, then stopped abruptly when she realized she might not be able to catch his scent. She put the shirt on, closed her eyes, and tried to conjure him up. Her eyes welled. She ached for Michael.

She went downstairs, turned the TV on low, and sat on the sofa rehearsing what she could say to Michael to get him to listen to her. The first few sentences were important. Her future with him depended on it – if indeed she even had a future with him anymore.

The doorbell rang and she looked startled as though she were being interrupted from an actual conversation. Maybe it was him. She went to the door with hope, but it was Tory.

"Hi," Tory said.

"Hi."

"Nice shirt."

She was swimming in Michael's shirt. It extended past her knees and she hadn't bothered rolling up the cuffs. They hung loosely past her fingertips. She'd forgotten she had it on.

"I saw Pop today," Meg told her.

"Yes, I know. I was just at the hospital. He told me. They're keeping him another day for observation."

"I was so worried last night."

"Yeah, me too. I'm glad you thought to go over. Michael was feeling a little guilty. After all, he moved home to keep an eye on him. But Luther and I are just as guilty for not helping. We've left everything in Michael's hands." She sat down on the sofa. Meg sat down on the opposite side, looking at her inquisitively. Tory licked her lips nervously. She looked at Meg and finally uttered, "I want you to tell me everything."

Okay, she wants it. Here goes.

Meg heaved a massive sigh. Where to begin? "Bill started physically abusing me about five years into the marriage."

"I *knew* it. I knew that son-of-a-bitch…"

"Prior to that, he was doing stuff like, you know…" Meg grasped for the words. "He'd play with my mind. He'd tell me he was going out to dinner, and then show up at dinnertime demanding that I cook. Or he'd say he was going to do something and then he'd say he never said it. It sounds stupid, but when you string all those incidences together…I thought he was trying to drive me crazy. For that reason, I started keeping a notebook, in case we ended up in counseling or divorce."

"That was smart, to document everything. Where's the notebook?"

"I don't know. I think the district attorney in Los Angeles has it. They have pictures and a video of my testimony, too. Anyway, the first time he hit me was over food again. He wanted dinner on the table every night. Never mind that he didn't show up half the time. I'd have chicken, filet mignon, pork roast sitting in the refrigerator going bad. He hit me for wasting food, but he refused to eat leftovers. He slapped me across the face the first time I talked back to him."

"Why did you stay? A man hits you once, you get the hell out, 'cause he's sure to do it again," Tory said strongly.

Meg repositioned herself on the sofa to face Tory more directly.

"It's hard to explain. It wasn't all bad, ya know? He could be so charming when he wanted to be. He was always so sorry afterwards. Sometimes he'd even cry. Then he'd wine and dine me, buy me things... We'd go to Lakers games and he'd introduce me to some of the players..."

Tory interrupted in order to get Meg back on track. "How often did he hit you?"

"It increased over the years. I don't know, maybe once a month toward the end."

Tory felt agitated. She couldn't relate to this abuse. She'd never experienced it and couldn't understand why any woman would endure it. "Why didn't you tell us, your family? You know we woulda come right out there to bring you *home*."

"Believe me, I must have picked up the phone a hundred times. All I could picture was Pop or Michael coming out to Los Angeles and killing him."

Tory sputtered, "You got that right!"

"Bill threatened me that if I ever left, he'd never leave me alone." Meg lowered her head and voice. "Then he threatened the whole family."

Tory sighed deeply and shook her head slowly. "Son-of-a-bitch..."

They sat for a moment, Meg letting Tory digest what she had just been told.

"So, what set him off that night? I mean, what made that night different?"

"I didn't know this until later, but he saw me at a bar with some of my teacher friends. I was with, like, six people. But apparently when Bill walked in, the others were dancing and I was left at the table with a very attractive male colleague, Matt."

"So, he thought…"

"Yeah. Bill's girlfriend, Jerri, told me that he saw me."

"His… Oh, my God. It just keeps getting worse."

"It sounds like a soap opera, doesn't it? Meg shook her head. "I mean, these things aren't supposed to happen in real life. Jerri thought I knew about her. She actually was helpful in the end. He'd hit her, too."

Tory shook her head. The lawyer's mind in Tory was racing and planning. But the sister in her was grieving for her friend. "I guess Michael is a far cry from Bill," she said softly.

"The farthest," Meg whispered. "That's the thing. I was so busy trying to protect what I had with Michael… Oh, Tory, how could I think that I could keep it from him? Why would I want to? I was so afraid."

Tory decided she didn't need to scold Meg. She was doing a pretty good job of beating herself up.

"So, what happened when Bill got home that night?" Tory probed.

Meg took a deep breath. She was ready to tell.

CHAPTER EIGHTEEN

Fifteen months earlier

Meg heard the car door slam in the driveway. These late nights with Bill were never good. Because his job of freelance sports writer meant that his hours were often irregular, Meg never knew his schedule from one day to the next, an aspect of his job that he quite enjoyed. He appeared at home or at Meg's work whenever he felt like it. He sometimes spent long nights out with the excuse that he was working on a column. She suspected that he was having an affair. He could hide a lot – and did. She could hide very little from him.

When he came home late, he'd be loud, aggressive, and abusive. Usually, he would have been drinking.

The moment he entered the house, he would start yelling something incomprehensible. Then there would be mumbling, tripping, then more yelling with expletives. Meg's body would grow tense as she pulled the covers up under her chin. Sometimes, if she faked being asleep, he'd leave her alone.

The night it happened, it began with the usual noises downstairs. Then he suddenly burst into the room, the doorknob banging into the wall behind it. Drywall crumbled to the floor. He was breathing heavily.

My God, he stinks.

The liquor and smoke smell instantly filled the room, making Meg gag.

I can't fake being asleep if I'm gagging...

He stood by the bed a moment, looking at her. This pause was excruciating. A psychologically frightening moment of nothing.

Meg heard a noise and took a quick peek. He'd started pulling off his clothes. He was pathetically clumsy, unable to keep his balance.

Still in his boxers, he pulled the covers off Meg, straddled her and started pulling at her nightgown. This was his favorite position because she couldn't go anywhere. He was in control. He was still mumbling words that she couldn't understand.

I hate him.

"No, Bill," Meg managed to utter in her best sleepy voice, as she clutched at the sheets.

"Don't tell me no. You're my wife, for crissakes," he slurred. "I'm not gonna beg for it."

It was obvious what that meant. But she had had enough. She leaned up on her elbows. "I said no."

He looked startled at first, surprised at her defiance. Even in his drunken stupor he noticed something different about her. He stood up by the side of the bed, the veins pulsing in his temples. Her breathing shallow, Meg braced herself. She tried to avoid eye contact with him, but it only left her unprepared for the first blow. He hit the side of her head with such force she flew sideways out of the bed, knocking the lamp off the nightstand. She lay crumpled on the floor in a fetal position. She felt the welt from his ring already rising on her cheekbone.

He was standing over her, panting. She started to uncurl her body in an effort to get up, trying at the same time to move away from him. He kicked her as hard as he could in her stomach. She screamed out in pain and saw bright white flashes of light, then stars, and instinctively curled back up. He raised his foot to kick again but stopped in mid-swing when he realized she was curled up too tightly and he no longer had a clear shot. He stumbled up against the wall.

I've got to get out of here!

She lost sight of him. Her vision was blurred. Suddenly it was quiet. Why was it quiet? She started to crawl toward the steps. She couldn't get up. Her mid-section throbbed. Whimpering in pain, she sat down on the first step and started sliding down one step at a time. Her left eye was almost swollen shut now. She was totally dependent on the blurred vision of her right eye.

I'll get some ice, my keys, and I'll slip out.

She was more than halfway down the steps when she heard him behind her, running down the steps. He kicked her with all his might right between the shoulder blades, then lost his balance and fell on top of her. She tumbled down the last few steps. This time she felt her ankle twist. The pain shot everywhere. Somewhere beyond the pain, she heard him cursing as he tried to get up.

Ice. She needed ice. She had to get to the kitchen.

Jesus, where are my keys?

Through sheer will, she pulled herself up and hobbled into the kitchen. Ice. She needed ice. She jerked the ice tray from the freezer and shuffled to the sink.

He had been abusive before, but this time it was different. He didn't care *where* he hurt her. He was kicking and swinging haphazardly. Usually, it was more calculated. Meg had a very bad feeling. She suddenly knew with absolute certainty that she had to get out right away – not just out of the house, but out of the marriage. She had to save herself.

All at once, she sensed him behind her. Before she could react, he grabbed her hair and suddenly, violently, her head snapped back. Ice flew in every direction. She felt blood trickling down her scalp. She screamed in pain, sobbing for him to stop.

Please, God, just let me get out of here alive.

Then, abruptly, eerily, he calmed himself. His breathing was still heavy, but he gently moved his hands up and down her arms. Meg shuddered and forced back the wail building up inside.

I'm not going to give him the satisfaction.

"What's the matter, baby?" he whispered.

Meg braced herself against the kitchen sink and closed her eyes. Then she turned to face him. Maybe he'd have some compassion if he were looking directly at her. He was so close he had her pinned to the sink.

Be brave. Say it.

"I'm leaving, Bill."

Bill's face tightened. "What do ya mean?"

"I'm leaving," she stammered. "I can't stand this anymore." She sounded much more pathetic than she wanted.

Through clenched teeth he spat, "All you have to do is give me what I want. I bring home good money, don't I? I let you buy whatever you want. Most women would love to be in your shoes."

"I make money too," Meg reasoned.

Bill threw his head back and cackled a horrid, nasty laugh. "You call what you make as a teacher *money*?" He laughed again. "You can't survive on your own with that kind of salary. You depend on me. Where would you live, anyway?"

"I'm going to move back home to Delaware."

"You mean home to that nigger family of yours? Over my dead body."

He leaned against her, pinning her. The edge of the formica cut into her lower back. Curiously, it didn't hurt.

"Move," she said.

"You'll never get away from me. I'll follow you and I'll find you no matter where you are. I'll never leave you alone. I can kill off your little family and make it look like an accident."

"Move!" Meg said. But the minute she said it, she got more scared.

His hands moved up and down her arms again, then rested on her shoulders as he stared coldly into her eyes.

"You will *not* leave me. I fought hard to get you. I even fought that nigger Michael for you. No one else will have you."

Michael? Fought him? What's he talking about?

Something changed in his eyes and his hands moved to her neck and started to squeeze. His face was vacant, dead.

"Let's hear you yell for help now, nigger-lover."

Meg whimpered and struggled uselessly. Bill was a big man. Meg was tiny, one hundred ten pounds soaking wet.

Then Bill imitated Meg trying to call out for help. "*Pop! Michael! Help me!*" he whined, then laughed horridly.

Meg could hardly get any air now, but those names...Pop...Michael...

My family loves me.

My family loves me...

Meg fumbled on the counter behind her for the kitchen drain board. She felt the cold blade of the knife cut her finger. She traced the blade to the rubbery handle and wrapped her fingers around it. She prayed he couldn't see what she was doing.

I hate him.

She could not miss. The consequences would be too dear. Her actions had to be swift. She brought the knife around and plunged it blindly into Bill's stomach.

Oh my God.

She felt the knife hit something. Bill's eyes widened, his mouth

171

gaped. His grip around her neck relaxed. She sucked in a deep breath. His face was so close to hers, she could taste his sour breath in her own mouth. She felt momentarily dizzy, outside her own body. Her mind raced.

What if he doesn't die?

What if I'm stuck with him in a wheelchair or he's a vegetable or something?

What if he can still attack me?

With that, she pulled the knife out and purposefully stabbed him a second time, as close to his heart as she could guess. The second time the blade went in a little easier. No hard obstruction.

Bill's eyes widened further and he moaned horribly. Blood trickled from his mouth as his body sagged toward her. Meg shoved him backward with strength she didn't know she had, screaming a sound that echoed as though it came from somewhere else in the house. He fell heavily to the floor and lay there quietly.

Meg stood there, breathing fast. Realization suddenly set in. Her hands shook and she began to sob. This was someone she had loved once. She started to raise her hands to her face, then saw they were blood-covered, especially the right one. She looked down at Bill's body. Blood was gathering in a large, dark pool at his side. The blood looked thicker than it did in the movies. And darker. There was so much blood that he had to be dead.

An eerie calm came over her in just a few short minutes. Her breathing returned to normal, except there was a whistle in her throat every time she exhaled. She walked over to the phone and called 911.

"Hello, my name is Meg Robbins. I've just stabbed my husband."

She caught a glimpse of herself in the microwave door.

My God, is that me?

She looked like a prizefighter who'd lost the big fight.

When the police arrived, it didn't take a genius to deduce what had happened. They took Meg to the hospital and she was released a few hours later. She voluntarily went down to the police station, where they took photos and a video of her statement. She was released under her own recognizance.

After a speedy preliminary hearing, the case was dismissed. Friends of Bill who showed up at the hearing didn't even stay until the end, realizing that they, too, had been Bill's victims.

Meg left for Delaware as soon as she got all of her affairs in order. She had avoided looking back. Until now.

CHAPTER NINETEEN

Days passed without word from Tory or anyone. Although Meg had been able to tell Tory everything that night, it hardly made her feel better. Instead, it had stirred up some deeply buried emotions, and with no contact from anyone, Meg fell into a deeper depression. She had stopped planning for the hearing with the school board, figuring that she'd wing it and answer the questions as honestly as she could. She stayed in her pajamas all day long. Her head pounded. Her eyes burned. Periodic waves of nausea rippled through her, so she lay there on the sofa, not up to moving around.

She was at her lowest low, beginning to give up now. Too many days had passed. Had Tory told Michael? Surely she had. He was her brother. Blood is thicker than water – and let's face it – Meg wasn't blood. Michael had reminded her of that fact in the hospital.

She fell asleep on the sofa with the TV on mute, punishing herself with the silence. She didn't deserve the joy of music, laughter, or conversation.

She was awakened by a soft melodic sound. Thinking that she was dreaming, she rubbed her eyes, and looked around. Had she left the radio on in the kitchen? No, that hadn't been on in days. The sound was coming from the porch. What was it? It was muffled. The song "Lida Rose?"

In a sleep-induced fog, she slowly rose from the sofa, walked to the porch door and opened it. The song rang out louder, the harmonies not perfect, but loud and strong.

She gazed upon the four beautiful faces of her students serenading her in the near perfect barbershop song, two of them kneeling on one knee, the other two standing behind them.

Meg beamed and her hands flew up to her cheeks in delight. She waited for them to finish the song, smiling, crying. Her kids had come to her rescue. She was overwhelmingly touched. She broke down crying, then sat down in one of the porch chairs.

The boys looked at each other, dumbfounded. Had they made her feel worse? They stood there not knowing what to do next. Maybe they had made a terrible mistake.

Finally, she smiled through her tears and said, "That was so beautiful!" Then they began grinning, quite proud of themselves. "Thank you so much," she whispered, placing her hand over her mouth to muffle yet another sob.

"Hey, Ms. Robbins, don't cry. This was 'sposed to cheer you up," Louis said.

"Oh, it did! I can't believe you did this for me!"

"We thought you'd be low, so we… ya know…" Jesse shrugged.

"Yeah. You made school fun, ya know? We miss you there," Geoffrey said sincerely.

There was a long pause. Then Meg asked them, "Do you want to know what happened?"

"We already made Mr. Burns tell us," Ronald said with authority, as though he hadn't given Leon a choice but to tell them.

"You don't look too good, Ms. Robbins. You look…all skinny and all," Jesse said.

"Shut up, man," Ronald scolded. "We came to cheer her up. You don't go sayin' that she don't look good!"

"It's okay, Ronald. It's true. I haven't been doing too well emotionally. I want to get back in the classroom, and my personal life is in a shambles. Anyway, I'm so glad you're here."

They talked for a long time in Meg's kitchen, eating microwave popcorn and drinking every can of soda in her house. They told Meg how they'd taken all her CDs so that they could find the song, not remembering which CD had a barbershop song on it. They updated her on all the gossip in the school, too.

While the boys were there, she received a call from Marcus. He and Leon had been on a senior class trip as chaperones and he apologized for not being in touch for a few days. They talked briefly about the upcoming hearing. When he told her that her friends at school were getting together the next day to plan how to help, Meg was cheered. People were coming to her rescue all at once.

Then talk with the "quartet" seemed to drift naturally into confidences. She learned that Ronald's mother was a prostitute, he called her an escort, and that he lived part of the time with Geoffrey since their mothers were sisters.

Jesse lived with his maternal grandmother because his mother had died of a heroin overdose when he was only six. Louis's mother worked two jobs and Louis barely saw her. He had no clue about his father. He'd never asked, and his mother had never told. They were children having to deal with very adult problems.

Meg felt overwhelmed that these students with so many problems of their own had worried about her. When they left, she hugged each one of them and kissed them on their cheeks. Even Ronald let her.

On the way out, Ronald said, "Oh, Ms. Robbins, I almost forgot. Andrew wanted us to tell you that Erika had some bruises again."

"Where?"

"On her arms and neck."

Meg guessed that because the weather was warmer, the kids were dressing lighter and Erika wasn't able to hide as much in short sleeves.

Her winter clothes had probably concealed everything.

"Thanks for telling me. Tell Andrew I'll do what I can."

"You gonna get her step dad arrested?" Geoffrey asked.

"I don't know what I can do since I'm suspended, but I'll make some calls – maybe to social services." She knew she had to do something for her – and soon.

Meg visited Travis early the morning after the boys' visit. Tory and Travis' house was a beautiful contemporary just outside the city limits, which Michael had designed for her. And it had a sprawling lawn, ready for a growing family.

When Travis opened the door to Meg, it was clear that he wasn't pleased to see her.

"Hi, Travis."

"Meg," he said coolly.

"Uh, I brought you some of Mootsie's sauce. You can freeze it if you want to."

He took the container, wordlessly staring her down. She was very uncomfortable. She swallowed.

"May I come in?"

"Tory's not here."

"That's okay. I came to see you."

"I have to leave for work soon."

"I know. I'll just be a few minutes. I really needed to see you before school. It's not like I can visit you *there*, you know."

"Yeah," he said as he stepped aside to let her in, then stood in the tiled two-story foyer, unwilling to let Meg get any further inside.

Their voices echoed.

"Some of the kids came to visit me at my house and they talked about Erika Woods. They're saying that she's bruised again."

"Then it's time to take action. I'll call social services."

Meg nodded. "I'm so afraid for her. I hope the stepfather doesn't take it out on her."

"This is the right thing to do. We have to protect the child."

She nodded again. "Okay." There was an awkward silence. Then Meg heaved a heavy sigh. "I guess I better go."

Travis avoided eye contact as she started for the door.

"Meg," he said, stopping her.

"Yes?"

"I would like you to stay away from Tory."

"What?" Meg whispered.

"It's just that I don't want anything upsetting her during her pregnancy. This whole thing has gotten her so upset…"

Meg stepped toward him, looking at him directly. "Travis, you know I would never do anything to intentionally hurt Tory."

"It's the unintentional stuff that I'm worried about. She also loves her brother and it's killing her to see him like he is."

Meg closed her eyes momentarily. "I love Michael – and I still have hopes I can make it right with him. I adore Tory. Please don't ask me to stay away from her. She's been coming to see *me* anyway."

"I know. I know. She would kill me if she knew that I was saying this to you."

"I know how much this baby means to you. I'll make sure I take special care not to upset her."

Travis nodded, knowing that it was probably useless trying to keep these two women apart. They were forever a part of each other.

After saying goodbye to Travis, Meg went to her church's rectory.

"I need to speak to Father Delaney," she told the secretary.

"May I ask what this is in reference to?"

Meg looked at her for a moment. "I just need to talk to him."

The secretary stared at Meg as though she had a third eye in the middle of her forehead. "Confessions are before the Saturday night masses…"

"Listen, I need to speak with him face to face, as soon as possible," Meg said firmly.

"You need to make an appointment. Let's see…" She ran her finger down pages in an appointment book, flipping the pages several times.

Meg grabbed the book from her hands and closed it. She leaned toward the secretary and spoke slowly, holding her eyes.

"I need to speak with my priest, now."

"I…I'll see if he's in," the secretary sputtered and disappeared through a door.

In a few moments, Father Delaney emerged from the door, smiling. "Hello." He extended his hand. "You are?"

Meg looked at the secretary, who had resumed her position behind the desk. Meg didn't want to say her name in front of her, so she said, "May I tell you in private?"

"Sure," he said, waving her into the lounge. The lounge was a spacious room off the office. Although it was heavy and masculine, full of dark paneling and books, it was filled with sofas and chairs.

"I'm sorry if I interrupted you in the middle of something. My name is Meg Robbins. I need reconciliation, Father, but I'd rather do it this way due to… the weight of my sins."

Father Delaney's curiosity was piqued. "All right. I'm glad you came to me."

Once Meg started talking, she didn't stop, sometimes crying, sometimes expressing anger, but mostly just relating events in a soft, little girl voice. Several times during Meg's confession, a buzzer went off inside the room. Finally, Father Delaney got up, excused himself and left the room.

After a few moments, he returned. "I'm sorry about that. I'm not used to having confessions in here. We won't be interrupted any more."

"I'm sure other confessions aren't this terrible either," Meg said.

"Oh, you'd be surprised." He smiled reassuringly.

Meg continued her story, right up to the present day. The priest's face had registered sympathy when she told him about the abuse, shock when she told him of the murder, fascination when she told him about Michael, and warmth when she told him about her students.

"First of all, Meg, you must be a very tough person to have endured what you have."

"I don't feel very tough."

"Of course you don't. From what you're telling me, you've been moping around feeling sorry for yourself, when you need to grab the bull by the horns and straighten out your life. Why did you come to me?"

"I don't know. Forgiveness? Someone impartial to talk to? A direct line to God?" said Meg.

Father Delaney chuckled. "Now, you are obviously a loving person, with Jesus in her heart and I think deep down you know what you need to do. You give love with no expectation of anything in return. What's your plan, Meg? Besides coming back to the church, of course."

Meg paused, not sure what to say.

"It's your life. What do you think?" he encouraged.

"Oh, well…I…I guess I should go see Michael first. Try to get him to listen."

"He will."

"I wish I had your confidence. Then I should plan more for the hearing on Saturday."

"Good."

"What else?" she asked, sighing.

"What about your health? You said you haven't been taking care of yourself."

"Yeah. I didn't see the point."

"More self-pity! Snap out of it!" he said not unkindly.

Meg raised her eyebrows and smiled. She chuckled softly. He smiled back.

"Thank you, Father. I really needed someone to lay it out like this, you know?"

"I could tell. I hope I was of some help. What do you say, Meg, let's go eat lunch – my treat!"

"Lunch?" She looked at her watch. "Oh my G… It's one o'clock! I've been here for four hours?"

"Uh huh. Did I mention that I charge seventy-five dollars an hour?" he joked. "And we haven't even talked about penance yet."

She smiled. "Yeah…" Then her smile disappeared. "Penance…"

"Start out with about a million *Hail Marys*…"

Michael busied himself with Pop in the days following Pop's release from the hospital. The memory of seeing Meg at the hospital ate away at him. He didn't know how things could go on the way they were. Busying himself with Pop, driving Pop crazy was a way of avoiding thinking about Meg.

"Michael, I'm all right," Pop said, rolling his eyes as Michael fluffed up his pillows.

"How about some eggs?"

"No, just some cereal. But not now. Besides, I want to go into the kitchen this morning and move around."

"There's no rush, Pop."

"Yes, there is."

Michael looked at him inquisitively.

"I love you, son, but you're hovering over me. Even Luther has been around too much. I'm okay now – just regaining my strength and getting used to the new diet."

It was true Luther had been around more, for both Pop and Michael. He and Michael had bonded after Luther learned of the split with Meg. Between that and Pop's illness, they'd grown closer. It was the only good thing to happen over those hellish days.

Michael's face relaxed. He knew that what Pop was saying was true. "Sorry, Pop. I'll give you a little space."

"Son, when are you gonna talk to Meg?"

Michael froze momentarily at the mention of her name. "I'm not sure."

"You need to do it, ya know?"

"I know. I will."

"When?" Pop persisted.

"I don't know," Michael said, sounding mildly irritated. "Soon."

CHAPTER TWENTY

The day after hearing Meg's story, Tory had put in a call to the Los Angeles District Attorney to request everything to do with the police investigation –the notebook, the photos, the video testimony.

Finally the package arrived at her office late one Thursday afternoon, two days before Meg's Saturday hearing.

"Just in time," she said out loud to herself. She peeked her head out and said to her secretary, "No interruptions, please, Bonnie." After closing the office door, she pulled open the tab on the large envelope. Inside was everything she'd requested. She took the videocassette of Meg's testimony and inserted it into the VCR.

An hour later, Tory splashed cold water on her face in her office bathroom. She held onto the sink for support, head bowed. She had just finished dry heaving. How in the world could Meg have put up with all that? That bastard!

"He didn't deserve to live!" she said out loud.

She hadn't even looked at everything yet, and had read only part of the notebook, but that was enough. It was time to show all this to Michael.

Tory drove to the house with both anticipation and foreboding.

Should she watch the video with Michael? No, she decided. She couldn't put herself through that again.

It was around six p.m. when she arrived, pulling in at the same time as Michael.

"Hey, Tory," he greeted her outside.

"Hey."

"Here to see Pop?"

"No. You."

"Oh, `cause he's on a casino bus trip."

"So you let him out of your sight for the day?"

"I made Luther go with him," he said sheepishly.

Tory snorted a laugh, trying to picture Luther on a bus with a bunch of seniors. They entered the house, Michael detecting some tension. His eyes examined her.

"What's wrong?" he asked.

She pressed her lips together, licking them. "You need to sit down and watch something."

"Oh, Tory, not now..."

"Now, Michael," she said firmly. She removed the tape from the envelope, waving it at him. "You are gonna watch this tape and you're gonna watch it now."

He stared at her. His sister was stubborn, but he'd never saw her quite so insistent.

"What is it?"

"Just...never mind. Sit down!" she commanded.

He obeyed, eyes round, mouth slightly open. She popped the tape into the VCR, and plopped the pictures and notebook on the sofa next to him.

"I'm leaving," she said. "Promise me you'll look at it all."

He nodded.

She pressed play and left.

❧

The tape contained everything. The sight of Meg with bruised and swollen face made Michael blink in horror. He was hypnotized as the story unfolded. First, the police interrogated her about that fateful night. She recounted the struggle in the bedroom, the blows to her stomach, the tumble down the steps, the near scalping, the attempted strangulation. The camera zoomed in on her bruised neck when she mentioned the strangulation.

The police asked if Bill had been abusive in the past. Meg appeared to sort through her memories, picking out typical behaviors to describe to them. First she told them how he'd mentally abused her, leading to her decision to keep the notebook. Michael glanced at the notebook next to him on the couch. His eyes went back to the TV screen, where Meg was speaking of particular abuses:

The everyday verbal abuse and humiliation.

The countless bruising.

The time he knocked her tooth out.

The time he shoved her down the stairs and caused a miscarriage, then blamed her for it.

The time he burned the soles of her feet with a lit cigarette.

The many times he raped and sodomized her.

When the tape finished, he looked at the photos. Michael's hands shook as he sorted through them. One of Meg's face. Another of the clump of missing hair. Another of her swollen ankle. Another of her bare, bruised mid-section. Several shots of her neck. His stomach churned.

Michael had never before wanted to kill anyone. But at that moment, he wanted to kill Bill with his bare hands. He had to keep reminding himself that he was already dead. How could anyone hurt his Meg like that? He sat tormented, ready to explode.

Tory was sitting on Meg's porch when Meg got to her townhouse at a little before seven. Meg waved, parked, and grabbed a bag of groceries from the car and went in through the kitchen. She was making good on her promise to Father Delaney to take care of herself and had stopped by the grocery store.

She ran to the front door to let Tory in.

"Hey!" she greeted her. "Look at you! That baby's coming sooner than you think!"

"Well, you sure look and sound better." Tory assessed her.

"Yeah, I had an epiphany today," she said, leading Tory back into the kitchen. "I'm going to see Michael tonight."

Tory guiltily looked at Meg and swallowed hard. "I'm glad. Um, Meg, there's something I need to tell you."

Hearing the distress in Tory's voice, Meg stopped unpacking the groceries. "What is it? Is everyone all right? Is the baby okay?"

"Yes. Yes. I…I did something you may be mad at me for."

Meg visibly stiffened. "What?" she asked, a little frightened. Then, "You told Michael, didn't you?"

"No, not exactly," she sighed. "I obtained your video and stuff from the district attorney. I thought it might be helpful to you on Saturday."

Meg absorbed this standing perfectly still, not even blinking.

Then she sat down at the kitchen table. "Did you watch it?" she asked, not able to look at her.

Tory sat down also. "Yes. Meg, I just can't believe it…"

"Stop. You're not supposed to be getting upset. Besides, I just went through the whole thing with my priest. I don't want to…"

"Your priest?" Tory interrupted.

"Yeah. You know, Tory, I don't mind that you did that for me, you know, how you went to the trouble and all, but there's no way I want the school board seeing that. Where is it now? Do you have it with you?"

Tory looked at her guiltily.

Meg waited. "Tory?"

Tory's eyes darted from the tablecloth to Meg. She picked at a thread.

Meg's face fell. "Oh, Tory. You didn't."

"You said you didn't want me telling him. It was killin' me, Meg! This way I didn't break my promise. If Michael watched the video, it would be as though *you* were telling him. In fact, you're…probably almost done…" her voice trailed off.

Meg inhaled sharply. Her hands flew to her mouth and she slowly shook her head. She stood up, her heart pounding. She groped for her keys and literally fell out the kitchen door.

❦

Meg ran into the house just as Michael picked up the TV and heaved it across the room with a primal yell that reverberated through the house. The screen shattered into a billion pieces, and then the cabinet bounced into an end table splintering it, then into the entertainment center knocking CDs and knick-knacks to the floor.

She stopped in the den doorway, frozen. He was breathing heavily, bent over at the waist, grunting, crying, beside himself, trying to catch his breath. He didn't even know she was there.

"Michael?" she said softly.

He suddenly stood upright, looked at her, his face contorted with grief. She rushed to him, unafraid despite the violence she'd just witnessed. She knew he could never physically hurt her. Gently touching his forearms, she looked into his face, then wrapped her arms around him.

He broke down in her arms, sobbing, "Meg, oh, Meg..."

"Shhh, it's gonna be okay..." she comforted, beginning to weep herself.

They held on tightly to each other, crying, nuzzling, each trying to console the other. It seemed so long since they had touched, they held on tight for a long time.

When they finally calmed, he released her and wiped his face with his hands. "If I ever needed a drink, I need one now. You want one?" he asked her.

"I'll take some wine."

He stood at the wet bar and poured himself a shot of whiskey and swigged it down, shuddering. After a moment, he poured each of them a glass of red wine and sat next to her on the couch. She curled her feet under her, examining him. He turned and gazed at her.

"I'm so sorry, Meg."

"What?" she whispered, shaking her head. "You? I'm the one to blame here. Oh Michael, look what I've done to you," she said breathlessly, her chin starting to waggle.

"But I should've let you explain. I mean what kind of person am I that I wouldn't even let you talk..."

"I should've told you the moment I got home." She thought about that night. "We got so close, so fast. The more time that went by, the harder it got to tell you. I was in too deep."

Michael stared straight ahead. "I don't understand why you didn't leave him."

"It's so hard to explain. Each time it happened, I thought that it would be the last time. But it wasn't, of course. He'd be so sorry afterward, crying, one time threatening suicide if I left him. Then he threatened you...and Pop, everyone."

He was transfixed.

"I couldn't risk it," she continued. "He told me he'd follow me and never leave me alone if I left – and I believe he would have done it."

Michael closed his eyes, shaking his head in dismay.

"Oh, Michael, I can't tell you how sorry I am."

"I wish you had said something when you first came back," he said, not accusingly.

She swallowed and closed her eyes. "As I said, you and I got close so fast. And I was afraid you'd look at me...differently." She felt a sob rising, but held things together. "You know how I hate to be pitied. When my parents died, I remember people coming up to me saying, 'Oh, you poor little lamb...' Or staring. It was awful. I hate that feeling." She met his gaze. "It's no excuse though, I know."

"And after all these years, I had you built up into some perfect person," he said.

"We sure know that's not true."

"I wouldn't allow you to be human." His thoughts were shifting quickly. "Oh, God, the way I yelled at you..."

She took his hand and held it tightly. "It's not your fault," she whispered. She looked down again, afraid to ask the next question.

She licked her lips and asked, "*Do* you look at me differently now, Michael?"

He looked at her, took the wineglass from her hand and placed both wineglasses on the coffee table. He held both her hands in his. "I can't help but look at you differently. I see a strong, loving woman who I admire and love even more than I thought I could."

She closed her eyes, feeling the tears welling up. "Oh Michael, I don't deserve you."

"You deserve a better communicator."

"I think you'll be better at that from now on." She gazed at him lovingly.

He caressed her cheek, looking into those familiar chocolate-brown eyes. She was overwhelmed that this incredible man could forgive her. His touch was so tender.

He could see that she was about to cry again, but he stopped her. "Shhhh. No more tears. We've shed enough for a lifetime. Enough," he whispered.

He kissed her softly, sweetly. They embraced, her head resting on his shoulder with her nose nuzzling his neck, her favorite spot. Michael smiled and held her tighter.

"It feels so good to have you there again," he said.

"I missed you so much," she whispered.

"Mmmm," he murmured in agreement.

After a few minutes she asked, "What are you thinking about?"

"I'm sorry. I can't stop thinking about what you endured."

She lifted her head and looked up at him. "It was nothing compared to the last three weeks without you."

She was able to touch his heart in ways no one could. They kissed again, lingering. "You know, if we can get through this, we can get through anything," he said.

"We're okay then, right? Aren't we?"

"Yeah, we're okay," he whispered, nuzzling her.

At eleven-thirty, Pop walked in the front door, not using his own entrance because he was alerted by Meg's car out front. He smiled when he saw Meg and Michael asleep in each other's arms on the sofa. But joy turned to shock when he saw the rest of the family room. He raised his eyebrows at the chaos. He shook his head in typical Pop-fashion, covered the couple with an afghan, stepped through the debris, and retired to his own room.

CHAPTER TWENTY-ONE

When Meg and Michael woke up achy at one a.m. from sleeping on the couch, they crawled into bed. They called Tory later that morning, knowing that she'd be chomping at the bit, wondering what had happened between them. She answered on the first ring.

"Meg?"

"Hey, Tory," Meg said peacefully.

"Is everything okay?" she asked, hope in her voice.

"Yes. Everything is fine."

"Better than fine!" Michael said loud enough for Tory to hear.

Tory laughed, not only pleased with herself, but for them as well.

"Thanks, Tory," Meg said sincerely.

"You're not mad at me?"

"No. Of course not. We talked for a long time. We're better than ever. But we do have to replace some furniture downstairs…"

"What? Furniture?"

"Yes. I walked in just as Michael was pretending the TV was Bill."

"So basically there's no TV left."

"None whatsoever."

"Let me talk to my brother."

Michael took the phone. "Yes, Tory?" he said in a singsong voice.

"So you smashed the TV?"

"Yeah, well, he had it comin' to him. I would've destroyed the whole house if Meg hadn't walked in when she did," he said, chuckling slightly.

"How are you now?" Tory asked him.

"Excellent."

Suddenly, Tory shifted into lawyer-mode. "I'm so glad. Listen, tell Meg that I'll be over later. I'm planning her hearing for her. I know that technically she doesn't need legal representation, but I want to be there and..."

Michael interrupted her, "Okay, just come over later." He leaned over Meg to hang up the phone and took full advantage of the position, tickling her, and smothering her with kisses before going downstairs to face the family room.

It looked even worse in the morning light. Michael scratched his head, trying to decide what to do with the carcass of the TV. If he put it at the curb, certain neighbors would ask questions.

"Maybe I can get the mess all in trash bags," he suggested.

"I'll go get some shoes and a broom," Meg said.

While they were cleaning up, Pop heard them from the kitchen, came in and smiled. "It's a glorious sight having my Meg back in the house."

Meg went to him and embraced him. "It's glorious to be here, Pop."

"How did... You didn't..." Pop groped for the words.

Meg and Michael looked at him, not understanding at first. Then Meg realized and laughed.

"Oh no, Pop! Michael did this before I got here!"

"Pop!" Michael scolded.

I didn't know..."he said defensively. "I hope you two don't fight too often. I'm fond of some of the furnishings in this house," he teased.

They chuckled. "Sorry Pop," Michael said sheepishly. "It was all me."

"We'll replace everything today, Pop," Meg said.

"No," Pop scoffed. "I don't care about that. I'm just glad that you two made it back together."

Meg wrapped her arms around Michael's waist and he returned her embrace, burying his face in her neck, delighting her.

Pop watched them, smiled appreciatively and repeated, "A glorious sight..."

When they were nearly finished cleaning, Travis called from school for Meg.

"Hi, Meg," he said, voice low and downcast. "Listen, I'm real glad about you and Michael. Tory is ecstatic."

"Boy, good news travels fast. Thanks. Obviously, we're happy, too. But you don't sound happy. What's wrong, Travis?"

He sighed. "It's Erika."

Meg had been waiting for this call. She was frightened to ask the next question. "What happened?" She sat on the sofa.

Noting the change in Meg, Michael stopped putting debris in garbage bags. He went to her and sat beside her. She looked at him and, placing her hand over the mouthpiece whispered, "It's Erika."

Travis paused. "She's in the hospital."

Meg swallowed and closed her eyes. "How bad?"

"She's going to be okay, physically. She had some internal bleeding, cracked ribs from blows to her mid-section."

Meg leaned her forehead on her hand. "Do I need to ask who did it?"

"No."

"What's being done?" Then she mouthed to Michael who was waiting to hear, "She'll be okay."

Travis continued, "They arrested the stepfather early this morning. Meg, you should know that it's probable that the stepfather went ballistic when the social worker called because of my report."

"That's what I was afraid of. It's not your fault, Travis. People like him are unpredictable. Poor Erika. How's her mother?"

"She got knocked around pretty good herself trying to stop him, but she refused medical treatment. Joe Woods is a pretty big dude. Her mother's going through some major guilt."

"I can imagine. I know how she feels."

"Meg, like you said, we did what we had to do. In most of these cases, the fact that they know they're being watched stops the abusers, at least for a while. You just never know. I gotta go. I'm meeting with the social worker this morning."

"Okay. Thanks."

She hung up the phone and looked at Michael, crestfallen.

"Stepfather?"

"Yeah."

He stood up in front of her, his hands on his hips. Something occurred to him. "Oh boy. Things are really starting to make sense now. Your obsession with Erika. Oh, Meg. You knew, not from suspicions, but from experience."

She gazed at him and nodded slightly. He paced in frustration. She was lost in her own thoughts. He stopped pacing and announced, "I want to do something for her."

Meg looked up, a little surprised. "We can just be there for her. I don't know…"

"Where's her biological father?"

"I don't know. Erika never knew him." Meg stood. "I want to go to the hospital. I'm sorry, we should be together today. Instead we're cleaning up broken glass and visiting abused children in the hospital."

He wrapped her in his arms. "It's okay. We have every day, now."

"I love you for wanting to help her."

"I'm so much wiser today. There was so much I didn't... This young girl is..."

She rested her head against his chest. "I know."

"Do you want me to come with you?"

"No, not today," she said apologetically. "Tomorrow or Sunday? Actually," she paused in thought, "I don't know if I'll have time tomorrow with the hearing."

"What time is that?"

"Ten."

"Okay. Call me on my cell later. I may go into the office for a couple hours. Maybe I'll buy a TV."

"Okay."

After the events of the past several hours, they kissed for a long time, not wanting to walk away from each other.

"I want you to think about something," he said. "Think about moving in here."

Meg gazed at him. "I wouldn't be back in my old room, would I?" she teased.

"Not hardly. I don't want to let you out of my sight," he whispered with a slight catch in his voice.

"Oh, baby... You can't follow me everywhere. No one is going to hurt me anymore. I love you so much for wanting to protect me."

"I love you," he said, finally releasing her. He pressed his forehead to hers, holding her hands. "So will you move in?"

"Of course I will. Will it be okay with Pop?"

"Are you serious?" Michael said with a smile.

"I'm going to have to tell him the basics about what happened without getting him too upset. I don't want him seeing that video."

"No, I agree. I'm sure you'll come up with the right words."

"Yeah. Well, I better go," Meg said.

Michael picked up the trash bags to take outside. "Let's go, Bill. Time to get rid of you once and for all."

❧

Meg got to the hospital too early for visiting, so she went to the hospital gift shop to buy something for Erika. She scanned the items, but nothing seemed right. Then her eyes went to the cutest brown bear she had ever seen. It looked so similar to her own brown bear from her childhood. When she touched the fur, it was soft, talc-like. It was perfect. She picked up a Mylar 'Get Well' balloon and tied it to the bear's paw.

When she got to Erika's room in pediatrics, Erika was watching TV alone. There were no flowers or gifts of any kind, but then it was her first day in the hospital. Although she was in a semi-private room, the other bed was empty.

"Hi Erika," Meg greeted her warmly.

"Ms. Robbins!" Erika breathed, eyes round, smiling.

Meg approached her bedside and took her hand. "How are you feeling?"

"Okay, I guess. I'm real sore," she said, attempting to sit up straighter, grimacing in pain as if to emphasize her point.

Meg sat down in a chair by the bed. "It'll go away. Every day will get better."

"We miss you so much at school," she said.

"Thanks. I guess you know the whole story."

"Yes. We all do. We don't care what you did. I mean…sometimes I wanted to…you know…do what you did to my stepfather."

"I'm glad you didn't. What I did was wrong. I should've found

197

ways to deal with him legally."

"But you got away with it."

"It was wrong, Erika. I have to live with that for the rest of my life."

Erika nodded looking downcast. Meg let her words sink in.

"He can't hurt you anymore," Meg said.

"I'm still afraid he'll get out of jail and come after me."

"We are going to take measures to make sure that doesn't happen."

"Have you talked to my mom?"

"No, but I want to."

Just then, as coincidence would have it, Donna Woods walked through the door. "Hello!" Her tone was extremely upbeat. Maybe a little too upbeat, probably for Erika's sake. Her cheek was bruised.

"Hi," Meg said, smiling. She rose out of her seat and embraced her.

"I knew you'd come," Donna said. Then to Erika, "I brought you some things from home. Some pajamas, a couple books, toiletries…"

Erika checked out the pajamas that she'd brought. "Oh no, mom! I hate these!"

"You have to have something that opens down the front. It's easier for the doctor to examine you – unless you want to wear the hospital gown."

"No!" Erika said.

Meg laughed. The pajamas Donna had brought were a little childish. Too frilly. Maybe Erika had some bad memories where those pajamas were concerned.

"Here, sit up. Let me help you," Donna said.

Meg pulled the curtain and waited out in the hall. She could hear Erika whimpering in pain as her mother attempted to help her dress.

After a few minutes, Donna joined Meg out in the hallway. "I guess we should talk, huh?"

"If you're up to it," Meg answered. They walked down to the end of the hall to a lounge. It was empty. They sat down next to each other on a sofa.

"I feel so horrible," Donna whispered. "I'm a terrible mother." Her voice cracked.

"No, no, you're not." Meg took her hands.

"How can you say that after what I put my child through?"

"You thought that being with him was your only option. I know. I've been there."

"I know. After Erika told me what happened to you, I understood why you wanted to help her…and me."

"You're gonna make it."

"I hope so. I really don't have a choice now. I'm worried about money."

"Is the social worker looking into things, financially?"

"She will be."

Meg nodded. "I want you to call a locksmith right away and change all the locks in your house as soon as possible. I'm gonna pay for it."

"Ms. Robbins, you don't even have a job."

"Don't you worry about it. Promise me?"

She nodded.

"There are a lot of people who are willing to help you. You just have to let us know. It's difficult sometimes because we don't want to invade your privacy. So, you need to let us know," Meg said, looking directly into her face.

"Okay."

Meg stood. "I guess I should let you spend some time with Erika."

"Ms. Robbins?"

"Meg."

"Meg, I really hope you get your job back."

"Yeah," she whispered. "I do love to teach."

"You can tell. Erika wants to be a teacher because of you."

"Thank you." That was something Meg loved to hear.

"Good luck tomorrow. You'll be in my prayers."

The two women embraced. "You've been in my prayers since we first met," Meg whispered.

Meg said goodbye to Erika and went straight to a nearby mall to buy Erika a new pair of pajamas, ones that opened in the front, but were more appropriate for a fifteen-year old. She went into the Limited and found a pair of purple silkies. Perfect. And no memories attached.

CHAPTER TWENTY-TWO

When Meg returned to the house, it was early afternoon and Michael wasn't home yet. She remembered he had asked her to call on his cell phone. Meg smiled at the prospect of hearing his voice.

"Hey sweetie," she purred when he answered.

"Hiiiii," he said softly. "How's Erika?"

"She's hurting, but she'll be okay."

"Good. Where are you?"

"Home. I mean *your* home. Oh, you know what I mean!"

He chuckled. "It's your home, too. I'm at work right now. I already bought a TV; it's in my car. I'm gonna leave now…"

"It's okay. You don't have to. I'm gonna be on the Internet looking up district policies about…you know…stuff."

"That's a good idea. But I still want to come home."

She smiled. "You won't get any arguments from me!"

"I'm stopping off at a site, then I'll be home. I love you."

"Okay. I love you, too."

Tory called Meg about the hearing while Meg was surfing the net.

"Don't bother looking anything up," Tory said. "I've already looked into it. I'm comin' over later and we'll plan."

"Tory, you amaze me. I'm sorry for everything I put you through."

"Oh, stop. It's nothing."

"I haven't had the chance to apologize to you. I really am sorry for keeping all this from you. You've been so great, considering…anyway, I love you."

"Oh shut up, you're making me cry. Everything's been making me cry. Even commercials on TV! I can't stand it!"

Meg laughed. "Plan on dinner here."

"Oooo, I hear that! Meg?"

"Yeah?"

"Love you, too."

As soon as she hung up, Meg called Michael back and asked him to meet her at the hospital. Now that Tory was coming over, she wouldn't have a chance to return to the hospital that night with Erika's new pj's. She wanted her to have them right away.

When Michael got to the hospital, Erika was alone.

"Oh hi, Mr…Michael!"

Michael smiled brightly. "Hi, Erika! How are you doing?"

"Okay, I guess. Ms. Robbins went to the gift shop to get me some candy."

"Oh, okay. You have to have candy when you're in the hospital. It's a rule!" he said.

Erika smiled, a smile that somehow seemed familiar. Michael looked at her seriously. "Is there anything Ms. Robbins or I can do for you?"

"Oh, Ms. Robbins has done so much. Look at these pajamas she bought me! Aren't they beautiful?"

"Yes, I think purple is your color," he said appreciatively.

"And she brought me this teddy bear earlier."

Michael smiled, then looked down. How was he going to approach this subject? He wanted to help, but he didn't want to upset her. He sat in a chair by the bed. "Erika, what do you know about your real father?"

"Only that he didn't want anything to do with me."

"So he knew your mother was pregnant with you?"

"Yes. I think so. He just didn't care."

"Was he young?"

"Yes. They both were. They were high school sweethearts, I think."

"And your mother never heard anything from him after you were born?"

"No. I ask about him, but she won't tell me anything."

"So, it's possible that he lives close by?"

"I don't know." She shrugged. "Oh, wait, there is one thing I remember. One time she let something slip."

"What was it?" Michael asked hopefully, eyebrows raised.

"I think my father's first name is Luther."

❦

Meg entered Erika's room just as the last drop of blood was draining from Michael's face. He stood from his chair too suddenly.

"Hi!" she said. Her face grew immediately somber when she looked at Michael. "What's wrong?"

"Nothing... nothing. We were just talking..." He avoided her eyes.

She studied Michael. Then her eyes shifted to Erika. "Here you go. All the kind you like!" She dumped ten candy bars from a brown bag onto Erika's lap. Erika giggled.

"Hon, we better go if Tory's coming over," Michael suddenly said. She looked at him, and picking up on his tone, quickly said goodbye to Erika. Walking out to the parking lot, Meg asked again, "What's wrong?"

"Where is your car?"

"Tory dropped me off."

"You drive. I can't," he said, handing her his keys.

"Michael, you're scaring me." She slid into the driver's seat and pulled the seat forward so she could reach the pedals. Michael stared straight ahead from the passenger side.

"Michael?" She touched him gently.

He looked at her and swallowed.

"I think Luther might be Erika's father."

Meg's mouth dropped open. "Why do you think that?" she managed to utter.

"Erika and I were talking and she said the only thing she knows about her father is that his first name is Luther. Think about it. She's —what? Fifteen? Sixteen? That would be about right and she looks a little bit like Luther did at that age."

Remembering something, Meg gasped, her hand flying over her mouth.

"What?" he asked.

"Her mother's name is *Donna*."

"Luther's old girlfriend was named Donna. Donna Wilson."

"I know. Erika's mother's name is Donna Woods. Woods has to be her married name."

"Oh, my God. She has to be Luther's Donna," Michael said, shaking his head in disbelief.

They both sat there in stunned silence.

"What do we do?" she finally asked.

"We have to tell Luther."

Meg nodded, starting the engine. "What do you think he'll say?"

"Who knows with him?"

Meg smiled slightly, thinking, her hands resting on the wheel.

"What?" he asked.

"You have a niece. Erika is your niece."

Michael smiled. At that moment he made the split second decision that if Luther didn't want to be a part of Erika's life, he would be.

Meg and Michael drove straight to Luther's apartment, which was part of a pricey apartment complex on the outskirts of town, near the developing waterfront. Michael knew that Pop was helping him pay for it. He could never afford it on his own. They heard loud music playing inside when they knocked. They knocked again, louder.

Luther answered the door, clad only in pants and laughing at something.

"Hey, hey!" he greeted them warmly. "I heard you two were back together. That's great!" He stepped aside. "Come on in. This is Mandy." He motioned to a girl sitting on the sofa, dressed only in one of Luther's shirts. The apartment was a disaster, and had been since Jessica moved out.

"This is Meg and my brother, Michael."

They exchanged cordial greetings.

"We need to talk with you," Michael murmured.

"What? Now?"

"Now," Meg confirmed.

His eyes shifted between the two of them. "This looks heavy. We can go into the bedroom."

Meg and Michael followed him. If possible, it was in an even worse state than the living area.

"Ya know, Luther, I can't help noticing the color of Mandy's skin," Meg needled.

"Yeah, well, she's pretty cute, ya know? And if it's good enough for my brother here…"

Meg shook her head, smiling. Leave it to Luther.

Luther shoved aside a clump of clothing on the bed. "Here, sit down," he said.

"No…thanks." Meg shot Michael a warning look. Who knew what had occurred on that bed?

"Suit yourself," he said, sitting down. "What's up?"

Michael took a deep breath. "Luther, one of Meg's students…we think she might be your daughter."

Luther looked at Michael, then Meg. He covered his face with his hands and flopped backward on the bed, letting out a huge sigh.

Michael and Meg exchanged looks.

Removing his hands, but staring at the ceiling, Luther said, "I've been thinkin' a day like this might come. What does she want?"

Michael paused and said gently, "She doesn't know who her father is, just that his first name is Luther. I don't know that she'll want anything. But she *needs* a father."

There was a long period of silence.

Luther sat up, shaking his head. "Man, I just don't know about this…"

Michael continued. "Luther, her stepfather is in jail for abusing her."

Luther looked up, startled.

"She's in the hospital because of him. You might consider just being there for her. She's just a kid."

"Donna might have a thing or two to say about that," Luther said. "I haven't done one thing for that kid since she was born."

Meg knelt down in front of Luther. "Maybe she'll let you. You should see Erika," she said, smiling. "She's so smart and sweet and pretty."

Luther smiled slightly. "That's her name – Erika?"

Meg nodded. "Just think about it, okay?" she asked.

"Yeah."

Meg and Michael left Luther in the bedroom. They didn't even think to say goodbye to Mandy. There was too much on their minds.

Michael and Meg decided to hold off telling Tory and Travis about Erika until Luther was ready to make some kind of a decision. That evening, the four of them sat around the dining room table eating Vietnamese take-out and discussing the upcoming hearing. What to say, what not to say.

"Tory, I can't remember everything that you're telling me," Meg complained. "I just want to tell the truth. I'm exhausted."

"But you might say things that will incriminate you," Tory said.

"But I'm not on trial."

"The hell you're not!"

Meg leaned her head on her hand, elbow on the table.

"You okay?" Michael asked.

"I guess."

"Honey, have you given any thought to what you'll do if you're not reinstated?" he asked gently.

"We'll take `em to court!" Tory announced.

"No, no. I don't think I can deal with that. Actually, I have been thinking about maybe writing. I've always wanted to write a series of books on Delaware history geared to middle school children or younger. I've never had the time for it before. I've always loved research."

Michael smiled at her. "Sounds like a plan."

"It's a non-issue," Travis said. "Victoria Harrington-Price is your lawyer. You *will* be teaching again."

"That's right, baby!" Tory said.

Travis rose from his seat. "I'm gonna see what Pop's doing." He squeezed Meg's shoulder and said, "Hang in there, kid." He then disappeared into the kitchen.

"Okay, Meg," Tory said as she flipped the page of a legal pad. "Tell me everything you remember about the interview with Dr. Gardner."

Meg sighed and recounted everything. Tory had brought a stack of papers with her that made Meg feel enormously guilty. Tory had obviously done much more in the way of preparation than Meg had. She'd been too busy wallowing in self-pity.

"Tory, I really should pay you for all your work."

"I'll pay her," Michael said immediately.

"No, honey…"

"I'm a forty-one-year-old man with no kids, living at home with my father. I break brand new TVs for fun. What else am I gonna do with my money?"

Meg and Tory laughed. Then Tory said, "Nobody's gonna pay me anything. I'll think of another way for you to pay me."

"Oh, great," Meg joked. "I'll be washing your car for the rest of my life."

Tory looked at them seriously. "How about the two of you being our baby's godparents?"

Meg's face immediately grew somber. She placed her hand to her heart. "Oh…" she whispered.

Michael got up and wrapped his arms around Meg, putting his cheek next to hers. "I think that's a yes, Tory."

CHAPTER TWENTY-THREE

Someone had alerted the press to the hearing. When Meg, Michael and Tory pulled up in front of the school, there were crowds of people and cameras. With his arm around Meg, Michael protectively pushed through the reporters.

"Ms. Robbins, can you tell us if you think you'll get your job back?"

"Ms. Robbins, what was it like stabbing a man in cold blood?"

"Ms. Robbins, do you think that you should be around children?"

Meg found it all embarrassing and overwhelming.

The hearing was in the school library. The auditorium seemed just too big and they also needed the tables. Wearing a conservative blue dress, Meg entered the library, visibly nervous. The room was set up so that Meg and Tory sat at one table facing a larger table with eight chairs. Pitchers of water and glasses sat within easy reach. Most of the audience seating was behind Meg and Tory except for a few seats to their left. Michael sat in one of them so that Meg could see him.

Various members of the school board arrived and chose seats, whispering to each other, looking at Meg. After several minutes, they were finally ready to begin. Six members of the school board, Dr. Gardner, and Lester Smith would conduct the hearing.

"Don't be nervous, Meg," Tory told her. "We'll get through this."

Meg took a deep breath. "It feels like it's eight against two."

"That's all right," Tory said, unshaken.

"Do they know who you are?"

"Yep. I called Dr. Gardner and told him that I wanted to participate as your lawyer."

"What did he say?"

"He said it was okay. I think he's on your side."

Meg glanced at Michael who winked at her. When she noticed Father Delaney behind him smiling at her, she went to greet him and introduce Michael.

"Father, thank you so much for coming. This is Michael."

Michael turned in his seat to shake hands with the priest.

"Everything's back to normal with us," she explained.

Father Delaney seemed sincerely pleased. "That's wonderful. I'm very happy for you. Would you like to say a prayer, Meg?"

Before she could answer, the president of the school board, Julian Adams, said, "It's not quite ten o'clock, but I think we're all here, so we might as well start."

Julian Adams was a middle-aged man with thinning salt and pepper hair. He wore reading glasses on the end of his nose, and he looked as though he enjoyed peering over them. He had a reputation for not smiling much, not because he was mean-spirited, but because he took his responsibilities very seriously.

As Meg returned to her chair she saw Pop slip into the back. He made eye contact and held up his fist in a "give 'em hell" signal. Meg smiled at him. She didn't recognize anybody else.

Julian Adams did most of the questioning. When everyone was seated, he said,

"This is a hearing of this school board to decide whether one Margaret Robbins should continue teaching here at Thomas Garrett High School. We would like this to be an informal question and answer session and although we are not in a courtroom, your answers,

Ms. Robbins, must be truthful or this school district could impose charges against you. Do you understand?"

"Yes, I understand," Meg replied.

"Okay. Let's start with a little background information about yourself."

Meg took a deep breath. "I was born in Wilmington. My father was a local doctor here. I attended this high school. My parents died when I was fourteen and I lived with Dr. John Harrington and his family until college. I graduated from the University of Delaware with a degree in elementary education..."

"Your discipline area?"

"Social studies. I finished secondary education later."

Mr. Adams glanced at a sheet on the table.

"Magna cum laude?"

"Yes."

Although several of the board members were taking notes, Lester Smith sat with his arms crossed, his jaw cocked to one side.

"Okay. Continue please."

"Uh...I married five years out of college and moved all over the country. Do you have a list of all the schools where I worked?"

"Um, yes. I believe so." They all shuffled papers. "Yes. Here it is."

"Oh, good. There have been so many schools that if you asked me to recite them, I know I'd miss one," Meg said with a nervous smile.

"Why *were* there so many?"

"My husband liked to move."

"We've read over some of your credentials from your previous schools and they appear to be in order. In fact they're all top rate."

Lester Smith rolled his eyes.

"Why don't you tell us what prompted you to move back to Delaware?"

She knew that meant they wanted her to talk about the stabbing. She looked to Michael and he nodded his encouragement. She swallowed hard, took a sip of water, then cleared her throat.

"My husband's death prompted me to move back. He was an abusive man. Extremely abusive." Meg found herself focusing on a water drop on the table in front of her.

She continued, "One night he was so abusive, I was convinced that I wasn't going to get out of the house alive."

"What did he do to make you think that?"

"Specifically?"

"Yes."

"He knocked me out of bed, giving me a black eye; he kicked me in the stomach; he knocked me down the steps; he pulled some hair out of my head..." Meg's voice wavered slightly.

Michael closed his eyes, the veins bulging in his temples.

"Then he tried to strangle me."

There was silence except for the scratching of pens and pencils.

"How did you stop him?"

Meg blinked and took a deep breath. "There was a knife in the kitchen drain board. I stabbed him with it."

There was an audible gasp from people behind her. Meg turned. The room had filled without her knowing it. Her friends were there: Marcus, Lynn, Leon, and Regina. Some parents. Other teachers. Jim Morrelli.

"You had a preliminary hearing?"

"Yes."

"What happened at the hearing?"

"They looked at the pictures the police took and they watched a video of my statement to the police. They read a notebook that I'd kept. Then there were statements from doctors describing the severity of my injuries, especially to my neck."

"And they determined that you acted in self-defense?"

"Yes."

"How many times did you stab him?"

Meg pressed her lips together. "Twice."

More gasps and murmuring. Meg blinked nervously.

Tory looked at her and whispered, "It's okay."

Meg studied the faces of the people before her. They were incredibly hard to read.

"This happened early last year?"

"Yes. February 3."

"Did you return to work that year?"

"No."

"Why not? If the charges against you were dismissed, then why wouldn't you return to work?"

Meg opened her mouth to speak, then stopped. She tried again. "They asked me not to."

"Why?"

She licked her lips, then took another sip of water. Her mouth was so dry. "They told me I was no longer a good moral example for the children."

More writing. Meg's heart pounded and she momentarily closed her eyes.

"When did you move back to Delaware?"

"August."

"And you interviewed with Dr. Gardner for a teaching position?"

"Yes."

"Did you disclose to Dr. Gardner why you left your last job?"

"No."

"Why not?"

"He didn't ask me."

"And your résumé?"

"On my résumé, I don't say why I left any of my jobs. I believe Dr. Gardner assumed I left my job because Bill died and I just wanted to move back home. Essentially that was true."

Dr. Gardner nodded in agreement.

"So you did not disclose during the interview that any of this had happened?"

"No."

"So you willfully withheld information during an interview because you knew if you said it, you would not be hired. Is that correct?"

Tory leaned to her and whispered, "Don't answer that." Then she stood and addressed the table of eight. "I need to step in here. I am Victoria Harrington-Price, Ms. Robbins' attorney. I think we've already established that Ms. Robbins avoided the circumstances of her return to Delaware during the interview with Dr. Gardner, but since that question wasn't asked, she didn't lie. People usually answer what is asked. I have a copy of Ms. Robbins' employment application, and under the line where it asks if she has ever been arrested, she doesn't answer. Where it asks if she was ever *convicted* of a crime, she says no. That's the truth."

"We are here today to determine whether Meg Robbins should teach at this school. May I suggest, with all due respect, that the questioning be continued with regard to her credentials, including any observations that were done of her teaching here this year? I have eight different observations in writing right here if you need a copy." She sat down. Her delivery had been rapid-fire, clear, and respectful.

Meg looked at her with admiration. She was good. She was redirecting the whole line of questioning.

The school board members started to whisper amongst themselves. Julian Adams nodded at Tory. "Yes, uh, perhaps later. Um...Ms. Robbins, you teach ninth and tenth grade social studies?"

"Yes."

More paper shuffling from the board members.

"I see here that your students are doing remarkably well."

"Yes."

Some of said students were out in the hallway. Although they knew they wouldn't be allowed in, they simply wanted to be there.

"I understand that your classroom is typically noisy."

"Yes," Meg said, smiling slightly, her back straighter.

"You seem proud of that fact," he said, peering over his glasses.

"I'm not uptight about a little noise. Most of the time it's good. I use music with my lessons. Since my classroom is far removed from most of the others, we don't disturb anyone."

"Some people would equate a noisy classroom with a teacher who doesn't have control."

"I'm not sure where you got your information, but I am in complete control. I'm just not a traditional teacher. When students are engaged, they tend to get a little loud. Most of the time, my students are engaged."

"Have you played music with profanity in it?"

Meg's jaw tightened. Dr. Gardner shifted uncomfortably in his seat.

"Yes."

"Do you think that it is appropriate that a teacher use profanity in her lessons?"

"First of all, I consider the maturity of my students, and due to the fact that they listen to far worse at home..." Meg stopped. She knew parents were in the room and she couldn't afford to alienate anyone.

"Were you asked to stop playing the song in question?"

Meg sucked her upper teeth in disgust. "Yes. And I did." She looked at Tory who wasn't doing anything except writing.

Tory leaned to her and whispered, "Don't worry. We'll get our chance."

"Did you compare skin color to crayons during a lesson?"

Meg hesitated. They'd spoken to some of the kids. "Yes."

"And what was your point?"

"Some of the students weren't grasping the fact that we aren't truly white or black. I used crayons because they were the one thing I had available that had varied color."

"Did you tell a student that he wasn't white?"

"Yes, that he wasn't white in the literal sense. That was why I used the crayons for illustration. My point was that all humans are some shade of brown. It was a uniting effort on my part. We tend to classify people by color. I mean, what's the point? I think that it is especially stressful for kids of mixed race. In my opinion, putting people in groups further segregates us."

"Some people are proud of their heritage."

Oh good God. Don't you get the point?

"I think that's great. I'm not asking anyone to forget his or her heritage. I'm asking them to be accepting of the people around them, to realize we can all be lumped into the same group if we want to be." Meg felt more in control now. She was handling things better.

"Ms. Robbins, some of your students stay in your classroom after school?"

"Yes."

"Why?"

She shrugged. "They like to. I have a piano and they like to play it. And they just like visiting…I mean, it's better than them getting into trouble."

"Amen to that," Julian Adams said, flipping a page on his legal pad. "Do you have any physical contact with your students?"

"Physical contact?"

"Yes."

"Like hugging?"

"*Any* physical contact."

"Yes. Sometimes we hug."

"Is this voluntary on the part of the student?"

"Of course!" Meg said firmly.

"How about kissing?"

"No. Absolutely not."

"We have documentation that you kissed a...Geoffrey King..."

"Oh please!" Meg all but shouted.

Tory touched her arm. "Shhhh, calm down," she soothed.

Meg looked at Michael who looked at her reassuringly, giving her the non-verbal palm down, take-it-easy sign.

"Ms. Robbins, have students ever spent the night in your home?"

Meg swallowed. *Erika.*

"One student slept on my porch..."

"So that's a yes."

"Yes. But I didn't even know she was there..."

"Did you have any...male company that same evening?"

Meg felt defeated already. "Yes." How did they know *that*?

Michael was shaking his head.

"Do you think that as a teacher you're responsible for setting a good moral example?"

"I think that I'm *one* of the people who should be, yes."

"And do you believe by allowing an impressionable teenage girl to see that you had male company overnight that you are a good moral example?"

Meg closed her eyes and shook her head.

Tory spoke again. "As Ms. Robbins said, she didn't know the child was there. Ms. Robbins did not take a vow of celibacy when she was hired here. Let's move on, please."

There were a few chuckles from the crowd. Tory was making the eight a little nervous. They kept looking at each other and writing.

"Ms. Robbins, have boys ever spent the night at your home?"

"No."

"Just a few days ago, four boys came to your home and stayed…"

"Are you watching my house?" Meg demanded, more than a little pissed off.

Tory rested her hand on Meg's arm.

"Those boys came to my house to cheer me up due to…all of this happening." She waved her hand around dramatically. "It was completely innocent – and they didn't spend the night."

"How did they cheer you up?"

Meg looked down. She knew this was going to sound strange.

Oh, hell.

She looked at them belligerently. "They sang to me."

"They *sang* to you?"

"Yes," she said boldly.

"It seems you spend a lot of time with your students outside normal school hours."

"Is there a rule against that, too?" Meg asked with attitude.

Tory touched her arm and stood. "We need a break," Tory stood. It was nearly twelve o'clock and Meg was on the verge of tears.

Julian Adams looked at his watch. "Um…okay. Let's take a forty-five minute break. I understand that there are sandwiches and drinks down in the cafeteria for anyone who is interested."

CHAPTER TWENTY-FOUR

During the break, Meg, Michael, and Tory went into an open classroom across the hall from the library. She didn't see her students through the maze of people.

"This is an ambush!" Meg cried.

"Calm down," Tory demanded. "Just wait for *my* questions. Don't cry, Meg."

"This is what I do when I get really angry!" Meg said through tears. "They're trying to revoke my teaching certificate!"

"Not going to happen," Tory said assuredly.

Michael held Meg. "Come on. You have to hold it together," he whispered.

She held onto him tightly. She didn't know what she would have done if she and Michael hadn't made up already. She needed him now more than ever. She cried openly on his shoulder.

Pop and Father Delaney came in together. They didn't say anything right away, taking in the sight of Meg and Michael. Pop approached Tory, looking at her inquisitively.

"It's gonna be okay, Pop," Tory said, writing without looking up. "We're just gonna regroup."

Pop retreated to a corner, talking softly with the priest.

"Hey, Meg," Marcus said, sticking his head in the door. "Don't worry. We're going to the cafeteria and havin' a powwow. *We're* talking the second half."

"I'm going to get us something to eat," Michael said, kissing Meg on the forehead.

"Ms. Robbins?" Ronald called from the door.

"Ronald!" Meg called. She wiped away some stray tears.

"Can we come in?"

"I don't know. Who's 'we'?"

"Me, Geoffrey, Jesse, Louis, Taahira, Maria…"

"Well…" Meg didn't know how much time she had. She needed to talk with Tory.

"Yeah, come on in, you guys," Tory said. Meg looked at her in surprise.

Tory approached the large group of kids who entered the room. "Hi, I'm Tory. We may need you guys to speak at the hearing…"

"I didn't think they were allowed," Meg interrupted.

"Yeah, we'll see. Now, pick someone to talk and decide what you want to say. I want you to think about what makes Ms. Robbins such a good teacher and why you want her back. Keep it short; they may not give you much time, if any. Okay?"

There were murmurs of 'yeah' and 'okay' from the group. She dismissed them.

Michael came back with a tray of food. He handed Meg a Diet Coke. "Hon?"

"Hmm?" Meg was in a trance.

"Maybe I should go home and get the video."

"What?" she whispered. He suddenly had her full attention. "No!"

"It could help you…"

"No, Michael." She was indignant. "I don't want all these people…if they reinstate me, it should be because I'm a great teacher, not because my husband used to beat the shit out of me." Her voice caught on the last few words.

Michael looked at, examining her. "Okay," he said softly, holding her. "Okay."

When they reconvened, Luther showed up, sliding into the back row, grabbing a seat next to Pop. He didn't notice Donna Woods right away on the other side of the room.

Leon sat by the door across the aisle from Pop. He purposely cracked the door so the kids in the hallway could hear what was going on inside. They were a part of this — why couldn't they hear?

Julian Adams announced that they didn't have any further questions and that it was time for Meg to present her case.

Meg breathed a huge sigh of relief.

Tory rose from her seat. "Ms. Robbins, how long have you been teaching?"

"Eighteen years."

"And in that eighteen years, have you ever gotten a bad evaluation?"

"No."

"Never?"

"Never."

"I'd like to submit all of Ms. Robbins evaluations from the…"

"Mrs. Price, this isn't a trial…" Julian Adams started to protest.

"Are you interested in the truth? A woman's lifework is hanging in the balance. I should think as educators you would want all the facts."

Lester Smith rolled his eyes again. The others stared at her in stunned silence. They already had more paper to look at than they wanted.

Renee King, Geoffrey's mother came in, huffing and puffing. She was a very dark, very large, very imposing woman. She grabbed the only seat left on the aisle.

"May I continue?" Tory asked.

"Yes."

They passed around Meg's evaluations and observation reports.

"Ms. Robbins, I just want to clarify a few things. These hugs you give your students... Would you say that they like them?"

"Yes."

"Would you go so far as to say that they *need* them?"

"Sometimes. Yes. Don't we all sometimes?"

"Yes, indeed. This kiss. Where did you kiss Geoffrey King?"

"On the forehead."

"And why did you kiss him on the forehead?"

"He answered a complex question – I wish I could remember what it was – and I was so proud of his answer that I kissed him on the head. He liked it so much he left the lipstick on his head all day."

There were chuckles in the crowd. Even a few board members smiled.

"The student that slept on your porch... Why did she go there?"

Meg didn't want to betray Erika, and Tory had been careful not to use names.

"There were some abuse issues with the child. She was frightened to stay in her own house."

Donna Woods looked down guiltily.

"You reported these abuse issues at the school?" Tory continued.

"Yes."

"And this child is now..."

"She's in the hospital. Her stepfather is in jail for abusing her."

Luther shifted, ill at ease in his seat.

There was murmuring and frantic paper shuffling on the part of some of the board members.

"And to your knowledge, did any other teacher at this school report that this child was abused?"

"Not to my knowledge."

"And you knew she was abused due to your experience in this area and because of your experience as a teacher."

"Yes."

Tory flipped through some pages on her legal pad. "These boys who sang to you… What else did they do at your house?"

"Ate popcorn, drank soda, and talked…a lot."

"Nothing improper happened, of course."

"Of course not."

"Ms. Robbins, you said that you are not a traditional teacher."

"That's right."

"What do you mean by that?"

"I just think that teaching is more than reading books and taking notes. It's also about life experiences. It's about understanding and enjoying the world we live in. And respect plays a big role in my classroom. We all try to respect one another. It's something I hope they take with them when they leave my class."

"Can you give us some examples?"

"I've told you about the music. It's played in my room every day. One time one of our Jewish children taught us a traditional Jewish dance. Another child brought in sweet potato pie because some of the white kids…"

"You mean light brown," Tory interrupted.

Chuckles came from the gallery.

"Yes," Meg said with a smile. "Some of them had never had it before. And current events. My kids always know what's going on and why, if there is a why."

Tory paused to go in a different direction. "Do you think that there are some teachers at this school who don't like the fact that you date a bi-racial man?"

"Objection!" Lester Smith yelled.

"This isn't court," Tory said. "But go ahead, you sound like you have something to say."

Marcus and Leon were stretching their necks to get a better look at Lester Smith.

"*Other* teachers aren't on trial... That is, this isn't about other teachers," Lester Smith said weakly.

Dr. Gardner finally spoke. "I'd like to hear the answer to that question." Lester looked at him in disbelief. "I would like to know if any of my teachers are racists."

Tory looked at Meg, lifting her eyebrows, encouraging her to answer.

"I know that some people aren't comfortable about it, but it's my business. I do believe there are teachers at this school who are racists."

"Do you have any proof?"

"No. Yes. One day I found a note on my car."

"What did the note say?"

"It said 'nigger lover'."

Michael looked around the room accusingly. Loud murmurs of discontent rose from the crowd. Marcus's mouth dropped open. Regina clenched her teeth together. Leon bowed his head, looking at his feet, shaking his head. Pop was rocking in his seat, eyes closed.

"Who was the note from?"

"I don't know. I have my suspicions..."

Regina couldn't stand it one more minute. She stood and shouted, "It was Jim Morrelli...and Lester Smith! You *know* it was you," she pointed at Lester. "I heard Jim Morrelli use the word 'nigger.' He tried getting Leon Burns fired last year just because he's gay and now he's trying to get Meg Robbins fired."

The whole room was buzzing now.

Tory sat down, smiling. She couldn't have planned this turn of events more perfectly. If Julian Adams had a gavel, he'd be using it. Instead, he had to yell at the top of his lungs. "Quiet, please!"

No one listened. The kids in the hallway poured in, joining in the screaming and yelling. It was utter chaos. Julian Adams was red in the face. Other board members tried to help him with their own yelling, to no avail.

Meg rose from her chair, catching the eyes of several people. She raised her hand and said in a calm, clear, voice, "Eyes on me, one."

Several people stopped and looked at her. All her students stopped immediately. They had heard this before.

"Eyes on me, two."

More adults stopped and looked, wondering what this was all about.

"Eyes on me, three."

By this time, everyone had stopped, seemingly hypnotized, and all were looking at Meg. The room was silent. Meg stepped toward the table of eight, looked at Julian Adams in the eyes and said, "*That's* what I call control."

Regina whispered, "You go, girl."

Lynn asked, "Why is it okay if *you* say it?"

"Oh, shut up."

Julian Adams was looking at Meg, stupefied. Tory was holding back the biggest guffaw ever. Michael was smiling ear to ear.

Julian Adams cleared his throat. "Well, uh…these children don't belong in here."

Tory stood again. "If you don't mind, these kids have come on behalf of Ms. Robbins. After all, they have a vested interest in this too."

"They don't belong in here!" Lester Smith said.

Tory nodded to Ronald. Ronald knew he had to speak before they got thrown out. "We want you to know how we feel about Ms. Robbins. She cares about us, ya know? She likes to make us think of things in a different way. We're learnin' without realizing that we're learnin', ya know? It's like she's trickin' us. And if somebody doesn't understand somethin', she keeps explainin' it in different ways 'til every single kid in the room gets it." Ronald smiled. "She's happy too. You can tell she likes to teach. Some of our teachers, we wonder why they're even here. Yeah, she loves to teach, and I think she loves us, too."

The room was silent except for a few sniffles. Meg smiled at Ronald.

Then a man stood, "I've got a problem with Ms. Robbins."

Tory looked at Meg, who shrugged her shoulders and shook her head, not recognizing him.

"And who are you?" Julian Adams asked, exasperated, realizing that he had lost control a long time ago.

"I'm Joe McHale – David McHale's father." David was conspicuously missing from the group of kids. "I don't like the idea of my kid being taught by a murderer."

People started catcalling. Leon stood, pointed and shouted, "You're a racist, too! And what's worse, you're raising your kid to be a racist, and you don't like Meg Robbins because she's anything but..."

Others were shouting the things that they had kept bottled up all year. Meg worried that they might be doing themselves occupational harm.

"Mr. Burns, that's enough!" Julian Adams called out. "Mr. McHale, we've been through all that. We are currently going through Ms. Robbins' credentials. In fact, folks, let's finish up. If anyone has a brief statement, and I do mean *brief*, now is the time."

Marcus stood and spoke. "I'm Marcus Taylor. I teach band. I know I speak for several of us. We feel Meg Robbins is about the finest teacher we know. She's kind and gifted and above all, she's turned some of these kids around. Firing her would be a huge mistake."

Murmurs of agreement floated around the room.

Donna Woods stood. "I'd like to say something."

Luther sat bolt upright, recognizing her. Pop noticed Luther's face and studied the standing woman. Pop hadn't seen her in years. Not since she married.

"I am Donna Woods, Erika Woods' mother. Erika is the child referred to earlier who was abused. Ms. Robbins has been so supportive of me and my daughter." Her voice broke. "I'm sorry. It's just that…she's a wonderful teacher. You can't do this to her…I'm sorry." She sat back down, crying and searching in her purse for a tissue.

Renee King rose to speak. She drew attention due to sheer size. Her voice was thunderous. "I've got something to say, but I'm afraid I cannot be brief."

"Mom!" Geoffrey whined in embarrassment.

"Hush up, junior. Let your momma talk."

People chuckled, including Meg.

"Now, I'm sorry to say that I've never met Ms. Robbins, but I swear that if you walked down the street, I'd know who you were." She spoke directly to Meg. She then addressed the table of eight. "My son and nephew never stop talking about her. 'Ms. Robbins this' and 'Ms. Robbins that.' I was getting sick of it. But from what I see and what I hear, she's the best thing that's happened to this school in a long time."

She pointed with her index finger, making her points. "My son and nephew got into more than a little trouble last year, but not so much this year, and I attribute that to Ms. Robbins."

"Geoffrey knows how to play piano now." She shook her head in amazement. "You people are trying to make something out of the boys going to her house. I knew where they were and why. Heaven knows I heard them practicing 'Lida Rose' over and over again! And the huggin' and kissin', that's okay with me too. Some kids don't get any affection. We should be thankful that Ms. Robbins is generous with her hugs. I feel that if Ms. Robbins wrote me a note sayin' Geoffrey needed a whoopin' I'd do it just because Ms. Robbins said so. Never mind why!"

Everyone laughed, including the whole table of eight. Meg's head was bowed. She smiled, but was becoming emotional.

Then Renee King got serious. "I don't care about what she did," she said quietly. She pointed around the room in sweeping circles and then, her voice escalating again added, "Any one of you would have done the same thing if someone was gonna kill you." She pointed to the table of eight. "You leave her alone!" And with that she gave one dramatic nod of her head and sat down.

Loud applause broke out all over the room. Pop was whistling. Luther was whooping. The kids were going nuts, high-fiving Geoffrey. Meg was overwhelmed and started to cry.

Julian Adams shouted, "Everyone! Everyone, please! Let me have your attention." This time they listened. "I think we've heard enough. The members of this school board will meet and discuss this matter on Monday morning. We should have a decision early in the week." Then he peered at Meg. "Ms. Robbins, do you have anything else that you would like to say?"

Meg thought for a moment, then rose from her seat. "Yes. I just want you to know how much I love to teach. It's the second most important thing in my life." She glanced at Michael. "Teaching is what I was meant to do. I also want to apologize to Dr. Gardner, my associates, parents, and students who were caught off guard by this...secret of mine. I am not a violent person. Anyone who knows me can attest to that. I've had enough violence in my life to last many lifetimes. I'm truly sorry for all the chaos I caused and I respectfully ask you to please reinstate me." Meg choked on her last words and sat back down.

There was a short moment of silence and Julian Adams said, "Thank you, Ms. Robbins, and thank you everyone for your thoughts." He heaved a huge sigh. He had a migraine.

As everyone made motions to leave, Meg rose from her seat and hugged her best friend. "Thank you so much," she whispered.

"Hey, it's what I do! I love this!" Tory exclaimed. She was pumped. "You did great! Are you okay?"

"Yeah. I think so."

"Good. Let's get outta here!"

Meg turned to find Michael standing directly behind her. "Oh! Hi!" She wrapped her arms around his neck and he kissed her and held her, scanning the crowd in hopes that Jim Morrelli would see.

"Good job, sis!" he said to Tory and hugged her warmly.

"Why thank you!"

Luther craned his neck to search for Donna Woods. She was one of the last people to leave. He sheepishly approached her, heart pounding. He tried to force his hands into his tight blue jean pockets.

"Hi Donna."

She looked up and her face registered recognition. "Luther!" Then she smiled slightly, smoothing back her hair with her hand. She felt old, a result of what she had been through, but he was still so good-looking and stress-free.

Luther looked down, shuffling his feet like a boy about to ask a girl to the prom.

Michael looked over Meg's head at Luther. Meg looked up at Michael, noticed his stare and turned to look too. They looked at each other, holding their breath.

"I didn't realize the connection between you and Meg Robbins until I saw your brother and sister today," Donna said.

"Yeah, Meg lived with us. She's like...a sister to me." He looked into her face. Gone was the carefree, pretty teenager he had had a fling with. She looked hardened and weary and so much older than he felt. It was hard to believe that they were almost the same age. "How's Erika?"

Donna tensed. "She's fine," trying to sound nonchalant. She avoided his eyes.

"Michael and Meg came to see me yesterday. They think she's my daughter."

"How..." she stammered. "I..." She searched for the words. Her eyes met his. "She is."

Luther looked down. He wasn't sure why he was there. He wasn't sure what he wanted. "Look, I know I wasn't the nicest guy. I mean, I was irresponsible, still am sometimes, to tell you the truth. But, I don't know...maybe I could meet her sometime."

She smiled slightly at his attempt at an apology. "We were both so young..." Luther had a way of putting women under a spell. Donna shook her head to break the spell. "I don't know. Um, let me think about this. I'd like to discuss it with Erika."

"Okay. I'm not going to interfere or anything. I just...ya know...maybe she'll need me."

"She needed you..." she started. "Never mind. That ship has sailed. I'll let you know." She walked away quickly, leaving Luther standing there feeling scared and suddenly much more grown up.

CHAPTER TWENTY-FIVE

The family congregated at the house feeling victorious even though they had no idea what the outcome of the hearing would be.

In the kitchen, where they were eating, drinking, and relaxing, Tory imitated Meg at the hearing, standing and gesturing with her finger. "And *that's* what I call control!" Then howling with laughter, she fell back into her seat. "Oh *girl!* I almost died! I was holdin' it in… I had tears coming out of my eyes."

Everyone at the dining room table cracked up. Meg covered her face with her hands in delighted embarrassment.

Michael raised his beer mug. "Here's to Meg. I knew you were a good teacher before, but I never knew the magnitude. You've touched so many young lives and no matter what happens, you'll still find a way to touch many more. We love you."

"Here! Here!" Everyone clanked glasses.

"Mootsie would be proud," Pop said.

Meg gazed at Michael, rose from her seat and sat on his lap, pressing her forehead to his and quietly said, "Thank you." He kissed her, forgetting that everyone was watching them.

Travis said, "Oh, here they go…" then started fanning them with a napkin.

Luther walked in the house sullenly. "Hey everyone."

"What's the matter with you?" Tory asked.

Luther drew up a chair and sat. "Did you tell them?" he asked Meg and Michael.

"No. We thought you should," Michael answered.

"Thanks. Uh, I've got to tell y'all something."

Michael and Meg looked at each other, slightly uncomfortable, slightly excited. Meg was relieved it wasn't about her for a change.

Luther continued, "Everyone know Meg's student, Erika?"

"Yeah, the one in the hospital," Pop said.

"Yeah, well, it turns out," he cleared his throat, "that she's my daughter."

There was silence, absolute silence for a moment. No one even moved.

Travis finally said, "Holy shit."

"Are you sure?" Tory asked.

"Yeah."

"What are you gonna do, son?" Pop asked.

"I'm not sure yet. I've been thinking a lot about it. Then I thought about Tory."

"Me? Why me?"

"You're about to have Pop's first grandchild. I don't know. I feel like if I get involved with Erika, that I'll be stealin' your thunder."

"Don't be silly," Tory said. "Besides, I'll have a perfect babysitter."

"I think it's real nice you thought about your sister, Luther," Michael said admiringly.

"Me, too," Meg added.

Luther nodded, uncomfortable with the rare praise from Michael.

"How involved do you want to get, Luther?" Travis asked.

"I don't know, man," Luther said in exasperation. "I talked to Donna. She's not sure. And I keep turning it over and over in my head and I haven't come to any conclusions."

"Maybe you just need to wait and see," Pop suggested.

Luther nodded. "One thing I don't need to wait about," he said as he stood and approached Meg.

"I was proud of you today," he said pressing his lips to her forehead. "You too, Tory."

There was silence then, and more than a few sniffles. "What's the matter with y'all? Am I that stingy with the compliments?"

"Yeah," Travis answered quickly.

"And you're still ugly," Luther shot back, grinning.

"Be that as it may, the ugly one's taking me home. I need to go put my feet up," Tory said, getting up. "Meg, party at my house next Saturday. Either we'll be celebrating your reinstatement or your new occupation as a writer."

"Tory, you've done enough..." Meg started to protest.

"I'm just supplying the backyard. Your man here is doin' the rest."

Meg shook her head in amazement at the man whose lap she still sat in. "It sounds like fun," she said, never taking her eyes off him.

"Will I be greatly rewarded?" he asked her softly.

"Oh, yeah," Meg giggled.

On Saturday, the family descended upon Tory and Travis's house to set up for the party. Michael hired a man to roast a pig and he was there at sunrise, already cooking. The delicious smell wafted throughout the neighborhood. The rest of the party was catered. It was a warm May day, not too hot, not too cold, with a pleasant breeze in the air.

Everyone else started showing up in the afternoon, most of them bringing food. Tory and Meg sat on chaise lounges next to each other, relaxing, drinking iced tea.

The entire week had gone by without word from the school

board. Meg had called Dr. Gardner on Thursday, only to be told that he was out of the office until Monday.

"This is unbelievable. We don't even know what we're celebrating," Meg said.

"We're celebrating *you*," Tory said simply.

"I just can't believe we haven't heard anything yet." Meg panned the crowd, smiling. "Hmmm."

"What?"

"Everyone I care about is here."

Most of Meg's students were there, as well as a handful of parents, including Renee King, who was the life of the party. Meg had made a phone call to her right after the hearing to thank her. Assorted faculty members showed up, including Meg's friends, of course. In Tory's two-acre backyard people were playing horseshoes, badminton, volleyball, board games, dancing, or just talking. Several students took turns as DJ. Not surprisingly, they didn't choose any of Meg's classroom songs to play. Meg enjoyed seeing these people she loved so much interacting with each other. Pop played chess with Ronald. Travis talked with Maria. Even Father Delaney found something to talk to Lynn about. Tory pointed out Michael sharing a huge laugh with Marcus. "Look at my brother."

Meg smiled. "Yeah."

"I don't think I've ever seen him so happy, Meg."

"I promise to keep him that way, Tory."

"Oh girl, I know you will," she said with a chuckle in her voice.

Luther roamed aimlessly around the party. The high school girls giggled as he walked by and normally he'd thoroughly enjoy it, shake his butt to amuse them, but today he was preoccupied. Erika and Donna were not there yet and he worried they might not come. Donna had called earlier in the week, okaying a meeting between the father and daughter and Luther had assumed it would be today. He finally settled on a bench under a tree, not far from Pop. Michael, seeing him alone, joined him.

"Whatever happened to Mandy?" Michael asked.

"Mandy? Oh, Mandy. Oh, that was just a... that was nothin'. I really blew it with Jess. I miss her."

"Have you tried talking to her?"

"Yeah. She's still hurt. I don't know, man. Sometimes I think she was the one. Then other times I think maybe not."

"Maybe you haven't found 'the one' yet. I mean, I was never very good at flirting, not like you, but all I know is that since I've been with Meg, flirting with other women doesn't interest me in the least. That's why I got on your case at the bar that night."

Luther thought a moment. "I'm sure Meg told you about what I said a while back about..."

"Yes. It upset her, Luther. It was ludicrous."

"I know, I know. I just...I was jealous. There I said it. I've had all these women, but you, you picked and chose so carefully. And it's pretty obvious Meg is your soulmate. I think you guys may be even closer than Pop and Mootsie were." Luther shook his head and looked at his brother. "I don't think I'll ever have what you guys have."

Michael looked at Meg who was smiling, talking to some parents. He smiled at her. "I hope you do, Luther, 'cause it sure is hard to describe."

The two brothers embraced for the first time in a long time. Pop didn't miss it and was touched to see his sons connecting.

Erika entered the party alone and was warmly greeted by several of her classmates, especially Andrew. But Erika walked right past them when she saw Meg.

Meg caught sight of her and drew in a deep breath, scanning the crowd for Luther. There he was with Michael.

Perfect. Stay right there.

She excused herself from the parents and went to Erika. "Erika! Hi! How are you?" Meg hugged her gently, in case she was still tender.

"Is he here?" They were the first words out of her mouth.

"Yes. Would you like to meet him?"

She smiled slightly. "I guess. I'm a little nervous."

"He's pretty terrific," Meg said to reassure her.

Erika smiled wider. She was excited. Nervous, but excited.

Meg took Erika by the hand and walked toward Luther and Michael. The two men looked up as they approached. Luther stood, knowing.

"Erika, I'd like you to meet...Luther. Luther Harrington. Luther, this is Erika."

Luther's eyes never left Erika's face. He felt as if he were staring into his own eyes. It was magical.

"Hi," he managed to utter. "You were right, Meg. She sure is pretty." When Erika smiled shyly, Luther thought it was the most beautiful sight he had ever seen.

"Oh, yeah, what's the connection between you two again?" Erika asked.

Luther looked at Meg, arms around the waist of his brother and said, "Meg?" He swallowed and said, "She's my sister."

Meg went to Luther and held him close. Erika looked at Michael, not sure what to make of the moment, not knowing what Luther's words meant to Meg. He winked at her reassuringly.

"Erika, can I get you a soda?" Michael asked her.

"Okay," she answered. Her eyes wouldn't leave Luther.

"I'll get it for her," Luther said. "Come on." They walked away slowly, talking.

The kids were checking out Luther with Erika, whispering to one another. The girls were jealous, as was Andrew. Meg suspected Andrew had a crush on Erika.

Michael took Meg by the hand and led her away. Someone put "Precious Love" on and Michael looked at Meg with lifted eyebrows.

"Never mind!" she laughed. But they danced to it, reminiscing as they did so, only without the X-rated parts.

Halfway through the party, Meg was making her rounds when she realized she hadn't seen Michael in a while. She found Tory filling her plate with food and asked, "Tory, have you seen Michael?"

"No. Oh, he's got to be around."

Meg had started talking to Regina when she saw Michael running toward her across the backyard with an envelope in his hand. He reached her, huffing and puffing.

"Where were you?" she asked.

Between puffs he said, "I…something occurred to me…What if they *mailed* their decision to *your* house?"

"But I was at your house."

He smiled. "Exactly."

"But I told them that."

"Someone screwed up," he said simply. He handed her the envelope.

By this time a crowd was gathering around Meg, understanding what was happening. Meg stared at the envelope, and held it for a long time. She then shoved it back to Michael.

"You open it. I can't." Michael looked at her and then to Regina.

"If one of you doesn't open it, I will!" Regina said.

Michael tore open the envelope. He scanned the letter for the words. His face registered nothing. Everyone around them was still.

"Michael?"

He looked up and simply said, "You start back in September – if you still want your job."

A deafening scream went up among the large circle of friends surrounding Meg. She threw herself into Michael's arms, her feet leaving the ground, the letter flying off in the gentle breeze.

On that lovely May afternoon, Meg felt wrapped up in her quilt of shades of brown. Parts of that quilt were old and other parts were new. Some were worn, some fresh and bold. Some were loud, and others weren't. Some dark, some light. Parts of that quilt she'd hold closer than other parts but she knew that, no matter what, all parts of the quilt worked to create a beautiful whole.

That quilt was her life.

AUTHOR BIOGRAPHY

Shades of Brown is **Denise Becker's** first book. Before beginning her writing career, Denise worked in banking and was a stay-at-home mom. She later returned to college to earn her Bachelor's of Science degree in Elementary Education at the University of Delaware.

A native of Delaware, she resides in Hockessin with her two children and teaches elementary school in Wilmington.

EXCERPT FROM
CODE NAME: DIVA
BY
J.M. JEFFRIES

Odessa Ripley walked rapidly through Athens Airport, dodging the tourists who filled the terminal. She was followed by her hand-picked team: Carl Gardner, helicopter pilot, and Jennifer North, communications specialist. Odessa rubbed at her gritty eyes. Four hours on the Concorde to Paris, courtesy of Raven's father because the bureau wouldn't pop for emergency funding, and then another four hours to Athens had left her exhausted.

"Rafi Yusuf is picking us up," Odessa announced as she scanned the crowd of people rushing back and forth through the corridors.

"He'll have what we need?" Jenny asked. She was small, thing woman with light brown hair that constantly fell in her eyes to be brushed back with a squarish, capable looking hand. Jennifer North was brilliant at her job. She had an almost mystical ability to pick out relevant information from what sounded like nothing by casual chatter.

"Helicopter, communications stuff and weapons. Ready to extract Raven when she shows up." Odessa shied away from the thought that

Raven might be badly hurt, or even dead. Not on her watch.

"Any idea what kind of helicopter?" Carl asked. Carl had been a navy pilot, and during the Gulf War had managed to discover vitally important information that had brought him to the attention of the CIA. When they had recruited him, they'd had a completely different assignment for him, but he'd proved he was more valuable flying the helicopters and safely extracting teams that had been compromised.

"Hopefully, one that flies," she retorted.

"That's a start," Carl said with a wry grin. "No help to us if it don't."

Odessa didn't respond. Carl had a quirky sense of humor that she didn't quite understand. But then Odessa wasn't known for her ability to spot something funny, which had made her the object of several practical jokes during her first years on the job.

Odessa, Jenny and Carl exited the airport to bright sun and blue sky that washed across the landscape and seemed to leach all the colors. Rafi Yusuf leaned against an illegally parked silver Range Rover. Though he looked around casually, Odessa could see that he was tense.

He straightened when he saw them and opened the front door with a flourish. He took Odessa's suitcase from her.

As she stepped into the Range Rover, her phone rang. Before answering, she checked the umber finding it was Senator Hathaway's private phone in D. C. "Sir, what do you have?" Odessa asked skipping the greeting.

"Hi to you, too, Odessa," the Senator said after a short laugh. "I have some interesting news."

Interesting good or interesting bad, she wondered. "I'm not going to like hearing this, am I?"

"Depends on interpretation."

What was it about CIA people and their cryptic shit, she thought. Even though she was CIA herself, she would never understand. "Then interpret for me, sir." Her voice was sharper than she intended, but she was too worried about Raven to temper her mood.

"Since you're Raven's best friend, I'm sure she's told you all about Derek Lange. Turns out Lange is out of the country for an unspecified reason doing a small job for General Miller. A military transport dropped him off at the southern Tabezistan border, and was seen driving north. He's been off the radar since. What do you want to bet that Raven his little job."

Odessa wouldn't bet anything. She knew all about Raven and Lange's past together. She also knew about Derek Lange's super commando rep. The Marines hadn't called him the Big Bad Wolf for nothing. This guy was the real deal demolition man. "Are we assuming that Derek Lange has something to do with the palace blowing up and Raven being out of communication?"

"You can come to any conclusion you want, but I can tell you that he works closely with General Miller who is in the pocket of Senator Warren, which makes me wonder if Raven's cover hasn't been blown, and they know we know that they're up to no good."

Resting her head against the back seat rest, she let the news digest. "You're telling me that Miller and Warren are after Raven."

"That's the way the wind is going."

Odessa's worries went into overdrive. Miller was a nasty one, but Warren was a piece of work. He'd done a few questionable things that should have gotten him slapped on the wrist, but the Senate ethics committee had done nothing. "I'm going to take a wild guess here, but they must have found out about the CIA's investigation into their illegal activities and how Raven is involved. Derek Lange is their bagman."

Six people, maybe seven people in the whole CIA knew that Raven worked for them. Beside herself, there were three people she could eliminate because they'd worked with her and Raven and adored Raven. They would never leak information regarding anything Raven did for the job. The other three were on the periphery with no direct contract to Raven, but did know what she did, which made them suspect. "Have you talked to Mr. Dinsmore?" Dinsmore and the Senator went way back to the golden days of CIA, when no one had a policies and procedures manual to play by, so they made things up as they went along.

"Not yet. I talked to you first because I trust you the most."

That made her feel good. She'd lost his only child and he still trusted her. She hoped she never found out what could happen when he stopped trusting her. "When you talk to Mr. Dinsmore, tell him I suspect someone in the department is on Miller's payroll."

"I was thinking the same thing. While you're out rescuing my daughter, I'm going on a mole hunt." Hathaway disconnected and Odessa bit the inside of her lip. A mole! Carlyle wasn't going to like this development.

Rafi drove through the city, staying away from the main, tourist thoroughfares. The side streets were narrow, crowded, and dirty. Rafi honked his horn at the congested traffic and yelled out the window accompanied by vulgar gestures and a great deal of swearing. He impressed Odessa by cussing in three different languages.

Odessa wanted to grab his hand and make him stop drawing so much attention, but she recognized that they needed to blend in, to look like they belonged.

The car skirted the harbor with its huge cruise ships anchored at the different piers. Odessa couldn't believe that so many cruise ships could fit so snugly against the piers. They looked like a giant maze.

They left the crowded, cramped downtown area for a quiet, almost suburban looking area with houses that kept their distance. The suburban area slowly gave way to farmland. Rafi turned down a lane and headed into a copse of trees that hid a farm house that looked more like a summer villa despite the air of neglect that hung over it. He parked the Range Rover under a giant tree and hopped out.

Odessa opened her door and sniffed. A foul stench invaded her nose. Her facial muscles went tense with distaste. "This smells like a frickin' barn."

Rafi laughed. "Good. This is an agricultural research station and it's supposed to smell this way."

Yuck! Odessa was a city girl and damn proud of it. "I'm in the country!" Who the hell had she pissed off to get this gig?

She turned in a circle staring at a dozen goats in their fenced pens, a flock of chickens pecking at the ground, and a small white dog sunning itself on the porch though it was probably called a veranda.

Rafi lifted luggage out of the back of the Range Rover. "We do legitimate research here. Your cover story is that you're a livestock photographer doing a story on the station for a national magazine."

Odessa rolled her eyes. "You are kidding. Raven," she said to the tree shading the car, "you owe me big time."

Jenny stepped out of the Rover with a frown on her face. "Do people really do agricultural study for a living? Don't you just drop seeds in the ground and watch them sprout. And what do you need to know about goats?"

"You'd be amazed." Odessa glanced around the villa and then turned to Rafi. "Where's your security? Who's protecting the perimeter. Where are the guards? Anyone could approach here. Who the hell came up with this cheap-ass idea?"

"The CIA." Rafi pointed at the pond. "See those geese."

About ten of the big white birds swam around the water. One of them was seriously eyeballing Odessa like it wanted to give her a serious smack down "That flock?"

Rafi gave her a look that spelled out just how dumb he thought she was. "Actually it's a gaggle of geese."

"Whatever." She crossed her arms over her chest "Who knew geese gaggled?"

"And when they fly, they are a skein. They are the best surveillance team. Nothing gets near the house at night without them squawking."

Well who the hell died and left him the Animal Planet channel? "So you're saying a gaggle of geese guards the safe house?" They were going to die before the day was over, she just knew it.

"Sometimes low tech is the way to go. But there are security cameras."

"Oh look," Jenny cried, pointing at the lawn where several peacocks danced around each other, tail feathers displayed. "It's a muster of peacocks."

"A muster of peacocks?" Odessa queried. Was that like a flock of those birds?

Rafi grinned and pointed at a wire enclosure. "That's a confusion of guinea fowl. We also have a parliament of owls in the trees, a pace of asses in the barn, a covert of coots, a husk of hares, and a murder of crows. And once a few years ago, we have a plague of locusts."

Odessa shook her head, defeated. "Show me to my room, I need a drink and a shower. In that order." She resisted laughter, though she was pleased that Rafi had a sense of humor. Humor was what kept them from going insane. And one of the reasons why Odessa adored Raven so much.

Rafi handed her her luggage and headed toward the house with Jenny and Carl following. Once in the villa, Odessa felt more at home.

Several ground floor rooms held computers and communications consoles. Thank God, she thought, she was still had technology at her fingertips. She could survive here with the machines.

2003 Publication Schedule

January	Twist of Fate Beverly Clark 1-58571-084-9	Ebony Butterfly II Delilah Dawson 1-58571-086-5
February	Fragment in the Sand Annetta P. Lee 1-58571-097-0	Fate Pamela Leigh Starr 1-58571-115-2
March	One Day at a Time Bella McFarland 1-58571-099-7	Unbreak My Heart Dar Tomlinson 1-58571-101-2

April	At Last
	
	Lisa G. Riley
	
	1-58571-093-8
		Brown Sugar Diaries
		  & Other Sexy Tales
		Delores Bundy &
		  Cole Riley
		1-58571-091-1

May	Three Wishes Seressia Glass 1-58571-092-X	Acquisitions Kimberley White 1-58571-095-4
June	When Dreams A Float Dorothy Elizabeth Love 1-58571-104-7	Revelations Cheris F. Hodges 1-58571-085-7
July	The Color of Trouble Dyanne Davis 1-58571-096-2	Someone to Love Alicia Wiggins 1-58571-098-9
August	Object of His Desire A. C. Arthur 1-58571-094-6	Hart & Soul Angie Daniels 1-58571-087-3
September	Erotic Anthology Assorted 1-58571-113-6	A Lark on the Wing Phyliss Hamilton 1-58571-105-5

October	Angel's Paradise	I'll Be Your Shelter
	Janice Angelique	Giselle Carmichael
	1-58571-107-1	1-58571-108-X
November	A Dangerous Obsession	Just an Affair
	J.M. Jeffries	Eugenia O'Neal
	1-58571-109-8	1-58571-111-X
December	Shades of Brown	By Design
	Denise Becker	Barbara Keaton
	1-58571-110-1	1-58571-088-1

Other Genesis Press, Inc. Titles

A Dangerous Deception	J.M. Jeffries	$8.95
A Dangerous Love	J.M. Jeffries	$8.95
After the Vows	Leslie Esdaile	$10.95
(Summer Anthology)	T.T. Henderson	
	Jacqueline Thomas	
Again My Love	Kayla Perrin	$10.95
Against the Wind	Gwynne Forster	$8.95
A Lighter Shade of Brown	Vicki Andrews	$8.95
All I Ask	Barbara Keaton	$8.95
A Love to Cherish	Beverly Clark	$8.95
Ambrosia	T.T. Henderson	$8.95
And Then Came You	Dorothy Elizabeth Love	$8.95
A Risk of Rain	Dar Tomlinson	$8.95
Best of Friends	Natalie Dunbar	$8.95
Bound by Love	Beverly Clark	$8.95
Breeze	Robin Hampton Allen	$10.95
Cajun Heat	Charlene Berry	$8.95
Careless Whispers	Rochelle Alers	$8.95
Caught in a Trap	Andre Michelle	$8.95
Chances	Pamela Leigh Starr	$8.95
Dark Embrace	Crystal Wilson Harris	$8.95
Dark Storm Rising	Chinelu Moore	$10.95
Designer Passion	Dar Tomlinson	$8.95
Eve's Prescription	Edwina Martin Arnold	$8.95
Everlastin' Love	Gay G. Gunn	$8.95
Fate	Pamela Leigh Starr	$8.95
Forbidden Quest	Dar Tomlinson	$10.95
From the Ashes	Kathleen Suzanne	$8.95
	Jeanne Sumerix	

Gentle Yearning	Rochelle Alers	$10.95
Glory of Love	Sinclair LeBeau	$10.95
Heartbeat	Stephanie Bedwell-Grime	$8.95
Illusions	Pamela Leigh Starr	$8.95
Indiscretions	Donna Hill	$8.95
Interlude	Donna Hill	$8.95
Intimate Intentions	Angie Daniels	$8.95
Kiss or Keep	Debra Phillips	$8.95
Love Always	Mildred E. Riley	$10.95
Love Unveiled	Gloria Greene	$10.95
Love's Deception	Charlene Berry	$10.95
Mae's Promise	Melody Walcott	$8.95
Meant to Be	Jeanne Sumerix	$8.95
Midnight Clear	Leslie Esdaile	$10.95
(Anthology)	Gwynne Forster	
	Carmen Green	
	Monica Jackson	
Midnight Magic	Gwynne Forster	$8.95
Midnight Peril	Vicki Andrews	$10.95
My Buffalo Soldier	Barbara B. K. Reeves	$8.95
Naked Soul	Gwynne Forster	$8.95
No Regrets	Mildred E. Riley	$8.95
Nowhere to Run	Gay G. Gunn	$10.95
Passion	T.T. Henderson	$10.95
Past Promises	Jahmel West	$8.95
Path of Fire	T.T. Henderson	$8.95
Picture Perfect	Reon Carter	$8.95
Pride & Joi	Gay G. Gunn	$8.95
Quiet Storm	Donna Hill	$8.95
Reckless Surrender	Rochelle Alers	$8.95

Rendezvous with Fate	Jeanne Sumerix	$8.95
Rivers of the Soul	Leslie Esdaile	$8.95
Rooms of the Heart	Donna Hill	$8.95
Shades of Desire	Monica White	$8.95
Sin	Crystal Rhodes	$8.95
So Amazing	Sinclair LeBeau	$8.95
Somebody's Someone	Sinclair LeBeau	$8.95
Soul to Soul	Donna Hill	$8.95
Still Waters Run Deep	Leslie Esdaile	$8.95
Subtle Secrets	Wanda Y. Thomas	$8.95
Sweet Tomorrows	Kimberly White	$8.95
The Price of Love	Sinclair LeBeau	$8.95
The Reluctant Captive	Joyce Jackson	$8.95
The Missing Link	Charlyne Dickerson	$8.95
Tomorrow's Promise	Leslie Esdaile	$8.95
Truly Inseperable	Wanda Y. Thomas	$8.95
Unconditional Love	Alicia Wiggins	$8.95
Whispers in the Night	Dorothy Elizabeth Love	$8.95
Whispers in the Sand	LaFlorya Gauthier	$10.95
Yesterday is Gone	Beverly Clark	$8.95
Yesterday's Dreams, Tomorrow's Promises	Reon Laudat	$8.95
Your Precious Love	Sinclair LeBeau	$8.95

Subscribe Today
to
Blackboard Times

*The African-American
Entertainment Magazine*

*Get the latest in book reviews, author interviews, book ranking,
hottest and latest tv shows, theater listing and more . . .*

*Coming in September
blackboardtimes.com*

Order Form

Mail to: Genesis Press, Inc.

1213 Hwy 45 N
Columbus, MS 39705

Name _____

Address _____

City/State _____ Zip _____

Telephone _____

Ship to (if different from above)

Name _____

Address _____

City/State _____ Zip _____

Telephone _____

Credit Card Information

Credit Card # _____ ☐ Visa ☐ Mastercard

Expiration Date (mm/yy) _____ ☐ AmEx ☐ Discover

Qty.	Author	Title	Price	Total

Use this order form, or call 1-888-INDIGO-1	**Total for books** _____ **Shipping and handling:** $5 first two books, $1 each additional book _____ **Total S & H** _____ **Total amount enclosed** _____ *Mississippi residents add 7% sales tax*